PATRICIA WENTWORTH

OUTRAGEOUS FORTUNE

WARNER BOOKS

A Warner Communications Company

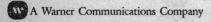

Visitor
At Midnight

Caroline drew back a little. She didn't want anyone from the village to see her leaning out of her window at midnight. The steps were coming toward the village, not from it. She wondered who it could be that was coming home so late. Hazelbury West kept early hours. She drew back until she was out of sight. When she stopped moving, the footsteps had stopped too. She waited for them to pass. She waited a long time, and there was no sound at all.

She leaned forward again with a shiver running over her. There was someone standing at the gate. Caroline could see nothing but a dark shape standing there quite still.

And then all at once the shadow by the gate did move. She heard the click of the latch, the gate swung, creaking a little, and a man came a few slow steps along the path. He stopped between the second and third rose trees and looked up.

In that moment Caroline thought that her heart had stopped. Everything seemed to stop, because, in the dusk that was neither light nor darkness, she thought it was Jim Randal standing there.

☆

OUTRAGEOUS
FORTUNE

Also by Patricia Wentworth

THE CASE IS CLOSED
THE CLOCK STRIKES TWELVE
THE FINGERPRINT
GREY MASK
LONESOME ROAD
PILGRIM'S REST
THE WATERSPLASH
WICKED UNCLE
DEAD OR ALIVE
NOTHING VENTURE
BEGGAR'S CHOICE
RUN!
MR. ZERO
THE LISTENING EYE

Published by
WARNER BOOKS

I

THE AUGUST SUN SHONE DOWN UPON THE ELSTON COTTAGE
hospital. After a week of every possible kind of bad weather
the English summer smiled its brief enchanting smile, charming away the memory of fog, cloud-burst, and storm. A
handsbreadth of hyacinth-blue sea showed where a green
cliff dipped and rose again. It was a blue halcyon sea.
Impossible to believe that only four days ago it had flung its
angry spray against that green hillside, had battered a ship to
matchwood, and engulfed the wreck in the deep treacherous
quicksands which lay beneath the sparkle and the ripple of
its waters. After the storm, fog. And then, on a sudden, this
exquisite perfect day.

The men's ward was on the ground floor, with a verandah
that looked upon the garden. At two o'clock in the afternoon the day sister was getting the convalescent cases out,
the light beds were being pushed along, and there was a
good deal of chaff and banter.

"Sister—can't I have the place by the wall? Billy Button's a-going to grow up it like a creeper if he 'as it much
longer."

"Sister—my 'air wants cutting something crool. What's
the young lady visitors going to say when they sees me on
the verandah looking like this?"

"You can have an umbrella," said the day sister. She had

a pleasant voice with a north country accent. She turned back to an old man with a merry wrinkled face. "Now, Mr Giles, you'd better have that shawl your wife brought."

"Don't want no shawl," said Mr Giles obstinately. "Hot as hot it is." He jerked his elbow towards the next bed. It had two red screens about it. A monotonous muttering sound came from behind them. "Keeps on—doesn't he?" he said.

"Has he been saying anything?" said the day sister.

Mr Giles screwed up his face.

"He've said 'Jimmy Riddell' twicet, and Jimmy 'tis, sure as 'taters are 'taters. D'you think there'll be anybody a-coming to identify him?"

"I hope so," said the day sister. "Now, Mr Giles—if you're ready—"

"I ain't," said Mr Giles. "I want to tell you something first."

"What did you want to tell me?"

"It wasn't 'arf funny listening to that there radio message last night, and him in the next bed. But Matron shouldn't 'ave put no more than just Jimmy Riddell—those other names was all nonsense. It's Jimmy Riddell he keeps saying, and I'll take my Bible oath to it."

"Now, Mr Giles, I can't stop talking here."

Mr Giles screwed up his face until it was all wrinkles.

"And I'll tell you something else he said too."

"Something else?"

"Um—" said Mr Giles. "Something most uncommon queer, sister."

"Well—what was it?"

Mr Giles chuckled.

"First he said, 'Jimmy Riddell,' and then there was something about being clever, and then he said, 'Green—like a kid's beads.' Plain as plain that was. And then off he goes muttering again."

"Oh well—" said the sister. "I can't stop talking here. I believe you're just trying to keep me, because you don't want to go out. You're a crafty old man, that's what you are—but out you go."

She pulled the bed away from the wall as she spoke, and taking it by the head, pushed it briskly down the ward.

Behind the two red screens the muttering voice went on. Outside, the sun streamed down.

Nesta Riddell got out of the car a little way down the road and stood for a moment with her hand on the door.

"Now, Tom, you'll wait here, and if it's Jimmy, and if they'll let him come, I'll come out and tell you."

"And if it isn't?" said the man at the wheel.

He was so like Nesta Riddell that strangers took them for twins. As a matter of fact, she was three years the elder and very much the better man. Tom Williams did as he was told, and with no more than sometimes a sulky look, and sometimes a jerk of the shoulders.

Nesta slammed the door and walked up the road towards the gate. It was going to be really hot. She had been in two minds about wearing her new blue voile, but in the end she had chanced it. For all she knew, it might be the last opportunity she would have, because if this man who had been picked up in the fog wasn't Jimmy, then it was a hundred to one that Jimmy was drowned; and if Jimmy was drowned, she would have to go into black.

She lifted the latch of the gate, pushing it open with a brisk jerky movement, and walked up the gravel path. The garden was bright with autumn flowers. Big heads of pink, and white, and purple phlox sunned themselves, but the cornflowers and Shirley poppies had been beaten down by the heavy rain and sprawled untidily on the drenched earth.

Mrs Riddell did not look at the flowers. She walked straight up to the front door, rang the bell, and then waited, with her hands clasped rather tightly upon the red handbag which matched her beret. She was rather a handsome young woman, with a high colour and dark hair that curled naturally. Her grey eyes were a little too small and a little too closely set, and there were lines between them, and other lines about her mouth which might spell temper. She wore large pearl earrings and the latest choker necklet, also of pearls—enormous white ones. They made her throat look brown and rather stringy.

She had rung the bell, but the door stood open. She could see across the small lobby and down a long white-walled corridor. Two other passages went off to the right and left, and in a moment a fat, rosy-cheeked girl of eighteen, with a white cap and blue print sleeves rolled up, came flying round the left-hand corner.

Nesta Riddell began at once.

"I've come about the message on the radio."

The girl opened blank round eyes.

Mrs Riddell's brows met in a straight line, a dark line like a frown.

"There was a radio message to say that a man had been picked up in the fog—"

The rosy girl became rosier, and her eyes rounder. She was desperately interested and very nearly inarticulate.

She said, "I'll tell sister," and bolted like a rabbit.

Nesta opened her bag, took out a sheet of paper, and waited. When the sister came, she would know whether Jimmy had been drowned or not. What did it matter if he had been drowned? She didn't care. There wasn't any manner of reason why she should care, only she wished that the sister would come and get it over. That girl was next door to a half-wit; she looked as if she didn't understand a word you said to her. She wondered at their keeping a girl like that—but then of course it was just a cottage hospital.

The day sister came round the corner—dark blue, and an apron, and a much more becoming cap—not young, but rather good-looking.

Nesta Riddell said her piece again.

"I've come about my husband. There was a radio message to say that a man had been picked up in the fog."

"Oh yes. And you think he is your husband?"

"My brother wrote the message down," said Nesta Riddell. "I haven't got a radio myself, but my brother wrote it down, and I've brought it along."

She raised the sheet of paper and read from it:

" 'Will the friends or relatives of Jimmy Riddell, Reddell, or Randal communicate with the Cottage Hospital, Elston, Sussex. This man was found unconscious near Elston and is believed to be a survivor of the wrecked coastal steamer *Alice Arden*. He appears to be suffering from loss of memory.' That's what my brother wrote down. Well, I'm Mrs Riddell, and I want to know whether it was my husband that was picked up, or whether it wasn't.''

''Well, Mrs Riddell—''

Mrs Riddell took her up sharply.

''That's the point, Nurse. Riddell—that's my name, and that's my husband's name—Jim Riddell—Jimmy to his friends. And what I want to know is, what's all this about Reddell and Randal? Didn't he say who he was?''

''Well—no.''

Mrs Riddell took her up again.

''Well, if he didn't say, who did? I mean, why Riddell, or Reddell, or Randal? I mean, where do you get any of the names from?''

The day sister frowned. This was a pushing young woman.

''Was your husband on the *Alice Arden*?''

''He might have been. I don't say he was, and I don't say he wasn't. What I want to know is, how did you get hold of those three names?''

The day sister wasn't going to be hurried. North country people take their own way and their own time.

''Well, he was found on a ledge on that cliff just to the left of the gap over there. That's where the *Alice Arden* broke up. She was driven in with the gale, and there the current got her and she smashed on the rocks. You must have read about it. It's a very bad bit of coast because of the quicksands. The lifeboat people picked up a few of the passengers, but this man wasn't found for getting on thirty-six hours. The gale went down very suddenly, and then there was a fog, one of the worst fogs I've ever seen. You couldn't see your hand before your face on the cliffs, and it wasn't till it lifted that they found him. He must have crawled up on to the ledge and then lost consciousness. Dr Sutherland thinks he's had a knock on the head. When he came round he didn't seem to know who he was or where he came from.''

''Then I don't see—''

The day sister just went on as if there had not been any interruption.

"But when he is asleep he keeps muttering, and one of the things he keeps saying is that name. The Jimmy is plain enough. That is to say, Matron says it is Jim—and she made out the message that was broadcast—but when it came to the surname, Dr Sutherland said it was Randal, and I thought Riddell—but Matron said Reddell, so she put in all the three. Anyway his linen's marked J.R.''

Mrs Riddell was folding the piece of paper with the broadcast message on it. She stopped for a moment, pinching the edge of the paper hard. Then all at once she asked what some women would have asked before.

"Is he bad?''

The day sister hesitated.

"He's not ill,'' she said—"it's just that he doesn't remember anything.''

Nesta folded up the paper with the radio message on it. She folded it quite small. Then she said,

"He hadn't any letters or papers on him, I suppose?''

"A note-case with some money in it—pound notes—seven or eight, I think.''

"Nothing else?''

The day sister hesitated. Then after a moment she asked in her slow voice,

"Do you know anyone called Caroline?''

"I might,'' said Nesta Riddell. "Why?''

The name went round in her mind. The only Caroline she knew was old Caroline Bussell. Had she written? What had she written?

"Why?'' she said sharply.

The sister hesitated again. She didn't want to make trouble between husband and wife. Then she gave way before the pressure of Nesta's will.

"Oh, it was nothing really—just the torn-off end of a letter with the signature.''

"Caroline?''

The day sister nodded.

"Nothing else?''

"No."

"Anything the other side?"

"No. It was really only the smallest scrap."

Nesta slipped the paper she was holding into her red bag and snapped down the catch.

"I'd like to see him," she said.

As she walked beside the sister along the left-hand passage, she was wondering about that marked linen. What would Jimmy be doing with his initials on his shirt and pants? Why, the last thing on earth he'd want when he was out on a job would be anything like that—and this had been the biggest job yet. If his things were marked, it wasn't any of her marking; and that was certain. All her muscles tightened up a little as they came into a light airy room with a row of windows down one side and a wide verandah at the far end.

The ward was rather empty. Half a dozen beds were out on the verandah, and the sound of cheerful conversation came back into the empty space and echoed there. Between two of the windows there was a bed with a couple of screens about it. The day sister pulled the nearer one back, and Nesta Riddell went past her and stood at the foot of the bed.

There was a man in the bed, and he was lying on his side with one arm thrown up across his face. She could see the line of his limbs, the hump of his shoulder, and the crook of the arm. Her heart began to beat very fast.

"Is it your husband?"

Nesta Riddell turned slowly round. The sister was behind her, with a hand on the screen.

And then all at once the rosy girl who had opened the door was there, full of hurry and importance.

"Oh, sister—Dr Sutherland wants you on the 'phone. There's been an accident."

The day sister was gone before the girl stopped speaking.

Nesta Riddell put up her hand and closed the screens. They made a sort of red twilight about the bed. She went past the foot and stood above the sleeping man. His head was not bandaged. She could see rumpled brown hair, and a bit of brown forehead, and a bit of brown unshaven chin. Her heart went on beating very fast.

She bent down and touched the arm that was hiding the man's face, and at once he said, quite clearly and distinctly, "The finest emeralds in the world."

Nesta drew back her hand with a jerk. A look of terror passed over her face. To lie here in an open ward and talk about emeralds! The man's voice lost its distinctness and fell to a mutter, but she could hear what he was saying well enough:

"Like a lot of green glass ..... like a kid's green beads .... funny to think you'd kill a man for a thing like that ..... kid's beads ... green ..... Jimmy Riddell ....."

Nesta took hold of his arm and dragged it down.

The man's face was brown and haggard against the coarse white pillow. A two days' stubble made him uncouth. His eyes were half open. He seemed between sleeping and waking.

"Jimmy Riddell?" said Nesta harshly.

His eyes opened—dark grey eyes with black lashes. He gave her back the name like an echo:

"Jimmy Riddell."

Nesta shook him.

"Yes—Jimmy Riddell?"

"I don't know ... no one knows ... nobody knows but me ..... and they're the finest emeralds in the world ..... the Van Berg emeralds ... and nobody knows where they are but me. ....."

His eyes began to close again. He pulled his arm away and flung it up across his face. She heard him mutter:

"Green ... like a kid's beads ..... Jimmy Riddell. ....."

She straightened herself and stood looking down at him— the long limbs, the rough brown hair, the sunburn, the arm thrown up to shield his eyes. Her face worked for a minute, then muscle by muscle it hardened. When she turned at the sound of hurrying steps, those short dark brows of hers made one straight line and her lips another.

The day sister had her question on her lips.

"Well? Is it your husband?"

Nesta Riddell nodded. It seemed as if her lips were set too close to speak.

II

"Tom!"

Tom Williams had been staring idly at that blue hands-breadth of sea and thinking that it was just the day for a dip. He hadn't had a proper swim this year, what with the weather and Nesta's affairs. That bit of blue water was just about right.

"Tom!"

He turned with a start. Nesta had the door of the car open. She was very much flushed, and her eyes were bright and hard.

"We're taking him back with us," she said.

"Then it's Jimmy?"

Nesta frowned and went on speaking in a hurried, jerky voice.

"Of course it's Jimmy. We're taking him back with us, and you'll have to drive right in, because he's pretty dicky. They wouldn't let me take him away, only there's been a charabanc smash at the cross-roads and the doctor's just run up to say they've got to take in six whether they've got room for them or not."

"What's the matter with him?" said Tom Williams.

"Crack on the head. Now look here, Tom—I've had to fight to get him away. If it hadn't been for this charabanc business, I wouldn't have got him. Even as it is, they wouldn't have let him come if they'd known it was the best part of sixty miles, so I've told them we've come from Marley."

"*Marley*?" said Tom. "Why Marley?"

"Because I remembered the name, and it's only about eight miles from here—and don't start asking questions or I shall scream."

She stepped back from the car, but kept her hand upon it. Tom Williams looked at her curiously. The flush which had covered her face had now drawn together into a brilliant patch high up on either cheek, leaving the rest of the skin white and wet.

"What is it?" he said. "What's the matter?"

That something was the matter was very certain. Nesta didn't look like that for nothing. Not for the first time, he felt as if her affairs were a sort of trap in which he was caught and from which he had no hope of ever getting free. If it wasn't for Nesta's affairs, he and Min might be as happy as the day was long. Yet for the life of him he couldn't keep out of Nesta's affairs. What had been happening to make her look like that? He felt a horrid pang of apprehension, and his voice shook.

"Nesta—what's the matter?"

Nesta Riddell's hand tightened on the side of the car. Just for a moment she had felt as if she were going to faint— "And a nice thing that would be!" she said to herself furiously.

"*Nesta*—"

She straightened up, leaning on the car, and said in a voice that was as low as a whisper but much harder.

"He's talking about the Van Berg affair."

Tom Williams felt as if someone had hit him in the face with a wet towel. His jaw dropped, and his eyes bolted.

"*What*?" he stammered.

Nesta's colour became the normal colour of an angry woman.

"Be quiet, you fool!"

"The Van Berg—"

"Will you be quiet!"

"But why?" said Tom Williams. "I mean why—I mean—"

Nesta jumped into the car, sat down, and held him by the arm.

"Because he's out of his head. Now shut your mouth and

listen to me, because I'm not going to say it twice! I went in, and I'd hardly got in when the sister was called to the telephone about this charabanc affair! She left me alone with him, and there he was, muttering to himself like she said he'd been doing all along. All they'd been able to make out was 'Jimmy Riddell'—and we may thank the Lord for that. He kept on saying it, but whilst I was there he said a pack of other things too—and my Lord, *what* things!"

Tom shifted away from her, moving round so that he could see her face. A chill of foreboding ran up his spine.

"What sort of things?" he said uneasily.

"Damned dangerous things."

"What sort of things?"

Nesta slipped her arm through his and brought her mouth close to his ear.

"He was talking about the emeralds."

Tom turned the colour of a tallow candle.

"The—the emeralds?"

"He kept right on about them—how he'd hidden them, and no one else knew where they were. I tell you he kept right on. I've got to get him away before anyone tumbles to what he's talking about."

Tom leaned back against the side of the car and fixed an alarmed gaze upon his sister's face. His eyes were of the same shape and colour as Nesta's; he had the same straight nose and short dark brows, the same line of cheek and chin. But the driving force was lacking. He felt the steel teeth of the trap, and struggled ineffectually.

"Look here, Nesta—"

She mimicked him.

"Look here, Tommy—"

" 'Tisn't fair to go bringing me and Min into this. You go off on your own and marry a man we've never so much as set eyes on, and then all in a hurry you come along and tell me he's a crook, and before I know where I am you've dragged me into this Van Berg affair, and there's a man shot and emeralds worth no one knows what missing—and why should I be dragged into it when all I ever get was to lend him my motor-bike? Why, all I saw of him was to hand it over in the dark.''

"Hold your tongue!" said Nesta sharply. "You won't come to any harm if you do what you're told. Now look here, Tommy, you're not to get rattled. It's not the first little job we've done together—is it?''

"I'm going straight now I'm married—I told you I was.''
She patted his arm.

"So you shall. But we've got to get Jimmy away from here. Listen! He came to himself yesterday, and he didn't know a thing—not his name, nor who he is, nor anything. When he's awake that's how he is; but when he's asleep he talks all the time, and the sort of thing he talks about is the sort of thing that'll land you and me in quod. Now you've got it straight—and now you know why I'm not leaving him here to talk. I want my share of those emeralds, and I bet you want yours. You can got straight afterwards as much as you like, but you've got to help me now.''

"*Nesta.*''
She gave his arm a squeeze.

"Buck up, boy! We'll pull it off. I'll get you safely back to Min—don't you worry. Now drive right in—and remember we come from Marley, and all you've got to do is to hold that wheel and keep your tongue between your teeth.''

III

"MISS LEIGH?'' SAID THE DAY SISTER.

"Oh yes,'' said Caroline Leigh in that warm, dark voice of hers.

Someone once said that Caroline's voice was like damask

roses. He was an infatuated young man who wrote poetry. Caroline laughed at him kindly but firmly, and all her friends chaffed her about her crimson voice. All the same there was something in it.

"We're up to our eyes," said the day sister. But she did not say it as firmly as she might have done if Caroline had not been gazing at her with the sort of melting intensity which very few people had been known to resist.

"I know," said Caroline. "And I'm *too* sorry to bother you, but I've come about the message that was broadcast last night, because I think the man who was picked up may be my cousin, Jim Randal. And oh, please may I see him?"

The day sister took the time to look at Miss Caroline Leigh. They were busy in the ward, but perhaps not quite so busy as she had said. The six charabanc cases were none of them desperately serious, and they had all been got to bed and had their injuries dealt with. She could spare a moment to look at Miss Leigh, who was a very easy person to look at—shining eyes and pretty hair, and a way with her. She was sorry to have to disappoint the eager creature. She didn't look as if she was used to disappointment; she was more like a child that puts out its hands and expects to have them filled with flowers or sweets. "Life isn't like that—well, she'll soon find out," said the day sister to herself.

"I'm sorry," she said aloud, "but I'm afraid it wasn't your cousin who was here."

"*Was*?" Caroline was the picture of dismay. "Has he gone?"

"The name was Riddell," said the sister. "And his wife came and took him away."

"Oh, his wife?"

"We let him go because she seemed so keen on it, and there was a charabanc smash we had to take in. Mrs Riddell's one of those people who will have it their own way—at least that's how she struck me. I'm sorry it wasn't your cousin."

"Oh," said Caroline—"so am I."

"He was on the *Alice Arden*?"

"I don't know. Oh, I hope he wasn't!"

"If you don't know, I should go on hoping," said the day sister.

Caroline looked at her with shining eyes.

"Yes, I can—can't I? You see, I haven't seen him for a long time—oh, not since I was about fifteen—and he's been all over the world—he's an engineer—and he came home in July, and I was in Scotland. Then he wrote from London, and I wrote back and said why not come and join us. And he said he would. And he was going to come by coastal steamer because he liked the sea."

"Then you don't know that he was on the *Alice Arden*?"

"No. But I'm afraid—because he hasn't written—and when I didn't hear, I came home—and then last night there was that S.O.S., and I thought—" She stopped and fixed pleading eyes on the sister. "You're sure it wasn't Jim?"

The sister nodded.

"I'm afraid so. Riddell was the name, though we couldn't be sure about it at first—Jimmy Riddell—and his wife has taken him away."

"Oh—" said Caroline. "And he hadn't any papers or anything of that sort?"

"Not a thing—nothing at all, except the torn-off end of a letter."

"Oh, that's something!" Caroline's voice thrilled. "A bit of a letter? Oh please what was on it?"

"Nothing but the signature," said the day sister.

"What? Your affectionate Uncle Alfred, or Aunt Maria, or Cousin Jemima?"

The day sister felt a little disturbed; she did not know why.

"No—it was only the name."

"What name?"

"Just Caroline."

Caroline put both hands to her head as if she were afraid that her hat would blow off in some violent, intangible wind. She felt giddy with the rush of it. It slapped her face and sang in her ears. She held on to her bright brown curls and opened her eyes as far as they would go.

"Caroline?" she said in her very deepest voice.

"That's all."

"It's quite enough. My dear thing, it's more than enough—because I am Caroline."

"Oh!" said the sister. Then she said, "Caroline—" in an experimental sort of way. Then she stopped dead.

"Caroline Leigh," said Caroline with a warm rush of words. "I told the girl who let me in, but I expect she forgot—or perhaps she just didn't like the name—lots of people don't. But I *am* Caroline Leigh, and I wrote to him and signed it just like that—just Caroline. And what do you think of that?"

The sister did not seem able to think at all. She took refuge behind Nesta Riddell.

"Mrs Riddell said he was her husband."

"Is her name Caroline?"

"I don't know. I did ask her if she knew anyone by that name?"

"And what did she say?"

"She said she might."

Caroline stopped holding her curls. The wind had blown past her and away. Her right hand took her left hand and pinched it hard.

"She said he was her husband?"

"Yes."

"She ought to know. What was he like? I ought to have asked that straight away—oughtn't I? What was he like?"

The day sister looked vague. Her mind didn't work as quickly as that; it did not in fact work quickly at all, except on the accustomed lines of routine.

Caroline's eyes sparkled and implored. They were bright, as deep spring water is bright—bright, and brown, and eager.

"Oh, what was he like? Aren't you going to tell me?"

"Well—" said the sister slowly, "it's not so very easy to say, you know."

"His age, height, weight, colour, hair, eyes?" Caroline flung the words at her like a handful of pebbles.

The day sister caught at the easiest question,

"Well, his hair was what you'd call betwixt and between—nothing very special, you know."

"And his eyes?"

"I never noticed them—he'd mostly got them shut."

Caroline picked up the rest of the pebbles and threw them one by one. She wanted to shake the sister, but she restrained herself.

"Age?"

"Oh, he wasn't old."

"About thirty?"

"He might have been."

"Height?"

"Oh, just ordinary."

"Colouring?"

"Well, he was sunburnt—we all noticed that."

"Where has she taken him?"

"Marley," said the sister. "It's only eight miles from here, and if it will set your mind at rest—"

"Yes—I must see him. I'll go there. Thank you very much—I'll go." She turned, and turned back again. "You haven't got that bit of my letter, I suppose?"

This was going too far for the day sister.

"I don't see how it could be your letter," she protested. "No—we left it in his pocket just where it was."

Caroline turned again. The signature would have told her everything at once. Now she'd got to wait and wait and wait. Eight miles, or eight hundred, were all the same when you wanted to know something at once—at once.

"Miss Leigh—"

Of course she hadn't said good-bye. How frightfully, unforgivably rude. She flung round with an impulsive hand out.

"Oh, please forgive me—you've been so kind!"

But the sister was taking something out of her apron pocket.

"That's nothing. But if you're seeing Mrs Riddell, perhaps you'll give her this." She held out a flimsy folded paper. "The nurse who let her in thinks she must have dropped it when she opened her bag. She's just given it to me, and though I don't suppose it's important, still if you are seeing her—"

"Yes, of course. What's the address?"

"She didn't say—but Marley's quite a small place."

"Good-bye, and thank you," said Caroline.

IV

TIDES RISING AND FALLING—WAVES ROCKING—AND A LONG dream that rocked with them—rocking—rocking. He was swinging like a pendulum between the dream and some vague waking state—swing, swing—out and back again— out and back again. When he swung out, there was a sense of light and women's voices; but when he swung back, there was the rise and fall of water, and black fog, and only one voice, that never stopped. He thought the voice was his own, and when he was in the dream he knew very well what it was saying; but when he swung towards the light the meaning drained away and was gone even before he lost the sound.

Presently the swing of the pendulum became uneven. There was a long swing out into the light, and a short swing back into the fog. The voice dwindled, and its meaning went from him. The light beat strong and warm against his eyelids. They opened, and up went an arm in an instinctive movement to shield his eyes. There was sunlight in the room, slanting across the bed in which he lay. As he moved, someone else moved too. There was a soft hurry of footsteps. A blind came down with a click and the sun was shut out. His arm dropped.

He rose on his elbow, and saw a girl turning back from

the window, a very pretty girl with silver flaxen hair and big pale blue eyes. She wore a blue overall, and she was looking at him rather as a small child looks at a tiger in a cage.

She said "Oh!" in a soft, breathless way and edged towards the door.

He sat up, closed his eyes for a moment, and then opened them again. The girl had almost reached the door.

"I say—don't go," he said in an alarmed voice.

The girl stood where she was.

"I'll tell Nesta," she said.

He repeated the name.

"Who's Nesta?"

She looked really terrified when he said that.

"Oh *please*—" she began.

"I say, don't look so frightened—I only want to know where I am."

This was apparently something that could be answered. A little modest pride displaced her timidity.

"You're at our place—Tom's and mine. I'm Min."

"Oh—" He was expected to know who Tom was. . . . Tom and Min. He certainly didn't, but it was obvious that he ought to.

The girl said again, "I'll tell Nesta," and got as far as turning the handle of the door, when he stopped her.

"No—do wait a moment. Can't you tell me what's happened? I don't know—I—" His voice stopped dead. He didn't know. What didn't he know?

He shut his eyes and tried to pierce the fog that filled his mind. He had had a dream about fog, and a dream about a voice. He had left the voice behind in the dream, but the fog had come with him. It filled his brain. He groped in it and found nothing.

At the sound of the closing door he opened his eyes again. Min was gone, and where she had been standing there was now someone else—an older woman with dark hair and a high colour. She came across the room, sat down on the edge of his bed, and smiled a ready-made smile.

"Well, Jimmy—so you're awake?" she said.

He felt an immediate prickle of irritation. Her eyes were too close together. Who was she? And what was she doing calling him Jimmy? He loathed being called Jimmy.

"Well?" said Nesta Riddell in her hard bright voice. "You look pounds better. You've slept round the clock, you know. Are you hungry? You ought to be. Min's getting you something."

He said, speaking slowly and with a sort of frowning intensity.

"Why did you call me Jimmy?"

Nesta Riddell stared.

"Isn't it your name?"

The frown became a sheer straining effort to find an answer to that. And it beat him. He didn't know—he didn't know what his name was. He knew that he hated being called Jimmy. That stuck out like a corner in his mind, but he couldn't get round it.

"Look here," said Nesta Riddell, "You wait till you've had something to eat. Here's another pillow for you. And if I were you I shouldn't go bothering my head about things at present."

The pillow was comfortable. He relaxed against it, conscious of a swimming head. Then Min came in with a tray, and he found that he was faint with hunger.

Nesta watched him eat and drink. When he had finished, she took away the tray and came back to her seat on the bed.

"Well?" she said, "feeling better?"

"Yes, thank you."

"Want to talk?"

"Yes."

"All right—go ahead—"

That was easier said than done. Where were you to begin when you had no landmarks? He went back to the question he had asked before.

"Do you mind telling me where I am?"

"You're at Tom's place—in Ledlington."

He opened his eyes upon her very directly.

"And who is Tom?"

"My brother," said Nesta Riddell. Then she laughed a

little. "Come, Jimmy—you're not going to say you've forgotten Tom?"

He put his hand up to his head.

"I can't remember. Have I had a crack on the head?"

She nodded, watching him.

"Do you mind telling me how I got here?"

"You really don't remember? Well, I'll go back to a week ago. You know what had happened. You said you'd got to get off the map for a bit. I was to come here, and you were going to work up the coast to Glasgow. I don't know what name you went under, but you were on the *Alice Arden* when she got driven ashore on the Elston sands. There was a gale first, and then an awful fog, and she broke up against the cliffs. Very few people were saved. They took you into the Elston cottage hospital, and Tom and I fetched you away yesterday. Can't you really remember anything about it?"

His hand went up to his eyes and pressed on them. He said,

"Tom—" His voice choked on the word. Then, in a dull whisper, "I remember—the fog."

For a moment it was the fog which was pressing against his eyes—the fog; not his own hand. And behind the fog things moved—vague, horrible things. He jerked himself out of the fog and flung out his hand.

"No—I can't remember."

"What—nothing?"

"No—no—"

"Not your own name?"

"I don't—know—"

"Your name's Jim Riddell," said Nesta sharply.

The name came back to him like a faint echo from somewhere in his mind. It was as if someone had spoken it from behind that deadening fog. She said, "Your name is Jim Riddell," and something in his own mind answered her.

He said the name aloud: "Jim—" Then with more confidence, "Yes—Jim."

He preferred Jim to Jimmy any day of the week. Jim

Riddell . . . He left the name and began to go over what she had said. He took the easiest part first.

"You brought me here yesterday? I can't remember anything about it."

"You needn't worry about that. They gave you some kind of a sleeping-draught to take you over the move, and when we got you here you had a good drink of hot milk and off you went again like a baby."

"Why did you bring me here?" His voice was quiet and direct.

Nesta's dark eyebrows rose.

"That's a funny thing to ask. Where else should I take you? We'd agreed to give London a miss, hadn't we?"

He groped for memories of London.

"London?"

"You're not going to say you've forgotten London!"

"I've forgotten everything. I—" His hand closed upon the edge of the bed. He shut his eyes for a moment, giddy with the sense of empty space all round him. There were no landmarks, nothing to steer by, no horizon line, no faintest, farthest star.

He opened his eyes, clutching desperately at this tangible present—the firm softness of the bed on which he lay; the sunlight at the edge of the blind; the brown linoleum on the floor, with its parquet pattern; the blanket with the three pink stripes across his feet; the texture of the twilled cotton sheet. These things were reassuringly actual.

The woman who sat on the end of the bed looking at him was also actual, but somehow not so reassuring. He didn't like her very much. He didn't like the way she was dressed, or the way she did her hair, or those near-set eyes of hers. He supposed she was handsome, but he didn't like her. She had a black dress with little magenta and yellow squiggles on it. The pattern hurt his eyes.

Her voice cut sharply across his thought—a bright voice with an edge to it.

"You're not going to tell me you've forgotten *me*, Jimmy!"

He looked at her with growing apprehension. There was no echo from the fog. But she called him Jimmy. She had brought him here. And she said "we." She said "we," and she called him Jimmy. His hand clenched hard upon the bed. He had to force his voice.

"Who are you?"

"Oh, come!" said Nesta.

"Who are you?"

"Good Lord, Jimmy—you don't mean—"

"Who are you?"

"You don't mean to say—"

"For God's sake!"

She began to laugh.

"My dear Jimmy—"

He looked at her with something so grim in his expression that the laugh broke off.

"Will you kindly tell me who you are?"

The colour rose in her cheeks. She looked away from him. "I'm Nesta."

"I'm afraid that tells me nothing."

"Nesta Riddell." She risked a sideways glance. That three days' beard gave him a savage look. . . . It wasn't only the beard. . . . She stayed where she was, but it needed an effort not to jump up and get nearer the door.

"And still that tells me nothing," he said in a carefully controlled voice.

Nesta sprang to her feet and flung out her hands.

"I'm your wife. Jimmy—you *can't* have forgotten me!"

He had known what she was going to say; before she said it he had braced himself to take the shock. When it came, it actually steadied him. He felt as cold as ice and as quiet as if he were dead. He said just above his breath.

"My wife—*no*—"

She burst into angry tears. Take it whatever way you like, it was a slap in the face. Nesta did not take kindly to being slapped. She felt no impulse to turn the other cheek.

"Yes—your wife! What else did you think? How dare you think anything else—and in my own brother's house!"

"I beg your pardon—you misunderstand me. I simply have no recollection of you at all." He should have left it at that, but he went on, his calm broken a little. "I can't—I can't—believe—"

"You can't believe—and you can't remember? Well, how much can you remember? How did you come here, if you're not my husband? Why, Tom and I went to the hospital and fetched you away!"

She dashed the angry tears from her eyes with the back of her hand. It was the gesture of a furious child. The tears were real, and so was the choke in her voice as she flung open the door and called,

"Min! Min! Come here!"

She stood aside as the girl in the blue overall ran in. Min came to a standstill about a yard inside the door, looking timidly from Nesta to the bed.

"Perhaps you'll believe Min, if you won't believe me." Nesta wasn't crying now, but her colour was high and her eyes bright.

"What is it?" said Min in a bewildered voice.

"Tell him who he is!" said Nesta sharply.

"Jimmy? Why, Jimmy Riddell."

"Tell him who I am."

Min began to look frightened.

"Why, Nesta."

"Nesta what?"

"Nesta Riddell." She took a step towards the bed. "What's the matter? Don't you remember?" She spoke sweetly and pitifully.

He shook his head, watching them both, holding himself in.

"Oh dear! Don't you know Nesta? Oh *dear*!"

He spoke then, quite quietly.

"I've lost my memory. I don't know either of you. You say I'm Jim Riddell?"

"Oh yes."

"And that is Nesta Riddell?"

"Oh dear, yes."

"What is she to me?"

"Oh, she's your wife," said Min, and burst out crying. Something began to roar in his ears. He felt himself slipping and fell back against the pillows. The room went round. He heard the women's voices as you hear voices in the roar of heavy traffic. They came and went, and they meant nothing. Actually he had done no more than lean back and close his eyes.

Min Williams said, "Oh, he's fainted!"

Nesta took her by the shoulders with a quick, "Run along and don't talk nonsense!"

After that the door was shut. Nesta stood waiting with her back against it, and in a moment he was looking at her. His eyes were of so dark a grey as to seem black. His brows frowned above them, making the shadow deeper. He went on speaking as if there had been no interruption.

"When were we married?"

"On the twenty-fifth of July."

"Of what year?"

"This year."

"This is—what month?"

"August."

"What date?"

"The thirteenth."

"We were married—here?"

"No—in London." She crossed the room, opened a drawer, and came to him with a paper in her hand. "There's the certificate."

A voice in his mind said quickly, "She had it ready." It was like what stage directions call a voice off. It didn't seem to have anything to do with him, but he remembered it afterwards. At the time, he was looking at the certificate, which set forth that James Riddell had married Nesta Williams at a registry office in Kensington on the 25th July 1931.

Nesta put out her hand to take the paper back. The hand shook, and all at once it came to him that, whether he liked her or not, it was hard lines on her. He didn't like her, but it was damned hard lines. Her hand shook. There was enough to make it shake.

He said in a constrained voice,

"I don't know what to say—I can't remember."

V

THERE WAS NO MORE TALK THAT DAY. IT WAS MIN WHO brought him his meals, and Min was much too scared to talk. She left the door wide open, put down the tray, and was gone. He guessed she thought of a man who had forgotten his name and his wife as well over the border line of insanity. Presently she would come back with a quick glance over her shoulder, pick up the tray, and hurry from the room. He could almost hear her breath of relief as the door swung to. Nesta never came near him.

He lay in the darkened room and wrestled with the thing that had happened to him. Presently the sheer blank horror passed. He wasn't mad. His head ached, but he could order and control his thoughts in a perfectly normal manner. He could repeat the multiplication table and the capitals of all the countries in Europe. He knew that there was a Labour government in power, and that Ramsay Macdonald was Prime Minister. He knew all the ordinary things which don't need thinking about, but he didn't know anything at all about himself. The minute he began to think about himself the fog came up and choked his mind, and, with the fog, the horrible panic sense of being lost in empty space.

He forced thought back to the things he knew. He had had a knock on the head. His memory would come back all right if he would let it alone. That was it—he'd got to let it alone—keep himself quiet, eat, sleep, say the multiplication table, conjugate French verbs, count sheep jumping over a hedge.

The sun went behind a cloud, the room darkened. Presently he did sleep, and, sleeping, heard again that voice which he took to be his own. Echoing it, he muttered and cried out.

Min ran half way up the stairs and called to Nesta shut in her room.

"Nesta! He's talking to himself!"

There was no answer.

"Nesta! He does frighten me. He just keeps right on. Can't you come down?"

Nesta's door opened. Nesta stood there, harshly contemptuous.

"What a baby you are!"

"He keeps right on talking."

"Well, you needn't take any notice, need you? Go into the kitchen and shut the door!"

With a frightened gasp Min took in the fact that Nesta was dressed for the street.

"You're not going out!"

"Why shouldn't I go out?"

"I can't stay alone here."

"Why, what d'you think he'll do to you?"

"Oh, Nesta, please don't go."

Nesta pushed past her.

"Don't be a fool, Min!" she said, and ran downstairs.

There were three rooms on the ground floor—kitchen, parlour, and bedroom. The two latter were at the back. Nesta stood for a moment at the foot of the stairs. The vague mutter of a man's voice came along the passage. After a moment's hesitation she walked to the bedroom door and stood there listening, with the handle turned and the mutter louder. Every now and then there were words.

"Green—beads—" said the muttering voice. "Finest in the world—no one knows but me—no one—green—like a kid's beads—" Then, with a change of tone, "They'll never find them—nobody'll ever find them—unless I show them how—Emily's dead."

Nesta had pushed the door ajar. If she spoke to him, would he answer, or would he wake? Old Caroline Bussell used to say that if you could put a sleeping person's right hand into a basin of cold water without waking them, they would answer you anything in the world you liked to ask. People said she'd done it too, and that was why she had such a hold over Mr Entwhistle—she'd certainly got something more than a housekeeper's place at the hall.

"Isn't it awful?" said Min's voice at her elbow.

Nesta shut the door and whirled round in a fury.

"Get into the kitchen and stay there!" she said, and banged out of the house.

It was a little house in a street of little houses on the outskirts of Ledlington. She turned her back on the town and walked in the opposite direction until the rows of houses gave way to fields and hedges, with here and there a cottage or a farmstead. She was walking to walk the anger out of her. She didn't care where she went or how far. She was walking to get away from the look in Jim's eyes when he heard she was his wife. If she couldn't walk away from the anger which was tearing her, she might just as well throw in her hand.

What did it matter how he looked at her as long as she got the emeralds? This was the cool, calculating Nesta who bossed her brother and meant to boss Jim Riddell.

"I'm not poison, for him to look at me like that! What'd he do if I chucked him out to go on the parish?" This was a curious incalculable Nesta who had seen herself refused. This Nesta's hot fancy played with the thought of taking Jim Riddell twenty, thirty, forty miles into the country and leaving him nameless, penniless. She could do it easily enough—another sleeping draught, Tom's car, a quick run out to the marshes or Winborough Common. "Wouldn't mind if he died either. If there was another fog—" She pulled herself up with a jerk. And throw away the emeralds? Not much! He knew where they were, and he'd got to say.

She walked on, her mind very busy. Min had got to be kept away from him. Fortunately she was scared to death. "She *is* a fool. But then Tom *would* marry a fool. He wanted a change after me—someone to make him feel the real he-man." She gave a laugh of affectionate contempt. "*Tom!* Anyhow he'll do as I tell him, or he'll know the reason why."

She walked for an hour, and came home with her plans made. Tom was back from the garage, and Min was all smiles again.

They left Jim Riddell to himself and turned on the radio in the parlour.

VI

HE WOKE IN THE MORNING TO THE SOUND OF TOM WILLIAMS clattering down the stairs and being softly hushed by Min. He was out of bed in a minute and at the door.

"I say, lend me a razor—there's a good chap!"

He found Tom embarrassed but friendly. The razor was produced, and Min brought him hot water and asked him timidly if he felt better. When he said, "I don't feel better—I fell well," she looked pleased; but when he added, "I expect I look like a cut-throat," she coloured and ran away.

He shaved, dressed himself, and was relieved to find himself no more than just a little shaky. His clothes he discovered in a neat pile upon a shelf screened by a chintz curtain. The suit had been pressed, but it still had a smell of sea-water about it; one or two rents had been neatly mended. He frowned at the clothes. They fitted him, so he supposed that they were his; but he couldn't remember them—he couldn't remember anything.

When he was dressed, he sat down on the edge of the bed and put his head in his hands. It was just as if a black gulf of nothingness were cutting him off from everything that had happened to him up till now. On this side of the gulf his mind was working in a perfectly normal manner. Yesterday, for instance, was on this side of the gulf, and he remembered all about yesterday; he could have repeated his conversation with Nesta *verbatim*. But as to what had happened to him on the other side of the gulf, he had only her statements to go by. He went over them with a sort of puzzled horror.

His name was Jim Riddell.

He was married.

He had married Nesta Williams at the Grove Road registry office on July 25th.

He had been on his way to Glasgow when the *Alice Arden* came to grief.

He had been going to Glasgow to "get off the map."

He ran his hands through his hair and asked himself why—and why—and why?

Why had he married a woman who hadn't the faintest atom of attraction for him? You may marry a woman for her looks, or for money, or for ambition, or for purely animal reasons, or for pity, or because you happen to love her. Not a single one of these reasons applied to Nesta Riddell. She was not an object of pity; the Williams were certainly not well-to-do; and mentally and physically she repelled him. Over and above all this, he had a sense of her strangeness. He could not believe that he had held her in his arms, that they had kissed. She was stranger to him than someone whom he had never met—far more deeply strange than any of the forgotten people on the wrong side of the black gulf which cut him off from his past.

He left that.

Why had he been going to Glasgow?

Nesta had given him the answer—to "get off the map."

Why had he got to "get off the map?"

The answer to that was somewhere on the other side of the gulf.

He went over everything that had happened yesterday down to the time when he had fallen asleep to the faint sound of Jack Payne's orchestra through the partition wall. He had slept without waking. He had slept without waking, but not without dreaming. He leaned his head on his hands, and knew that those sleeping hours had not been spent in unconsciousness. The shadows of swift clashing events moved in them. They were like the shadows of fierce darting fish seen through waters veiled by mist. Mist—fog. Fog came into it—fog, and a voice. His voice? Behind the fog, strange violent things, happening at an incredible speed, flashing through his mind too quickly to be grasped..... like beads of light, strung on a dark chain . . . . . like a kid's green beads. For an instant he saw a small brightly lighted picture. The light came from above, and swinging to and fro beneath it was a string of square green stones. They swung from a man's hand. There were eight of them—big, square, green stones; a double chain of pearls between every two. He saw the man's hand, and the square green stones, and the light shining down on them. The voice said, "Like a kid's green beads," and everything went dark.

Some time after this Nesta was at the door. He thanked heaven that he was up and dressed. If he had had to lie there whilst she sat on the edge of his bed and talked, he might not be able to hide the violence of his recoil. Women always bullied a man when they had him at a disadvantage. The thought of yesterday set his teeth on edge. To-day they would meet on equal terms, and he would try and remember that the situation was a horrible one for her. For himself it was very nearly intolerable. He hadn't a job, and as far as he knew, he hadn't a penny in the world. What was he to do? Live on Nesta—borrow from Nesta? The situation was not only nearly, but quite, intolerable.

These thoughts went to and fro in his mind as they sat at breakfast in the small hot kitchen.

Tom Williams bolted a couple of rashers, gulped down his tea, and was off, saying that he would be late. The chug-chug of his motor-cycle came back through the thin walls of the little house.

It appeared that Tom has a partnership in a small garage. The car that had gone to Elston was out of stock. Tom was hoping to sell her to-day; there was a customer coming in at nine. That was why he was in such a hurry. Tom was a wonderful salesman.

With recovered confidence Min began to tell him how

wonderful Tom was at almost everything—"Why, he can cook as well as I can. And every bit of paper in this house is what he hung himself." It was a great relief to have Min's prattle to get them through the meal. She had shy smiles for him now and no longer kept her eye on the door. So much for a shave!

When breakfast was over, he spoke to Nesta directly.

"Is there somewhere where we can talk?"

With no more than a nod she led the way into the parlour, with its saddle-back suite in bright shades of red and blue, its crimson Axminster square, and its silver photograph frames. There were three pink geraniums on the window-sill between blue plush curtains, and on the mantelpiece there was a green vase and a blue vase, and a pink and blue china clock supported on either side by a cherub with pink roses in its hair, and a pink ribbon round its waist. The fireplace was full of white shavings in imitation of the white shavings in Min's mother's parlour at Southsea, and the lace curtains which hung together inside the plush ones where also a pious copy. Presently there would be an aspidistra. Min was saving up for one. She had already saved enough out of her housekeeping money to buy a white woolly hearth-rug, and the aspidistra was to come next. The paper so fondly hung by Tom displayed a trellis covered with very large sweet peas in shades of sky-blue, lavender and grey. They crowded in upon the little room and narrowed it to the dimensions of one of those boxes with gay linings which are sold to hold sweets or fancy stationery.

Into this room, so new, so garish, so commonplace, there came these two angry, incongruous people; and at once its slight emptiness became charged with strain, pressure, resistance.

Nesta waited for him to begin. She stood with her back to the window, leaning forward over one of the red and blue chairs in a would-be easy attitude. He walked to the woolly mat, turned his back on the cherubs, and said what he had planned to say.

"This is a rotten deal for you. I want to tell you I'm awfully sorry about it."

Heavens! How incredibly difficult she made it! His words, his efforts to get her point of view, slipped back from the hard surface she turned towards him. It was like seeing a fly slip on a pane of glass. She was angry, hard, resentful, cold. But there was something else. He could feel the pressure of her will. Why should she be putting out her will against him like this? It got his back up. It made it too damned difficult to feel or say the decent thing. What was she to him after all, but a stranger whom he disliked? If she pressed him like this, he would let her see it. But of course he would try not to do that—only she was making it damned difficult.

He said, "I really am sorry," and the room filled again with her scornful silence.

She stood there leaning over the back of the chair with bright close-set eyes and just a hint of an angry smile breaking the straight line of her lips. There was something secret about that smile, something that said, "Take care— I can be even with you if I like." Behind his resentment he felt a creeping fear. What was there between them to make her look like that? What was there between them anyhow?

He spoke before he knew what he was going to say.

"Why do you look at me like that? What's behind all this?"

"Ah!" said Nesta very softly. "You'd like to know— wouldn't you?"

"Yes, I should."

"I wonder whether you'll like it as much when you do know?"

"I shall know more about that when you've told me."

She nodded.

All at once the tension was less. She said in an easy, ordinary voice,

"Sure you can't remember anything, Jimmy?"

"I've told you I can't."

"Then why do you talk about the emeralds in your sleep?"

It was exactly as if she had come towards him with a smile and then thrown a knife. He had seen knives thrown like that—a dago trick—he didn't know where or when, but he'd seen it. All right—he'd teach her to throw knives at him.

He looked at her with an effect of wooden surprise.

"Do you mind saying that again?"

She said it again, louder this time.

"Why did you talk about the emeralds in your sleep?"

"What emeralds?"—but in his mind there was a lighted space where eight square green stones swung from a man's hand—eight square green stones, linked two and two with pearls.

" 'Like a kid's green beads—' " said Nesta with her eyes upon his face.

A pulse hammered in his temples. Where did she get that? Someone had said that before . . . a voice . . . his voice?

"You talked in your sleep," she said. Then she dropped her voice. "Jimmy—where are they?"

He wrenched away from the picture of the square green stones.

"Will you tell me what you are talking about?"

"Will you tell me you don't know?"

"Yes, I will. I haven't an idea what you are talking about."

Nesta was smiling. When she smiled, she showed sharp uneven teeth, too small, too close, too pointed. Her brows still frowned, and her eyes were as cold as steel. He had never seen a woman with a sharper, colder look. And all the time she was putting out her will against his. It angered him, like being pushed in a crowd.

"You wouldn't know an emerald if you saw one, I suppose?" Then, with a change of voice, "Jimmy, we've been partners all through—you simply can't go back on me like this. Where have you put them?"

He stuck his chin in the air.

"What's the good of talking like that? I don't remember anything. You say, where have I put them—and I keep on telling you I don't know what you're talking about. How much farther do you think that's going to get us?"

"You don't know what I'm talking about?"

"No, I don't."

Something hung in the balance. He saw her checked, hesitating, uncertain. Then with an impatient movement she came round the chair.

"You want me to tell you things?"

"If there are things I ought to know."

She laughed then.

"Well, we might as well sit down."

"Thanks—I'd rather stand."

"And I'd rather sit—and I'm hanged if I'll get a crick in the neck talking up to you."

She dropped into one of the blue and red chairs, and rather unwillingly he took the other. Nesta threw herself back, lit a cigarette, and smoked for a minute in silence. He was determined not to speak to her. At last she said, with an edge to her voice.

"If you're playing a game with me, you'll be sorry for it."

He lifted his hand from the arm of the chair and let it fall again.

"I've got nothing to say to that. I thought you were going to explain what you were talking about."

She said, *"Explain!"* on an acrid note of scorn.

"If you're not going to explain—" He made as if to rise.

"Oh, I'll explain. I hope you'll like the explanation! Do you really need one? If you do, it may come as a bit of a shock to you."

"Do you mind coming to the point?"

Nesta laughed.

"Have you never heard of the Van Berg emeralds?"

He shook his head.

"Sure? Because you've got them somewhere. You took them, you know."

He experienced a horrible sliding sensation. It was as if the room had tilted. The chair in which he was sitting tilted. His thoughts slid, but only for a moment. Then he was looking fixedly at a point a little to the left of Nesta's head and saying quite quietly,

"Hadn't you better begin at the beginning?"

She drew at her cigarette and blew out the smoke.

"The beginning? That's before my time. I can't go any farther back than March."

"Then perhaps you'll begin there."

She hesitated again, bent a suspicious glance upon him, and said angrily.

"If you're making game of me—"

He leaned back and closed his eyes. This was the sort of woman who might very easily get herself brained. She exasperated him as much as she repelled him. And he had *married* her! In heaven's name—why?

"All right, I'll begin. And don't blame me if I'm telling you what you know already. Every heard of a place called Packham?"

He shook his head, and then was aware of the name playing hide-and-seek with his thoughts.

"Well, that's funny—because that's where we ran into each other. You don't remember that?"

He shook his head again.

"Well, we did. Mr Entwhistle was abroad, and the Hall was let to Mr Van Berg—Mr and Mrs Elmer Van Berg. That doesn't mean anything to you?"

"No." The hide-and-seek went on.

"Mr Van Berg had just given her the emeralds. His uncle, old Peter Van Berg, left them to him. He was the second richest man in America, and he'd spent half his life collecting emeralds. His nephews got the lot, and he took Packham Hall and gave them to his wife, and she was going to be presented in them and splash about London with the most valuable set of emeralds in the world. She was crazy about them." She stopped, tilted up her chin, blew out a cloud of smoke, and added, "So were you."

He did not allow himself to move.

"Well?" he said.

Nesta laughed.

"Well, that's where I came in. You tried pretty hard to make me believe you were crazy about me, but you needn't imagine I was such a fool as to believe you. You were crazy about the emeralds, and you needn't have troubled to make love to me, because I'd taken the length of your foot in the first five minutes.''

"But you married me."

"Did you think I was going to trust you? I married you because I meant to get my share.''

"And why did I marry you?" said Jim Riddell pleasantly.

Nesta coloured high.

"For what you could get out of me," she said. "You wanted my help, and you thought it was safer.''

"It's very interesting," said Jim. "Won't you go on?"

"*Interesting!*" She struck her cigarette against the arm of the chair and sent the ash flying.

"Very. Do you mind telling me how you helped?"

"I was staying with old Caroline Bussell. I've known her all my life—she's some sort of twenty-eighth cousin. She's been housekeeper at the Hall since the year one, and she does what she likes with Mr Entwhistle. When you spoke to me that day in the drive—''

"Yes?"

"I was going to go next day, because the Van Bergs were coming. I will say you had a nerve.''

"What did I do?"

She stared at him resentfully.

"Why you got me to work it so that I stayed on. It was quite easy for old Caroline. She said I was her cousin and the Van Bergs didn't care. And then—''

"And then?"

She reached out for another cigarette, struck a match, and looked at him over the little yellow flame.

"Are you trying to make me believe I'm telling you something you don't know?''

"I can't *make* you believe anything," said Jim.

She threw the match into the grate just short of the spangled shavings.

"Oh, have it your own way! Do you want me to tell you how you pinched the emeralds?''

He had himself well in hand. He said coolly,

"I stole them?"

Nesta laughed.

"You make me tired, Jimmy Riddell! *I stole them*!" She tried to mimic his voice. "Do you think you can act the innocent with me like that after the way I've heard you talk in your sleep? Why, you've never stopped talking, and if I hadn't got you out of that hospital in double quick time, we should all have been inside." She laughed again at his blank look and flung out, "Jug—quod—stir! Haven't ever done time, I suppose? Well you will over this if you don't cure yourself of talking at night."

He leaned forward with his elbow on his knee and his chin in his hand.

"You say I took these emeralds?"

"I say you did—and I'll say it was a pretty nippy bit of work. Pity you shot him, though."

He jerked away from the word.

"What are you saying?"

"You shouldn't have carried a gun," said Nesta maliciously. "I said so all along."

He got up. His spine had gone cold. He felt the sweat break out upon his temples.

"What's that you're saying?"

Nesta got up too.

"I'm saying that you shot Mr Van Berg."

He went over to the mantelpiece, leaning on it with his two hands, his head bent between them, his eyes staring blankly at the spangled shavings in the grate. What damned nightmare was this? He had broken into a house, stolen property, shot a man for a handful of green stones . . . . . eight square green stones—chained two by two with pearls—swinging from a man's hand. Whose hand? Van Berg's hand? He could see it under the light. It was as plain as anything he had seen in all his life—a powerful hand, with spatulate fingers and an old healed scar running from the lower knuckle of the first finger to the root of the thumb. He didn't see Min's carefully polished grate with the dazzle of shavings and the small bright blue tiles; he saw Van Berg's hand with the scar on it, and he knew how the scar had come there. Out of all the things that he had forgotten he remembered this one—that Van Berg had got that scar playing with a pet monkey. No, it wasn't a bite. The monkey had got fooling with a razor. It was a clean cut. He had forgotten everything in the world, but he hadn't forgotten Van Berg's monkey.

His head swam for a moment. Then he straightened up and half turned, still leaning on the mantelpiece. He caught a curious look on Nesta's face, a watching look, but it went past him.

"Is Van Berg dead?" he said.

"Not *yet*," said Nesta.

"Is he bad?"

She shrugged her shoulders.

"If he doesn't die for a year and a day they can't hang you."

His voice came at her with an angry leap.

"Is he bad?"

"So so." And then, "It's not your fault he's not dead. You let him have it all right."

He went over to the window and threw it up. He had to push past the pink geraniums; one of the bright blooms snapped off. The room had suddenly seemed crowded with used air. Outside, a light wet wind blew veeringly. There was rain in the wind, but it would not fall yet awhile. It struck damp and cool against his face, and he was glad of it.

Nesta's voice came from close behind him.

"Where did you put the emeralds, Jimmy?"

He turned blindly, pushed past her, and went blundering through the door and out into the street.

VII

CAROLINE DROVE TO MARLEY, WHICH, AS THE DAY SISTER had told her, was only eight miles from Elston. She found a charming little village with stone walls and thatched roofs. The cottage gardens were full of white and crimson phloxes, and bergamots, and marigolds, and home-painted signs with the word tea printed on them in tall straggly letters. The thatched roofs were doubtless a refuge for earwigs, but though Marley contained some six hundred inhabitants, with the usual allowance of cows, cats, pigs, hens and children, it did not, so far as Caroline could ascertain, conceal Mr and Mrs James Riddell.

At first this made Caroline angry. A very bright colour bloomed in her cheeks, and she thought of several things which she would have liked to say to Mrs Riddell. Later on, whilst she was having tea in the prettiest of the cottage gardens, she had what she called a brain-wave. There *were* earwigs in the thatch. She had just fished the third out of her tea, when the brain waved and she wanted to know why Mrs Riddell had said she was coming to Marley when she wasn't coming to Marley.

Caroline had, of course, taken the greatest possible dislike to what she described as that snatching woman. But even people whom you dislike very much don't as a rule tell entirely purposeless lies; so why had the Snatcher said she was coming to Marley?

Caroline drank some of her tea hastily, because she was very thirsty and she wanted to get in before the next earwig.

She had a feeling that there were going to be more earwigs, and sure enough when she put down her cup there was one in the saucer. She never killed anything, so she just said, "Shush!" and tipped it on to rather a moth-eaten marigold. Then she thought very seriously about Mrs James Riddell. And the more she thought, the less she could think of any reason why she should have told that lie—*unless*—

The "unless" was so exciting that Caroline felt quite dazzled by it. Why does anyone give a false address? Because they don't want to give a real one—and they only don't want to give a real one because they've something they're ashamed of or something they've got to hide. Mrs Riddell had come and fetched *him* away from the Elston cottage hospital. She had *said* that he was Jim Riddell, and she had *said* that she was going to Marley. Well, she hadn't told the truth about going to Marley, so why should she have told the truth about *Jim* being Jim Riddell? There may be people whose minds do not work like this, but Caroline's mind worked this way.

She deflected a spider from the milk-jug, drank the rest of her cup of tea, and was quite, quite sure that Mrs Riddell was not only a Snatcher but a Lying Snatcher, and that for some irrelevant reason of her own she had disappeared into the blue with Jim Randal—"Because if it wasn't Jim, how did he have a bit of my letter in his pocket? You can't get away from that—nobody can." She could see the twirl with which she had written Caroline—quite an extra one because she was so thrilled about Jim. When you've got one man in your family, and have made rather a special hero of him, and haven't seen him for seven years, it just naturally runs to twirls. Why should anyone but Jim Randal have the torn-off end of a letter with Caroline on it? She ought to have asked the day sister whether it was Caroline with a twirl, because that would have settled it—not that it needed settling, because she felt quite, quite sure. On the strength of which she drank another cup of tea, and was glad that her name was Caroline, and not a name that just anyone might have. She had, of course, never heard of old Caroline Bussell who was housekeeper at Packham Hall.

Well, if the snatching Mrs Riddell had stolen Jim Randal, she had got to be found. The bother was that Caroline hadn't any idea of where to look for her. She didn't even know what sort of car she was driving or anything. She supposed she would have to ring up the hospital and find out—and then it would probably be a Morris, or a baby Austin, or something that was as thick on the roads as—as—earwigs. Here Caroline brushed away no less than three.

And then she remembered the folded paper which the day sister had given her to take to Mrs Riddell. "The ward maid picked it up. We think it must have dropped out of her bag." That was what the day sister had said. And Caroline had just let it go right through her head and out at the other side. She opened her bag in a hurry, found the paper, and spread it out. It was a bill—one of the flimsy black-lined sort that a girl scribbles on in a carbon-papered book and then gets the shop-walker to sign.

Caroline tingled all over with excitement as she looked at it. It was, in her vocabulary, "absolutely stuffed with meat." To start with, there was the name of the shop—Smithies, Ironmongers. And then there was the address—29 Market Street, Ledlington. Lastly there was the bill itself—One purdonium, 19/11.

"For the love of Mike—what's a purdonium?" said Caroline solemnly, and then all at once remembered Mrs Pocklington's sale. Coalscuttles became purdoniums—or was it purdonii—or purdonia when they got into an auction. They evidently started life in iron-mongers' shops under the same classic alias. Anyhow Mrs Riddell had bought a purdonium at a shop in Ledlington. Now, you might buy sweets, ribbons, tapes, or cotton anywhere, or a hot wherever it took your fancy; but if you bought a coalscuttle in Ledlington, the chances were that you lived somewhere near by and that you made them send it home. Of course you might take it away in a car—but coalscuttles do have the most revolting corners, and what would be the sense of scratching your car when Smithies might just as well deliver the blighted thing? After all, Smithies had got to do something to keep his end up.

She paid for her tea, went down six moss-grown steps to the car, and pored over a map. Ledlington was a good fifty miles. She looked at her watch . . . . getting on for six. It was a clear impossibility to reach Mr Smithies before his shutters went up.

Caroline slapped the map together and jammed it back in the pocket. She did hate not doing things at once. And it was waste of petrol too, because she would have to pass within twenty miles of Ledlington anyhow. It was not until she had run a dozen miles that she reflected on the state that Pansy Ann would have been in if she had gone off to Ledlington and not come home till midnight.

The village of Hazelbury West is like a good many other English villages. There is a pond, and a green, a big house with stone pillars crowned by pineapples and a long neglected drive, a church, a parsonage, two or three houses of the better sort, a butcher, a baker, a general shop which is also the post-office, and a straggle of cottages.

Miss Arbuthnot, who was Caroline Leigh's first cousin once removed, lived in the last cottage on the left. Caroline lived there with her. Sometimes she wondered whether she was just going to go on living in Hazelbury West with Pansy Ann for ever and ever.

Miss Arbuthnot had been christened Ann, but preferred to be called Pansy. She sketched a little, and gardened a little, and painted a little on china. She also wrote minor verse and belonged to a society under the rules of which all the members read one another's compositions. Caroline called it The Vicious Circle.

It was half past seven when she ran her car into the shed which did duty as a garage and went up the flagged path with the red standard rose-trees on either side of it.

The cottage was really two cottages thrown together. The front door opened directly into a sitting-room, out of the corner of which a steep curly stair went up to the bedrooms.

Caroline stood on the door-step and said, "Golly!"

All the furniture had been pushed back, and there was laid out upon the floor a short length of brightly flowered chintz, a longer piece of sage-green serge, and a remnant of navy-blue crepe de chine with a pattern of green and yellow daisies. Some strangely shaped pieces of newspaper were disposed like islands and peninsulas upon the serge, whilst, kneeling with her back to the door and holding a pair of cutting-out scissors in a hesitating, hovering manner, was Miss Pansy Arbuthnot.

"Pansy Ann—what are you doing?" said Caroline.

Miss Arbuthnot sat back upon her heels and slewed round. She had very pretty dark hair, and it was obvious that she had been running her fingers through it. She was about ten years older than Caroline, and she had just missed being as pretty as her own romantic picture of herself. She had melting dark eyes and enormously long lashes; she had arched eyebrows, a straight nose, and a fine if rather colourless skin; she also had a tiny mouth, rabbity teeth, and a lisp. She wore a rather tired crimson smock stuck dangerously full of pins, and a yard-measure trailing round her neck like a scarf.

"Oh, I'm so glad you've come!" she said.

"Did you think I'd been abducted?"

"This won't come out." Caroline came nearer and surveyed the mess.

"What are you trying to do?"

"It's those three remnants that I got. There isn't enough of any of them, but I thought if I could cut out the chintz flowers and *appliqué* them on to the serge—"

Caroline gurgled.

"It'd look exactly like boiled greens served up with asters."

Pansy gazed at her with a worried frown.

"Do you think it would? And even then there wouldn't be enough, with these long skirts. And I don't see how I can work in the crepe de chine whatever I do."

"You can't," said Caroline with great firmness. "And, darling if we don't have some food soon, I shall probably swoon. I've got a feeling that I shall see those asters going round and round in about half a minute. What are we having?"

"Scrambled eggs."

"Go and scramble them. I'll put the mush away. You can make a knitting-bag out of the chintz, and a tablecloth for

Mrs Vickers out of the serge—if you keep it here, I'll leave home. I daresay I'll have a brain-wave about the crepe de chine some other time. Now go and cook. I simply must wash."

When Caroline came down again she had taken off her hat. She laid the table, and presently Miss Arbuthnot came in with a flushed face and a smoking dish of eggs. As she put it down, she shot a hesitating questioning glance at Caroline—

"It wasn't Jim?"

"I don't know?"

"You don't know?"

"He's gone to Ledlington. I'm going there tomorrow. He's lost his memory. I don't awfully want to talk about it, Pansy Ann."

Pansy looked a little offended. She loved Caroline dearly, but she thought her odd. It was odd of Caroline to be so reserved about Jim Randal. Pansy could have talked about him all day. It had always been her cherished belief that when Jim Randal went abroad he had taken with him a romantic passion for herself. She would have simply loved to hint at this to Caroline; she had in fact done so once, but somehow or other she had not felt as if she could do it again. Perhaps she was too sensitive. But there it was— Caroline had not responded, and Pansy required response. It was so hard to have to live one's emotional life without anyone to confide in. If Uncle James had died six months earlier, it might have made all the difference. Jim wouldn't have quarrelled with his uncle and gone abroad; and if he hadn't gone abroad, no one knows what might have happened. As it was, every time she went through the village there were the stone pillars at the entrance to Hale Place a little more covered with a green mould, and the drive a little more neglected. And Caroline wouldn't talk about any of it. She probably wouldn't even have said she was going to Elston if Pansy hadn't heard the radio message with her own ears.

Of course this man wasn't Jim Randal, and of course Caroline was disappointed. But then why not say so, and have a good cry and let Pansy comfort her? It must be terribly bad to repress one's self like that.

Caroline did not feel in the least inclined to cry. Her thoughts were full of a warm, delicious excitement. There were little slants of light and mysterious hide-and-seek shadows, like the glints and shadows in a wood. Far away amongst the trees a bird sang. But it was her wood, her trees, her sun and shadow. If she let anyone in, it would all be spoilt. Jim was her secret playfellow. She never talked to people about him, and he wasn't any real relation to Pansy Ann, though they had all been brought up together.

"I think you might talk about something," said Pansy in an aggrieved voice.

Caroline was quite ready to talk about anything except Jim.

"What shall we talk about?"

"You might have brought an evening paper." Pansy was still aggrieved.

"I wasn't near one. What did you want it for?"

"I wanted to know whether there was anything more about the emeralds and Mr Van Berg."

"Why should there be?"

Caroline wasn't really attending. She was thinking that she could get to Ledlington by eleven. She was thinking that fourteen hours was a very long time to wait.

"Well," Pansy went on, "he'll either be better or else worse. Won't it be dreadful if he dies? Jim having known him seems to bring it home so. You know, of course it must be wonderful to have the finest emeralds in the world—and I simply adore emeralds—don't you?—but just think of the anxiety. Even if they get them back, I shouldn't think that Mrs Van Berg would ever want to wear them again—anyhow not if he dies. I should think she'd always feel as if there was blood on them."

Caroline winced, not visibly, but deep inside herself. She couldn't talk about a woman who was waiting to know whether her husband was going to die. Jim had written about the Van Bergs from New York—they had been awfully good to him—Mrs Van Berg was pretty and kind. The emeralds were like a fairy tale. Now it was spoilt. She couldn't bear to think about kind, pretty Susie Van Berg with everything fallen to bits around her. A shot in the night had broken the fairy tale. She wished that Pansy Ann would stop picking over the pieces.

VIII

CAROLINE LEFT HER CAR IN THE MARKET SQUARE AT Ledlington next day, fitting it in neatly between a ten-year-old Daimler and a brand-new Hillman. Then she walked round the corner into Market Street and penetrated into Mr Smithies' ironmongery. The day was damp and rather muggy, and the shop was full of the mingled smells of paraffin, turpentine, varnish, tin-ware, and creosote.

Caroline asked for coalscuttles, and having been led into the corner which they shared with patent wringers, lawn-mowers and wheelbarrows, she produced Mrs Riddell's bill and smiled trustingly upon a freckled young man whose red hair rose a sheer three inches from a rather pallid brow.

"I do wonder if you can help me," said Caroline, her voice very soft and deep. "It would be so very kind if you would."

The young man blushed. He was a susceptible young man.

"Was it anything in the way of a purdonium?"

Spoken, the word was completely awe-inspiring. Caroline found herself echoing it in a rapt mental recitative: "Cadmium—chromium—euphonium—harmonium—purdonium......" She withdrew herself from this fascinating exercise with a start.

"Oh yes—if you'd be so awfully kind. No, I don't want one for myself."

"We've got some very nice ones, miss."

Caroline looked politely at a black purdonium with a wreath of pink roses, and a hammered copper purdonium trimmed with gun-metal tulips, and at a very refined oxidised silver purdonium with a bas relief of angels' heads. She looked, and looked away, controlling an inward shudder.

"I think Mrs Riddell bought one here. And this is the bill—she dropped it, and I'd like to give it back to her, but I don't know the address, so I thought perhaps you would be very kind and let me have it."

The young man asked nothing better than to be very kind to Caroline. He made a number of most helpful suggestions, such as, why bother about the bill, as it was a cash payment and no chance of its being sent in again; and "Let us have it, miss, and we'll see it's posted to Mrs Riddell, and no need for you to trouble."

Caroline handed all these suggestions back with gentle tact. She thought the red-haired young man was rather a lamb. She succeeded in making it quite clear that she wanted Mrs Riddell's address. When it came to the point, the young man had to go and ask Miss Smithies, a pale angular young woman in pincenez, and after some wrinkling of the brow Miss Smithies, recollected that Mrs Riddell was staying with young Mrs Williams out at Ledlington End. Yes, that was it, because the purdonium had been got for a wedding present and Mrs Williams came and helped choose it—"and—let me see—what's the name of the house? Not The Nest, nor Cosy Corner, but something after that style." Miss Smithies was afraid she'd have to look it up, and having looked it up, gave the address as ℅ Mrs T. Williams, Happicot, Sandringham Drive—"and you go right out to Ledlington End and straight past the War Memorial, and Sandringham Drive's the first turning on the left after you pass the Kosy Korner tea-house—and you needn't mention it, I'm sure; it's no trouble."

Caroline drove past the Kosy Korner tea-house, which displayed rustic seats and orange and chocolate striped umbrellas. Then she turned into Sandringham Drive. It was a bright, clean little road full of bright, clean little houses, all new and shiny like the toys off a Christmas Tree.

Happicot was the seventeenth house on the left, and it was not as up to date as the other sixteen. They had for the most part casement curtains in shades of orange, scarlet, rose-pink, or delphinium-blue; but the parlour windows of Happicot were hung with blue plush and Nottingham lace. The garden was raw earth, with a scarlet geranium surrounded by a circle of lobelia set out in the middle of it.

Caroline lifted the latch of the rustic gate, walked up a bright yellow gravel path, and knocked upon the front door. It was Nesta Riddell who opened it. She looked at Caroline with a mixture of surprise and suspicion. "Flag-day, or something of that sort," she said to herself, and prepared to shut the door.

"Mrs Riddell?" said Caroline.

Nesta nodded. If she wasn't collecting for something, what on earth could she want? Suspicion deepened.

Caroline felt as if there were strong invisible bars between them. She lifted her chin and took a step forward. All the bolts and bars in the world weren't going to keep her from Jim.

"May I come in?"

Nesta stood where she was, the door half closed.

"I'm Mrs Riddell—but I don't know who you are."

"I'm Caroline Leigh. I've got a message from the Elston cottage hospital. May I come in?"

Nesta Riddell had no intention of talking about the Elston cottage hospital at Min's front door. She stepped back, let Caroline pass her and, shutting the door, showed the way into the parlour. Caroline turned to face her, flushed with success. There, beside the hearth, was the coalscuttle, as bright as a new penny. She held out the bill.

"I think you dropped this bill. Sister asked me to give it to you."

Nesta glanced at it, frowned, and crushed it in her hand.

"Thank you—you needn't have troubled; it didn't matter."

"Oh, but I was coming to see you anyhow."

"You were coming to see me? What for?"

Caroline stayed silent. Her feeling of success drained away. She felt as if she were on the edge of saying something very important. Once she had said it, she would not be able to take it back. Yet she must say it. Only what it was that she must say she did not really know.

Then she said it.

"Where's Jim?"

Nesta's hand closed hard upon the crumpled bill. Jim—
Jim . . . Jim wasn't here, thank goodness. It was no more
than ten minutes since he had barged out of the house. *Jim!*
She'd teach other women to come after her husband. She
repeated the name in a most offensive voice.

"Jim?"

Caroline coloured brightly.

"Mrs Riddell—*please* I must see him—because I think
he is my cousin, Jim Randal. The sister said—"

"What does she know about it? He's my husband."

"Are you sure?"

Nesta laughed angrily.

"What do you suppose?"

"The sister said—"

"And I say, what does she know about it?"

"Please let me speak. The sister said there was a piece of
a letter in his pocket with the signature Caroline. I'm Caroline,
and I sent him a letter signed just like that, so you see—"

Nesta's manner changed. She smoothed away her frown
and said in her best company manner,

"It's a pity you've had so much trouble for nothing. The
letter was from a Miss Caroline Bussell, who is a cousin of
mine."

Dejection flowed in upon Caroline like a fog. It all came
out so pat—Miss Caroline Bussell—a cousin of mine. . . . . She
couldn't have invented a name like Caroline Bussell all in
one flashing instant.

She lifted her head as if to get above the fog and asked,

"Have you got the letter here?"

"No, I haven't. I don't keep old torn bits of paper."

"If I could have seen it—" said Caroline very earnestly.
She was pressing her hands together, palm to palm, and
finger to finger. Her eyes under her little brown tweed cap,
the bright clear brown of peaty water, gazed pleadingly at
Nesta. Her hair was the same bright colour.

Nesta did not answer in words. She smiled a little.

"If you would lend me a pencil—if I could write my
name—you'd know if it was the same."

"Do you think I don't know my own husband?" said Nesta.

What did one say to that—what could one say? Of course she must know her own husband. Caroline's hopes was a pricked bubble. She had made a fool of herself to a woman with a rasping voice and eyes like bits of tin.

She began to go slowly towards the door. She was wearing a loose brown tweed coat. She hugged it round her as if she were cold.

Nesta stood aside to let her pass, but just on the threshold Caroline turned, her colour changing brightly.

"Have you got a photograph of your husband?"

"No, I haven't."

"Not even a snapshot?"

"I've said no, haven't I?"

Caroline rested her hand upon the jamb of the door. Something in her would not take Nesta's no; she couldn't tell why. Eager words came hurrying to her lips.

"Mrs Riddell—I don't feel as if I could go away without seeing him. Won't you try and understand how I feel about it? It's such a strong feeling—I can't shake it off. If I go away like this, I shall keep on thinking about him, and about my letter—the one I wrote and signed Caroline. And I shall keep on thinking, 'Suppose it was Jim.' But if I were to see him, I should *know*."

The hard colour rose in Nesta's cheeks.

"Are you calling me a liar?" she said. "Because if you are, I've had about enough. Jim Riddell's my husband, and I've got my marriage lines to prove it. I don't know who you are, and I don't care. Calling yourself a chap's cousin's as good a way of getting off as any other—and you may be one of Jim's fancy girls, or you may be touched in the head. But this is my brother's house and I can do with your room instead of your company—coming here after another woman's husband and giving me the lie about him to my face! Let me tell you that you'll not see him, not if you were to stay here all day. He's got something better to do than sit about at home waiting for his lady friends to drop in. He's got our keep to earn and a job to go to. And I'll thank you to be off out of this."

Caroline's hand dropped from the door. She looked taller. She was pale.

She said, "Good morning, Mrs Riddell," and walked out of the house and down the gravel path to the car.

IX

Nesta Riddell had time to wonder what had happened to Jim during the hours that followed. When at last an uncertain step sounded on the gravel path, she ran to the door anxiety flaring into anger.

"Where have you been?" she began, and then stopped as he lurched past her into the parlour.

She thought at first that he was drunk, but it was fatigue that sent him reeling to the nearest chair.

"Where have you been?" she repeated. "You look all in. What d'you want to go walking about till you're fit to drop? Six hours you've been gone, and you couldn't have had a bite or a drop, because you hadn't a copper on you. Hold on and I'll get you something—Min's got a kettle on."

She brought him cold meat and vegetables and a cup of strong tea, and followed up the meat with bread and cheese. When he had eaten and she had taken the things away, she came back and looked at him sharply.

"Been a bit of a fool, haven't you? What d'you want to go flinging off like that? You've been ill, you know—and you get up out of bed and go walking about for the best part of seven hours on an empty stomach! Batty, I call it!"

He was lying back in one of the red and blue chairs, his face sharpened, his eyes fixed and heavy. He had the look of an exhaustion which was something more than physical. His body had moved mechanically whilst thoughts which he could not out-distance pursued and threatened him. They drove him, and he was driven without hope of escape. He did not know where he had been; only as he lifted the latch and felt his feet upon the new gravel which Tom Williams had laid down fatigue came upon him like an insupportable weight. The food had done him good. Now there was a dullness on him. It was like the fog. He frowned at the recollection of the fog.

"You'd better get to bed," said Nesta briskly.

And presently he was in bed and sinking, sinking down, into the depths of sleep.

Happicot kept early hours. Min tired easily, and on the days when Nesta was in one of her moods she would count the minutes till she and Tom could go off to their own room and be alone together. To-night Nesta was most certainly in a mood, not answering when you spoke to her, or if she did answer, fairly snapping your nose off.

Min couldn't help wondering how much longer she was going to stay. Of course, she paid towards the house-keeping and gave a hand with things, and she'd given them a lovely copper coalscuttle; but still, when you've only been married six weeks you do want your place to yourself.

Min sighed over the pale blue silk which she was making into a blouse, then coughed to hide the sigh, and said,

"Blue's my favourite colour. What's yours?"

This time Nesta bit her nose right off, and a couple of tears splashed down on the pale blue silk.

Tom got up and switched on the radio.

When the rest of the house had settled into darkness and silence, Nesta Riddell still sat on in the parlour. She sat leaning forward with her cheek propped on her hand and her eyes fixed. It was being difficult—he was being difficult. Would he be any easier if she waited? Or was her best chance now, before he had got back his strength?.....
Everything in her said *now*. She hadn't risked so much and come so far to lose everything for the want of a little pluck. The emeralds were half hers. If Van Berg died, they'd bring her in accessory after the fact. She'd risked that, and she

wasn't going to be done out of her price, not much she wasn't. She'd have her share of those emeralds whatever she had to do to get it.

It was a long time now since the footsteps overhead had ceased. For a little while there had been the faint whisper of voices, but it was a long time since they too had died away.

She wondered if there was anything in that stunt of old Caroline Bussell's. It was whispered in the village that Caroline knew a good many things that she hadn't any right to know. People in Packham said she had a hold over Mr Entwhistle and could do what she liked with him. Suppose she had tried this stunt of hers on him. Suppose she had gone into his room at the dead hour of the night, the hour between midnight and the first hour of the day, slipping in on her stocking feet with a bowl of water in her hand. . . . . You'd have to tread like a cat and keep yourself almost from breathing so as to know by the breathing of the sleeping man whether he were deep enough asleep. Old Caroline always walked quietly. She gave you the creeps in broad daylight the way she'd come on you without the least sound, with her neat upright figure and her prim starched collar, her face that always put Nesta in mind of a plump floured scone, and her brown front that never had a hair out of place. *There*—it was all nonsense, and creepy nonsense at that. Only, if a man *could* be got to talk like that in the dead of night with no power to hold anything back . . . . .

She sprang up suddenly and looked at the clock between the china cherubs. The hands stood at half past twelve. Nesta kept her eyes fixed on them for a moment. Then with a jerk of the shoulders she stooped, undid her shoes, and stepping out of them, went to the door and opened it. There was no light in the passage or on the upper landing. The linoleum was cold under her feet as she went through into the kitchen and switched on the bulb in the ceiling.

Min's big mixing-bowl would be about the right size. She reached it down off the china shelf and filled it half way at the tap. The water had to be cold—that was what old Caroline said. But how cold would it have to be? You could call anything cold water so long as it came out of the cold water tap. This wasn't very cold—no bite in it so to speak. Perhaps a drain out of the hot water tap wouldn't do it any harm. She let in a little and dipped her hand into the bowl. Would that wake you up if you were asleep? Not if you were really fast. Was it near enough cold to do the trick? You couldn't tell that till you tried; and it was long odds that it was nothing but a pack of rubbish anyhow.

In her heart of hearts Nesta did not believe that it was rubbish.

At the kitchen door she hesitated, and then put out the light. Now the house was all dark and silent with the warm, breathing silence of sleep. Even the newest and rawest of houses is a haunted house in the dead of night. The bodies of those who live there are unaware, but their thoughts fill the silence.

Nesta was not thinking of this, but as she stood with her hand on the door of the room opposite the kitchen, a little chill just touched her and her heart beat audibly. She had the bowl in her left hand, and she had to keep it steady. The door swung in and she followed it, taking three or four steps forward and then standing still to listen. The bedroom was on the left—the fireplace straight in front of her, the chest of drawers across the corner, and the window on the right.

She listened, and at first she could hear nothing at all because of the drumming in her ears. Then, after she had stood there for a while, it passed and she could distinguish his slow, deep breathing. The window was open and a light, cool air came in.

Nesta turned and closed the door with a steady hand.

There should be a chair at the foot of the bed. She frowned to find it heaped with his discarded clothes. When she had slid them off on to the floor, she brought the chair to the bedside and set the bowl of water down upon it. By this time she could see the outline of the window and the black jutting corner of the chest of drawers. The bed was just visible, and when she had looked a little longer she could see that he lay facing the window with his right arm clear of the bed-clothes.

She kneeled down by the bed and reached for the bowl.

The chair was too high. It hampered her, and she pushed it away. She could hold the bowl in one hand and have the other free. Yes, that was better. She put out her hand and felt for his, bringing her fingers down upon his wrist by the slowest of degrees. It seemed as if an interminable time passed before her hand lay on his, and he had not moved. There was something almost terrifying about this contact. His hand was heavy, inert, and warm. It was warmer than her own. She began to guide it very slowly towards the edge of the bed, and all the time she listened for a change in his deep, slow breathing.

The change came with an extraordinary suddenness. He cried out and flung over towards her, startling her so much that she jerked sharply back, letting go of his wrist and slopping some of the water over on to the floor. Her heart thumped hard, and through its thumping she heard him say in a rapid mutter, "Eight of them—the finest in the world—no one knows—"

After the first recoil she stayed quite still. The mutter died. The bowl of water became heavier and heavier in her hand. He lay now almost on his face, his left arm under him and his right hanging over the edge of the bed. His breathing became slow and deep again. She let the time go by.

At last she put her hand on his and slowly, slowly brought the bowl of water up to it. This time her fingers covered his. Hers touched the water first. And then almost imperceptibly their two hands sank into the bowl. He did not move. He breathed in the same deep, slow way. His hand was heavy and still.

She said, in a voice that was just not a whisper,
"Where are the emeralds?"

And at once he stirred in his sleep. His head moved on the pillow; his hand moved in hers. He said, as if repeating her words,

"The emeralds?"

"Where are the emeralds?"

There was the same movement again. He said, "No one knows."

"*You* know."

This time there was no movement and no answer.

"You know where the emeralds are."

He lay still and said, muttering,

"I know."

"Where are they?" She felt a fierce excitement, a fierce demand.

His hand pulled on hers. She forced her will, and felt that he resisted it.

"Where are they?"

He said, "No one knows but me." The resistance hardened.

"Tell me where they are."

He wrenched his hand from hers. The water ran over the lip of the bowl into her lap. Then, before she could recover herself, he reached out and caught her by the throat.

X

NESTA WAS A BRAVE WOMAN, BUT SHE WAS TAKEN MOST utterly by surprise. She tried to call out, to push him away, but her voice choked under his grip. The blood sang in her ears, and the darkness was full of fiery sparks. Then quite suddenly she was free. She sat back on her heels, gasping for breath. The sparks died out, and she heard him say in a sharp, bewildered voice,

"Who's there?"

He repeated the question again at once.

"Who's there? Speak, can't you! What's happened?"

Nesta stumbled to her feet.

"You've done your best to strangle me."

She heard him say, "I'm drenched"; and then, "What are

you doing here?" And with that, he was out of bed and switching on the light.

All Nesta's nerve had not kept her from a sharp recoil which took her back to the mantelpiece.

He stood against the door and looked first at her and then at the bed. He might well say that he was drenched. When Nesta threw up her hand to try and push him away she had still held the bowl of water. It struck his shoulder, overturned, and sent a cold cascade down his back. The shock of it brought him broad awake. His hands let go their hold. He'd been strangling someone. Who? Good Lord—where was he? What a nightmare! He'd been dreaming. But this wasn't a dream, for there was Nesta with her hand at her throat; and there, tipped up on the bed, was a yellow china bowl. The bed itself showed a large wet patch where the clothes were flung back.

He swung round on Nesta.

"What's the meaning of this?"

She had been frightened, and now she was angry. She could not bridle her tongue.

"You dangerous brute! You might have killed me!" Her voice broke on a sob of pure rage.

"I'm sorry—but what were you doing in my room?"

"I'm your wife!"

"I don't think you were here as my wife."

Nesta flung up her head.

"What d'you mean by that? You half kill me one minute and insult me the next!"

"I don't think it's as bad as all that. You can talk all right—" He stopped and ducked sharply. There was a rough lump of pink and grey quartz in the middle of the mantelpiece. Nesta had swept it off and pitched it at his head. It missed, crashed against the door, and fell heavily.

Next moment he had her by the wrists.

"Look here, that's enough of that! Pull yourself together. If you don't, I'll empty the water jug over you—and you can explain to your sister-in-law why I did it. Take a few deep breaths and count a hundred! I'm sorry if I hurt you, but I've been knocking about in some fairly rough places, and if anyone creeps into my room in the dark and puts a hand on me, it's their look out—I don't stop to think—I shouldn't be here now if I did."

Nesta had ceased to struggle. Now she suddenly leaned towards him.

"*Where* have you been?"

He dropped her wrist, stepped back, and looked at her, frowning.

"I—don't—know."

"You must know. You said—"

He passed his hand across his brow.

"What did I say?"

She laughed, half angrily.

"You said you'd lived in some pretty rough parts the last few years. I believe you too, the way you tried to strangle me. My lord, Jimmy—you've got a grip!" She broke off suddenly. "D'you mean to say you don't remember what you said?"

He shook his head.

"No—it's gone."

She looked at him curiously.

"You don't know where you lived or what you did before I met you? Honest Injun?"

He shook his head again.

"Well, I'm blessed!" She began to laugh. "It's a rum start, isn't it? The man without a past! And I can't help you; because you were always most uncommon close and never told me a thing, and as far as I'm concerned you start in where you stepped out from behind the bush in the drive going up to The Hall at Packham. And if I've got to guess, I'm going to guess that getting away with the Van Berg emeralds wasn't your first job by a long chalk. Rough places? Yes, I believe you—places where you shoot first and ask questions afterwards. Lucky for me you hadn't got a gun to-night—wasn't it? And it'd have been lucky for you if you hadn't taken one to Packham. Couldn't you have got the emeralds without shooting? You know what sort of sentence you'll get if you're caught. I tell you you'd better get out of the country as quick as you can. But you must tell me where the emeralds are before you go. I won't touch them—it won't be safe to touch them yet awhile—but I must know where they are, so that I can bring them over to you when the coast's clear and it's all safe." She came up close and slipped an arm about his shoulders. "Come, boy—it's nothing but common sense, and you owe me something."

Whilst she had been speaking, he had stood there looking past her, straining to recapture the flash of memory which had made him speak with certainty, of the past years. Years spent how—spent where? This was the under-current of his thought, but he heard what Nesta said as well. When she stopped, he put a hand on her arm.

"You haven't told me what you were doing here."

She looked at him coolly.

"You called out in your sleep—I came in to see what was the matter."

"What were you doing with the bowl?"

"I had it in my hand." She laughed. "Lucky for me I had! If it hadn't been for the water waking you, you'd have done me in." She pulled away from him, and picked up the lump of quartz. "Scratched the door a bit. Lucky it didn't break—Min sets a heap of store by it. It'd have spoilt your beauty a bit if it had caught you where I meant it to! You're a good dodger—I'll say that."

She put the quartz back on the mantelpiece, stretched her arms over her head, and yawned.

"Well, I want some sleep. You've had yours. Oh lord—my throat's sore!" She came up to him, tilting her chin. "Like to kiss the place to make it well? You can if you like."

His hand fell on her shoulder.

"There's nothing the matter with your throat. I want to talk business."

She looked up at him—a sideways glance, anger in it, and something else.

"Come along then."

He said, "How much money have I got?"

"You know what was in your pockets, don't you?"

He said, "No." And then, "But I could easily find out."

He felt her shoulder jerk.

"What d'you mean?"

"I could ring up the hospital."

A scalding rage swept over Nesta. If she had had anything to strike him with, she would have struck with all her might. She had nothing. She stiffened against the rage, and it went by.

"It would be quite easy to find out," he said; and then, "Do you want me to ring up in the morning?" He laughed a little. "I don't think you do. How much was it? Fifty pounds?" He was watching her eyes. "Forty? Thirty? Twenty?"

All the lines showed in her face.

"Five—if you must know."

"*Five*? To take me abroad?"

She laughed harshly.

"You were going to Glasgow—that's as much as you told me. You'd money to splash about as long as I knew you, but you never told me where it came from. If you want to know, you gave me ten pounds when you went away, and said you'd send me some more. And five pounds was what was in your wallet. That's straight. And I'm keeping what I've got. You can ring up the hospital if you like."

He thought she was speaking the truth. He said,

"I'll take the wallet."

Nesta hesitated, made a step towards the door, and turned again.

"What do you want it for?"

"It's mine."

"I'm going to bed."

As she passed the threshold, she was aware that he was following her. She swung round angrily.

"What d'you want?"

"That wallet."

"What—now?"

"Yes, now."

"If I say no?"

"I shall come and take it. You'd better hand it over—you haven't got a leg to stand on."

He thought she was going to strike him, but she governed herself. After a moment she spoke.

"You think a lot of yourself—don't you? Suppose I go to the police."

"Suppose you do."

She turned with a jerk and went along the passage and up the stairs. He heard her go into her room, and a minute later he heard her come out again.

He was at the foot of the stairs to meet her. She snapped on the passage light as she came out, and when she saw him she stood still about half way down.

"There's your case!" she said, and threw it at him.

XI

LEDLINGTON HAS QUITE A GOOD PUBLIC LIBRARY. AT A quarter past nine in the morning Jim sat at a solid wooden table and turned over the leaves of a fat pile of newspapers. He had asked for the file of *The Daily Surprise*, because it could be trusted to leave nothing out. Every available detail of the assault of Mr Van Berg and the theft of the Van Berg emeralds would certainly be found in its columns.

Jim turned the pages. He wasn't quite sure when it had happened. Nesta had been rather vague, perhaps purposely. . . . . Ah! Here was a piece about the *Alice Arden*! He had better read it. But it didn't get him anywhere; there was nothing he hadn't gathered from Nesta. He must go back a bit. . . . He came on a headline:

SERIOUS CONDITION OF MR VAN BERG

He frowned, hesitated, and went on turning the leaves backwards. Better begin at the beginning.

He found it at last—great sprawling capitals:

AMERICAN MILLIONAIRE SHOT—AMAZING GUN-MAN CRIME—INCA'S EMERALDS STOLEN.

He leaned forward and read, his face hard and expressionless.

"The charmingly rural village of Packham, twenty miles from Ledlington, has been the scene of a most amazing crime. Has Elmer K. Van Berg, the American millionaire gem collector, been the object of an attack by a transatlantic crime-king, or are the methods of Chicago spreading to this country? Mr Van Berg, an acknowledged connoisseur of precious stones, was discovered shortly after midnight in his library at Packham Hall in unconscious condition. He had been shot at close range, and it is doubtful whether he will recover. The room was in perfect order, but the safe in which Mr Van Berg kept his valuables was unlocked, and a unique chain of emeralds, said to have belonged to the Emperor Atahualpa, last of the ill-fated Inca chiefs, was missing. These emeralds, which had been recently inherited by Mr Van Berg, are eight in number, perfectly matched, flawless, and of immense value. Mrs Van Berg has fortunately been able to furnish the police with a detailed description of the missing jewels."

Jim ran his eye rapidly down the column. . . . . An interview with the housekeeper at Packham Hall, Miss Caroline Bussell. Bricks without straw. Miss Bussell had retired early, and had not known that anything out of the usual was happening until Mrs Van Berg ran into her room between one and two in the morning and said something dreadful had happened. She then woke the other servants, and when she got downstairs, Mrs Van Berg had telephoned to the doctor and was ringing up the police.

He turned to the next day's issue:

WILL MR VAN BERG RECOVER CONSCIOUSNESS?

This is an all important question, since it is probable that he, and he alone, saw his assailant, though it appears that Mrs Van Berg was within an ace of doing so.

"Elmer always sat up late," Mrs Van Berg told our representative, "I would go upstairs, and sometimes I would hear him come up, and sometimes I wouldn't hear a thing. Last night I came up as usual at about eleven o'clock, but I couldn't sleep. At twelve I went downstairs to get a book. As I passed the library door, I could hear voices. Elmer was talking to someone."

"You didn't go in, Mrs Van Berg?"

Mrs Van Berg shook her head. She is a platinum blonde with grey eyes and the slimmest of modern figures.

"No, I didn't go in. Oh, how I wish I had! It might have saved my husband's life."

"Were the voices raised? Did it sound as if they were quarrelling?"

Mrs Van Berg shook her head again.

"Oh no—they sounded just ordinary."

"Could you distinguish anything that was said?"

Mrs Van Berg appeared to hesitate for a moment.

"Oh no—I wasn't listening of course. I just got my book and went upstairs again."

"And then?"

"I don't know—I guess I was drowsy—but all at once I thought I heard a shot."

"Was that long after you came upstairs?"

Mrs Van Berg hesitated again.

"I don't know. It seemed to rouse me up."

"And then?"

"I ran downstairs, and as soon as I opened the library door I saw Elmer lying there."

Here Mrs Van Berg was overcome.

"Oh, it was dreadful!" she said when she could speak again. "I was afraid to touch him. I ran up and called Miss Bussell, and telephoned to the doctor and the police."

"And when did you miss the emeralds?"

Mrs Van Berg's eyes flashed.

"I wasn't thinking about the emeralds—I was thinking about my husband!"

"But you must have missed them some time."

"Yes—when the police came and began to ask questions."

"And was anything missing besides the emeralds?"

"There was nothing else there—nothing else of value. My other jewels were up in my room. I was going to wear the emeralds that week, so my husband had got them out of the bank. He always kept them in his own safe when I was going to wear them, because they were so valuable."

"Then it looks as if the thief was acquainted with his habits?"

"Yes, it does, doesn't it?"

That was all that really signified, though there was a lot about the emeralds, and the Incas, and the Mr Van Berg uncle who had started the famous gem collection.

Jim sat staring at the page. One thing hit him between the eyes. Elmer Van Berg had sat talking in his library with the man who had robbed him. Why had he done that? He had the odd feeling that he knew Elmer Van Berg, and that what he knew of him made it difficult to believe that he would have engaged in talk at that hour with any chance-come stranger. And if he knew Elmer Van Berg, and if it was he who had talked to him in that library at midnight, then there was no question of its being a stranger. And he did know Elmer Van Berg. He knew the way the straight iron-grey thatch of hair stood up above his forehead, the way the shrewd, pleasant eyes looked out under the iron-grey brows, the way the gold filling showed in that left-hand tooth when he laughed. He had only to shut his eyes to see these things, and the hand and the scar, and the emerald chain dangling from it under the light.

All of a sudden his temples were wet. It was true! He had sat and talked to a man as a friend and shot him down!

It was a damned lie.

He got out a handkerchief of Tom Williams' and wiped his forehead. If it was a lie, why could he see that hand with the scar, and the emeralds hanging from it?

With a dogged determination he went on reading. . . . Irrelevant interviews with servants . . . . Statements from the lodge-keeper, who had been in bed and asleep all night . . . . Interview with Susie Van Berg's maid, who described her mistress' state of prostration. . . . How did he know her name was Susie? He did know it. . . . . Description of the library and the terrace by which its French windows could be approached. . . . . He went on turning pages. . . . .

In the end he knew very little more. The police were said to have a clue. Elmer Van Berg had not recovered consciousness. His condition was extremely grave. There was no trace of the emeralds.

He sat back in the hard upright chair and stared straight in front of him. What next? He had left Happicot, and no power on earth would take him back there. He would have to make that quite clear.

He had bought some sheets of paper, a pencil, and a couple of stamped envelopes as he came along. He wrote a few lines of thanks to Min. A nice little thing—kind, pretty, timid. He hopes for her sake that Nesta wasn't stopping there long. It was quite easy to write to Min.

It wasn't at all easy to write to Nesta. How did you write to an unpleasant stranger who happened to be your wife, and make it perfectly clear that you never intended to see her again? It had got to be made perfectly clear. He hadn't the slightest intention of pursuing any path mapped out for him by Nesta. He couldn't imagine how he had ever come to be mixed up with her. Or with this Van Berg affair. According to all the available evidence, he had shot Elmer Van Berg and taken the Inca's emeralds. Unless or until he got his memory back he could neither rebut nor explain this evidence. All he could do was to try and get away from it.

He might remember why he had gone to see Elmer Van Berg. He had gone to see him, and they had talked and had drinks. . . . . That was a funny thing—there was nothing in the paper about those drinks. But he remembered drinking with Elmer. That is to say, he *had* remembered it. It had come and gone like a flash. Elmer standing up, with his hand on the syphon. If he could remember that, he ought to be able to remember the whole thing. He *might* remember it at any time. Remember? What? Shooting Elmer Van Berg and taking the emeralds? That was what he might remember. It was utterly damnable. He'd got to get away out of Ledlington—out of the country if possible.

It came to him that there had been no mention of those drinks, because they were a police clue. His finger-marks would be on the glass that he had used. The incident hadn't been given to the press on purpose.

He leaned forward with determination and wrote:

"I am going away. When I am in a position to do so, I will come to some arrangement with you."

He signed, J.R., and fastened the envelope and addressed it to Nesta.

Five pounds is not a very large sum. Carefully husbanded, of course, it will go quite a long way. If you tramp the roads, sleep out, and live on bread and cheese, your lodging costs you nothing, and your food not very much. On the other hand, a toothbrush, a cake of soap, and a razor are necessaries, and so is a change of linen. Money melts as soon as you begin to buy clothes. How long would his suit last if he slept out on it? It was none too grand now.

He pushed all these things away. He had got to get out of Ledlington, and he was lucky to have five pounds to take the road with.

As he passed a newspaper shop at the corner of the Station Road, a poster stared at him from a yard away:

VAN BERG CASE—IMPORTANT CLUE—MAN
WANTED BY POLICE.

A mile out of Ledlington he left the high road for a footpath across fields. It took him into a lane which climbed to an open heath.

He sat down to rest on the stump of a tree and looked about him. The day was fine, but not clear. The blue of the sky was misted over, and the sun came palely through.

There was a purple bloom of heather as far as the eye could see. He stared across it at the veiled horizon. A hill like a cloud stood up against its northern edge—a hill with a double top. He sat looking at it for a long time, and for as long as he looked at it there were pictures in his mind—broken pictures that came and went, forming, dissolving, and reforming. When he tried to think about them they were gone. He was left with a sense of things most deeply familiar.

He walked on towards the hill.

He had bought food in Ledlington. At mid-day he sat on a sunny slope and ate. Afterwards he fell asleep and dreamed about the emeralds. It was the same dream every time he slept, but it was getting clearer. At first it was just as if all the things which he knew about the emeralds had been smashed into splinters and mixed together like the pieces of coloured glass in a kaleidoscope. There was a sense of colour, and light, a rapid movement; there was a sense of confusion. In the dream he always knew where the emeralds were, but as soon as he woke up the knowledge faded. Sometimes he could hold it for a moment by shutting his eyes and keeping his mind empty; but as soon as he *tried* to keep it, it was gone.

The dream always began the same way. He could remember the beginning—Elmer's hand with the scar, and the emeralds dangling from it under the light—eight square green stones with pearls between them. They were as green as fire—sea logs split on a stone hearth and burning green—green fire spitting salt. The emeralds were as green as the green flame. Then the dream broke up into a rush of coloured fragments. There was a voice in a fog. There was the sound of a shot a long way off. There was the voice, and there was a picture in his mind of tall stone pillars with pineapple tops, and a drive that wound between them out of sight. The voice said, "Like a kid's green beads," and, "Nobody knows where they are." But in the dream he knew. A round room with five little windows like slits—a place where you might look for a year and never find them.

He woke up, the sun hot on his face. The dream was

gone, but the hill still broke the horizon. In some strange way he associated the hill and the dream. He made a pillow of bracken for his head and lay on the slope watching the hill. Presently he would get to it—presently. . . . .

He slept again.

XII

"IT'S ELEVEN O'CLOCK," SAID CAROLINE.

Pansy Arbuthnot ran a pencil through her hair and turned a page. The gate-leg table at which she sat was strewn with sheets of manuscript. Ernest Hughes Mottson's last poem lay on her left, Alicia Spence-Lely's last short story on her right. Verses and essays by other members of the Vicious Circle occupied the rest of the space. In her hand she held a single sheet of what looked rather like packing-paper.

Caroline was curled up by the fire. It had been a very pleasant fire. One can almost bear a cold August for the sake of old apple-wood burning on a low brick hearth. This particular log came from the crabby Worcester Pearmain which had blown down in the gale a week ago. Its logs were a great deal better than its apples had ever been. Caroline's grandmother used to say that,

> *An applewood fire*
> *Will show you your heart's desire.*

The log had broken into red embers, and the embers were turning grey. No one likes to see their heart's desire turn grey.

Caroline twisted round.

"It's ever so late, Pansy Ann."

"Caro—"

"Are you going to read those things all night?"

"Some of them," said Miss Arbuthnot, "are very striking." She sounded a little vague and she ran her pencil through her hair again.

"You look struck."

"Very striking *indeed*! I *would* like to read you this one."

Caroline sat back against the warm brick of the chimney arch and clasped her hands about her knees.

"Why?"

"It's so very striking."

Caroline's eyes danced.

"All right—get it over!"

"It's by a new man who's just joined the Circle. He signs himself 'Abaddon.'"

"How bad is it?" said Caroline.

"It's very striking," said Pansy in rather a dazed voice. She held the sheet of brown paper farther off and said, "*Query*." Then she stopped. "That's the title—only he hasn't written it like that, which is rather puzzling. He has just put an enormous question mark, so I don't quite know how to read it. Would you say Query, or would you say Question-mark?"

"Question-mark," said Caroline.

Pansy brought the paper a little nearer and read:

> *?*
>
> *Illimitable maximum*
> *Star glutinous space cataract*
> *Crushed platinum*
> *Inevitably wracked*
> *A tortuous torment of lamenting gloom*
> *Till lightning cracked*
> *The whole steep firmament*
> *Tilts shrieking blindly its impermanent*
> *Resistless unresisted blast of doom.*

"Golly!" said Caroline.

Pansy looked a little awed.

"There are no stops!" she said.

"There wouldn't be—not in a star glutinous space cataract. You don't have time—you're too busy tilting and shrieking."

"I like this one better," said Pansy. She paused, and then added—"*really*. It's quite different."

She picked up a neatly written sheet and read:

> *I went to look for violets,*
> *There were no violets there;*
> *But every single widowed leaf*
> *Had shed a shining tear of grief*
> *For violets that were.*

> *I went to look for roses,*
> *The roses all were fled—*

Caroline went off into a gurgle of laughter.

"That's not a poem—it's a foregone conclusion! I can tell you exactly what the other rhymes are going to be before you come to them. It's not another 'Abaddon,' I suppose?"

"No. She signs Gwendoline, but her name is really Dobbs."

Caroline scrambled to her feet.

"Sorry, Pansy Ann, I'm going to bed—I don't think I can bear any more Gwendoline."

She went up the stairs, which ended on a tiny landing with a door on either side. Her room was on the left, and you went down two steps to it. Both the steps and the floor of the room were odd polished boards, very wavy and uneven. The window, which looked to the front of the house, was set in a deep embrasure. Caroline had given it curtains of green sprigged chintz, a pattern of little holly leaves on a shiny white ground. There were green rush mats on the floor, and an old hand-quilted bedspread worked with pink and green flowers on the wide, low bed.

Caroline was very fond of her room. The bedspread had

been worked by her great great-great-aunt Caroline, who had been called after Caroline of Anspach. The bed had belonged to her too, and it was much too big for the room. Caroline had slept in it ever since she was six years old.

She shut the door and turned on the light in the lamp beside her bed. Hazelbury West had had electric light for the last eight years and considered itself very up to date in consequence.

Caroline turned down her bed, folding the quilt carefully and laying it on the chest in which she kept her hats. She had said she wanted to come to bed, but she wasn't really sleepy. If the fire had not died, she would have gone on sitting there beside it; but it is the saddest thing in the world to sit by a dying fire. And as for Pansy Ann's Circle and their appalling balderdash—with the least encouragement Pansy would have read her the whole lot.

She opened the bottom drawer of the chest of drawers which faced the window and took out a bundle of letters tied with a twist of pale blue knitting silk. Then she went over to the bed. Sitting down on the edge of it, she untied the bundle and turned the letters over. There were not a great many of them. Two the first year after Jim went out—one for her birthday, and one for Christmas—and two again the second year, and the third. In the fourth year he only wrote for Christmas. The pain of that missed birthday came across the three years interval and hurt her still. She had counted on her letter, and it hadn't come. Her birthday was in June, so it was six months since Christmas, and it would be six months before it was Christmas again. Six months is a most frightfully long time when you are nineteen.

In the fifth year there was no letter at all. On her birthday and on Christmas day Caroline read the old letters and tried to make believe that they had just come. It was not a very successful make-believe.

In the sixth year there were still no letters.

And then in the seventh year—this year—they began again. He had written at Christmas from New York.

Caroline got out the letter and read it again. It was a very nice letter. She hugged herself a little over it. It began, as all his letters always had begun, "Darling Caroline"; and it was quite long. He had been in lots of exciting places. He had been building a bridge in Mexico, and he had been in Chile, and Peru, and up in wild places in the Andes. He had also been inventing something which he hoped would make his fortune. He was burnt pretty nearly as dark as an Indian. And he had become a pretty good shot, because you needed to be. He was hers, Jim. He always signed just like that—"Yours, Jim."

That was the Christmas letter. Caroline answered it at once. She told him she was living with Pansy Ann, and she told him just how dreary and lonely and neglected Hale Place was getting to look—weeds in the drive, and green mould on the pineapples at the entrance—"and if you don't come home soon, Jim, the trees will meet across the drive, and the cedar and the copper beech will grow in at the west windows. There's ivy across the glass already, and the wisteria is over the old schoolroom. Aren't you ever coming home? I do so want you to come. Your loving Caroline."

She had always signed like that to Jim from the time that she wrote him her very first letter when she was seven years old and he had sent her a doll for her birthday. It had real hair, and brown eyes that opened and shut. Jim was sixteen. He loomed heroic to little Caroline. He could climb trees. He could swim two miles—as far as from Hazelbury West to Packham. He could make a swing. He could make a kite. He could swing you right up into the air over his head and hold you there. He wasn't a grown-up. Grown-ups said, "Don't—" and "You mustn't!" Jim was just Jim. She was his loving Caroline.

He wrote again in February. He was very hopeful about his invention. He couldn't tell her about it, because it was all extremely confidential. Elmer Van Berg might be going to back it. If he did, the thing was made. He wrote at length about Elmer Van Berg, for whom he seemed to have a high admiration—"The bother is, he's interested in too many things. He takes turns at them. Whilst he's riding one, the others might as well be dead. Just as I thought I had brought my job off, his uncle, old Peter Van Berg, died and left him an extraordinary collection of jewels. Elmer's too busy with them to have time for me and my affairs." There was a lot more about the Van Bergs. Susie Van Berg was awfully pretty, and awfully kind. They were great friends.

In March he wrote that the Van Bergs were coming to England for the summer—"Susie wants to go to Court in as many of old Peter Van Berg's jewels as possible. There are some emeralds which beat the band. They are said to have belonged to Atahualpa, the last of the Incas. I shouldn't mind having what they would fetch—you can't launch an invention without capital. If this thing of mine can only get a start, it's bound to go big."

After that there was nothing for a couple of months. Then he wrote again, still from New York. The Van Bergs were in England. He was half thinking of coming over after them. Susie thought it might be worth his while—she thought Elmer was working up for a change of hobbies. They had taken Packham Hall for the summer—"You might go over and call as it's so near."

Caroline had gone over to call with Pansy Ann; but it was June, and the Van Bergs were taking their London season very seriously and only coming down for week-ends. Caroline and Pansy had been asked to lunch on a Sunday—and of course it had to be just that one particular Sunday which Robert Arbuthnot had already commandeered. he was a distant cousin of Pansy's, a still more distant cousin of Caroline's, and trustee to both of them. He was an able solicitor, and a blinding bore. Caroline maintained that he only came to see them when he had something unpleasant to impart with regard to their investments. On this occasion he left Pansy the poorer by about twenty pounds a year, and made it impossible for Caroline to meet the Van Bergs.

In July Caroline went north to visit her father's sister, who kept open house every year in the Highlands. It was whilst she was at Craigellachie that Jim wrote to say he was in London. He was given a warm invitation to join Mrs Ogilvie's party.

Caroline passed quickly over the time when they waited for his answer. He would come—of course he would come.

They would go for tremendously long walks, and tell each other all the things that you couldn't put into letters. If he got Aunt Grace's letter on Wednesday morning, he might catch the night train and come right through. Caroline had gone about in a queer warm dream of happiness which it hurt her to think about now. Because Jim hadn't come. He hadn't written for three days, and then it was just a few lines to Grace Ogilvie. He thanked her very much, and he hoped perhaps he might be able to get up later on, but just at the moment he was afraid he couldn't spare the time. He didn't write to Caroline at all, not until the beginning of August, and then it wasn't what you could call a letter; just half a dozen lines, all scrawled in a hurry:

"I may be able to get off on the 8th if Grace can still have me. I shall probably take a steamer up the coast."

And that was all. That was the very last letter. It might have been written to anyone—to a hotel, or to someone you disliked, or to a Mere Acquaintance. It wasn't the kind of letter to be Jim's last letter to his loving Caroline. It gave her a very desolate, grey, hopeless feeling. It made her feel, quite illogically, that Jim was drowned. The *Alice Arden* had sailed on the eighth of August and had gone to bits on the Elston rocks. If Jim wasn't drowned, where was he? The only address they had ever had was his bank. She had been to the bank, and had been told that they had no address, and that Mr Randal had not called for his letters since the sixth of August.

That was a very frightening thing to hear. It seemed to make it certain that Jim had sailed on the *Alice Arden*. A cold shiver passed over Caroline. She put the letters together again with hands that moved a little stiffly. When she went over to put them away, the room felt very cold. She drew a sobbing breath as she shut the drawer. It felt as if she were shutting Jim away. The tears began to run down her face, and all at once she couldn't bear the light any more. It is only happy people who want to stand in the light. Caroline pushed down the switch, and was glad of the dark.

She cried bitterly, crouching down by the bed and pressing her face into the pillow lest Pansy Ann should hear.

Pansy had come upstairs and was moving about in the room across the tiny landing. Caroline cried all her tears away. She had held them in for a long time; now they were all gone, and she felt rather like a ghost, weak and light and insubstantial.

She went to the window and opened it, kneeling on the deep window-ledge and leaning out to get the air. It was a still night that would come near to frost before morning. There was moonlight, but the moon was not visible. The elm-trees opposite rose up dark and vague as smoke. All the shadows were soft and formless. The white phloxes in the border looked like spilled milk.

Something in Caroline's mind said quickly, "It's no good crying over spilled milk." She thought that was very odd.

She leaned out farther. There was something strange about the night. Or perhaps the strangeness was in herself. She felt as if everything was a very long way off and out of reach. A ghost might feel like that if it came back. There is a ballad in which a dead man comes to his lover's window an hour before the day:

> *"Are ye sleeping, Margaret?"* he says,
> *"Or are ye waking presentlie?*
> *Give me my faith and troth again,*
> *I wot, true love, I gied to thee."*

The verse came into Caroline's mind. It seemed to float there giving out a peculiar atmosphere of eerie strangeness. It would have been on just such a night as this that Margaret looked from the shot window and saw the dead man come tirling at the pin—no lighter than this and no darker—moon-shadow—moon-dusk. Even a living man might look like a ghost. A faint damp breath moved the trees across the road. Over the edge of the silence came the sound of footsteps coming nearer.

Caroline drew back a little. She didn't want anyone from the village to see her leaning out of her window at midnight. The steps were coming towards the village, not from it. She wondered who it could be that was coming home so late.

Hazelbury West kept early hours. She drew back until she was out of sight. When she stopped moving, the footsteps had stopped too. She leaned against the side of the recess and waited for them to pass. She waited a long time, and there was no sound at all. If the footsteps had passed, she would have heard them. They had not passed.

She leaned forward again with a shiver running over her. There was someone standing at the gate. She could see no more than that. A hornbeam hedge divided the garden from the road. It was cut into an archway over the gate, and under this arch someone was standing. Caroline could see nothing but a dark shape standing there quite still

The little breath of air had died away. None of the shadows in the garden moved. And then all at once the shadow by the gate did move. She heard the click of the latch, the gate swung, creaking a little, and a man came a few slow steps along the path. He stopped between the second and third rose-trees and looked up.

In that moment Caroline thought that her heart had stopped. Everything seemed to stop, because, in the dusk that was neither light nor darkness, she thought it was Jim Randal standing there. He had stood like that a hundred times, looking up at the old school-room window when he wanted her—calling, "Caroline!" He didn't call now. It wasn't Jim—it couldn't be Jim. Oh, Jim was drowned. How could it—how could it be Jim? Did anyone ever come back like that in the dead of the night? She felt as if she were drowning too, because she couldn't take her breath.

And then quite suddenly he turned and went down the path and out at the gate. The gate clicked, and everything went on again.

Caroline found herself taking deep choking breaths, whilst her heart raced furiously. The next thing she knew she was on the stairs, running down; and then the door was open and she was on the brick step, listening. There was no sound behind her in the house. Pansy Ann slept deep. There was no sound in the garden, not the rustle of a leaf or the stirring of a bird; but from the road there came the faint sound of footsteps that were going away.

She ran down the path and out of the gate and followed them.

It was cool in the road, and dark because of the elmtrees. The moon was somewhere behind the trees. Caroline ran a little way, and then stopped to listen again. The footsteps were just ahead, and presently she could see a something that was darker than the shadow of the elms moving before her at a steady pace.

> *It's hosen and shoon and gown alone.*
> *She climbed the wall and followed him*
> *Until she came to the green forest,*
> *And there she lost the sight of him.*

The words came and went, and came and went again. What was she doing? She didn't know. Where was she going? Wherever Jim went. It wasn't Jim—it couldn't be Jim. Who was she following? Jim was drowned. *What was she following?* Her mind shuddered away—

They went past the churchyard and past the church. They came to the green, with the pond catching the moonlight like looking-glass. There were trees still along the edge of the road, trees with spaces of moonlight in between. When he crossed the moonlight patches, Caroline was afraid. She could see no more than a tall man walking as if he were tired. It was when he was only a shadow that she felt most sure that he was Jim.

They passed a little row of silent, empty shops. They passed Mrs Grainger's cottage. It had one pale lighted window. Mrs Grainger slept badly, and was inordinately proud of the fact that she often read until past midnight. It was past midnight now.

Caroline looked back over her shoulder and saw the window very small and far away. The village world, other people, firelight, lamplight—the whole of everyday life—they were all small and far away and left behind. The ballad verse drummed in her head:

> *It's hosen and shoon and gown alone.*

> *She climbed the wall and followed him*
> *Until she came to the green forest,*
> *And there she lost the sight of him.*

But it should be *dark* forest—dark; not green—

> *Until she came to the dark forest*
> *And there she lost the sight of him.*

And with that the gate-posts of the Hale Place stood up in front of her in the ghostly light. There was no gate between them, nor ever had been since Caroline could remember. But the posts had always been there—tall pillars of grey stone with a stiff stone pineapple on top of each. The moon shone on the posts and on the pineapples, and on the man who passed between them into the black shadow which lay beyond.

> *And there she lost the sight of him.*

But she mustn't lost the sight of him. She had lost the last light of the village. Whatever happened, she mustn't lose Jim.

Jim was drowned.

She stood for a moment on the edge of the moonlight. The elms stopped here, and the light shone clear across the green. Something clamoured in Caroline's ear: "Jim's drowned—it can't be Jim." And then she was running through the moonlight and into the shadow.

The trees that bordered the drive had been growing together for thirty years. Old Mr Randal wouldn't have anything cut. It was as dark as the darkest tunnel. It was dark even when the sun was shining. Now it was like a tunnel hung with black velvet. The gravel was so overgrown with moss that it was like running on a soft carpet. Caroline's feet made no noise at all, nor, when she checked and listened, could she hear the sound of any other foot. She went on again, not running now, and with her hands fending out before her. The tunnel under the trees had an empty feeling. It went right on to the corner of the house and there ceased.

Caroline stood still and listened again. She couldn't hear anything at all. It wasn't dark any longer, but all the light came barred and chequered through the branches of the great cedar which stood up against the moon. The house seemed vague and unsubstantial, its tangled creepers dappled with silver. It wasn't a place where people lived any more. There was no fire on its hearth, no light in its chambers. It was a house of dreams.

Until she stood in the black mouth of the drive and looked at the house, Caroline had been afraid. Part of her had been very much afraid, but she had gone on because she had to go on. Now the part that was afraid stopped being afraid any more. The empty house drew her into its own dream, and she stopped being afraid. She began to run across the bars of moonlight and shadow, and as she ran she called,

"Jim! Jim! Wait for me!"

XIII

CAROLINE CAME TO THE CORNER, AND SAW THE WHOLE front of the house and the gravel sweep before it unshadowed in a faint moony light. In the middle of the sweep the man whom she had followed stood looking up at the house.

Caroline had done with hesitating and being afraid. Those were things which she had left behind, outside the dream. She came to him, running lightly, and as he turned at the sound of her running feet, she caught him by the arm.

"Jim!" It was her very warmest, softest, deepest voice. He stood there and looked at her. He had come here because his feet had brought him. At every turning, at each cross-road and bend, he had known his way, yet he could not at any time have said where he was going; he could only have said that he didn't know. Yet all the time he knew that his feet were following a familiar path. In the dark this feeling strengthened. It took him into Hazelbury West with the sure sense of a homing animal, and it had brought him here.

As he stood staring at the house, the strangest sense of forgotten things came to him from the shape of the three pointed gables, the half seen chimney stacks, the blank windows, the ivy, and the falling curtains of Virginia creeper.

And then feet running lightly over the gravel, and a girl holding him by the arm and saying, "Jim!" She said it again, softly, with caught breath. She was bareheaded. The moonlight had stolen all her colour. Her hair was shadowy and dark, her face just a half seen paleness, her eyes dark but catching the light as water does, her hands holding his arms, small and yet strong, her breath coming quickly, quickly, her parted lips dark where daylight would have shown them red.

"*Jim!*"

He went on looking at her. The hands on his arm began to shake.

"Jim—why don't you speak? Jim—you're not drowned!"

He said, "I'm not drowned—"

That was an easy thing to say. The pressure of those half remembered things increased. It was like the intolerable pressure of water. It was easy to say, "I'm not drowned." Just for a moment it eased the pressure. He looked down and saw that her eyes were wide and piteous.

"Jim—what's the matter? Why do you look like that, as if you didn't know me?"

He said in a heavy, shaken voice,

"I—don't—know you."

The hands let go of his arm; she stepped back. He had a sense of emptiness and loss.

And then she was laughing—such a pretty laugh, low, and full of something that was very young and innocent.

"But I'm Caroline! Darling—didn't you *guess*? I don't call that a bit bright of you. Who did you think I was?"

He shook his head.

"I don't know. . . Caroline?"

Caroline stopped laughing, because something in the slow tentative way in which he said, "Caroline?" made her stop.

"Jim—what's the matter? Jim darling!"

"Why do you call me that?"

And all at once Caroline began to feel cold. The dream was changing in the way dreams do. One minute she had found Jim and her heart was singing with joy, and the next there was a vague something that was cold and frightening. She didn't know what it was, and that made it worse. She said,

"What do you mean, Jim?" and he caught her up in a loud harsh voice.

"Why do you call me Jim? Jim what?"

Caroline said, "Oh!" and backed away.

"Jim—What's the matter?"

"Jim what?"

"Aren't you well?"—That was just a whisper.

He controlled his voice.

"Tell me why you called me Jim."

"Because it's your name. Don't you know?"

"No."

"Jim darling, don't you know that you're Jim Randal?"

He went past her in a blundering sort of way—right past her and as far as the stone steps which led up to the heavy door. He sat down on the second step and leaned over his knees with both hands covering his face. It was just as if a dam had broken. All those things which had been battering against his consciousness came flooding in through the breach. He was giddy and buffeted. He sat there, and knew that he was Jim Randal, and that this was Hale Place where he had grown up. This was Hale Place, and he was Jim Randal. But of course he was Jim Randal. Who was Jim Riddell? "You're Jim Riddell, and I'm your wife." Who had said that? Nesta—Nesta Riddell. "I'm Nesta"—"I'm

Caroline" . . . . . . Nesta—Caroline—Jim . . . . Jim Riddell—Jim Randal.

He lifted his head like a man coming up out of deep water.

"I'm Jim Randal, and this is Hale Place."

Caroline was sitting on the step beside him. Her hand came out and touched his.

"Didn't you know?"

"No."

"Oh, Jim! But you know now."

"Yes." He gave her hand a squeeze. "It's awfully odd—" He stopped, laughed a little uncertainly, and let go of her.

"Odd? It makes my head go round!"

Caroline did not speak. She didn't really want to speak. She wanted to sit quite still and let the knowledge that Jim wasn't drowned soak right down into her. It was like silver water coming in with waves of joy. It was like a tide of light and happiness. She didn't feel dizzy like Jim; she felt safely, blessedly secure and fixed. Everything was right again, and Jim was here; if she put out her hand, she could touch him. But she didn't really want to put it out. Just for the moment she had all the happiness that she could hold. One drop more, and it might brim over the drain away. When he got up, she leaned her shoulder against the stone baluster which flanked the steps and watched him with shining eyes.

He walked to the edge of the grass and, turning, looked again at the house. That was just how she had seen him from her window. How long ago? Half an hour? It was very strange to think that the world could change and be quite a different world to you in half an hour.

Jim stood and looked at the house. He looked at it for a long time. Then he walked to the edge of the gravel sweep and back again. He did this several times, and just at the end a little whispering dread stirred in Caroline's mind. It was like birds talking before daylight. You never know what it is that the birds are saying, or what sort of day they are waking you to. The whisper gave Caroline this feeling, but almost before she recognized it she saw Jim coming back.

She pulled herself up by the balustrade and stood on the step above him. He said,

"Caroline, I'm in a mess."

So that was why she had begun to be afraid. She said, "What sort of a mess, Jim?"

There was a pause.

"I don't know that it's fair to tell you—in fact it's not. I'm confused still, but I do know that. You oughtn't even to be here."

"How *dreadful*!" said Caroline. "Where else ought I to be?"

"In bed—and you'd better be getting along, my dear. I don't know how you came here at all."

"Oh, I followed you. All romantic, darling—it really was. I looked out of my bower window, and you lifted up the latch and came into the garden and stood looking up. And I knew you at once, so I followed you, and about half way I began to think supposing it wasn't you at all, or supposing it was a grimly ghost like the ballad says—so it was most awfully, awfully brave of me to keep on. I've never really liked even hide-and-seek in the dark, and in some ways moonlight's worse, because almost anything might be a grimly ghost by moonlight. And if you think, after that, I'm going back to bed without hearing all about everything, well, you've just got to think again, darling— and quite *differently*."

This was a Caroline he knew—a sweet, imperious, gently obstinate Caroline, with a laugh in her voice and a coaxing hand on his arm. Since she could speak at all he had been "Jim darling." He said heavily,

"All the same, you'd better go."

"As if I would! Jim—tell me—what's the matter?"

"Go home, Caroline!"

"*You're* home."

He pulled away from her roughly.

"Don't talk nonsense!" Then, on a changed note, "Caroline—go!"

The laugh went out of her voice as she said,

"You know I won't go. You *know* I won't."

"I know you ought to."

"We ought to do lots of things that we don't do—lots, and lots, and lots of things. And this is one of the things that I'm not going to do—not if the Prime Minister, and the Archbishop of Canterbury, and Robert Arbuthnot all stood in a row and said go. Darling—wouldn't it be funny if they did? And I should just blow them each a nice kiss—you know, the sort you put on your palm and push up to the top of your middle finger like this." She pushed a kiss delicately into position and blew it at him. "And then I should say, 'The answer is in the negative'; or in other words, 'I'll be Jericho'd if I do!' I've put it very tactfully because of the Archbishop, though I don't suppose he's half so easily shocked as Robert is."

She came down from the steps and slid a hand through his arm. Her voice dropped on to a deep loving note.

"It's no *use*, darling—you've got to tell me. Better get it over. You can't make me go."

"I ought to be able to make you."

"Come and sit down," said Caroline seriously. "Now, Jim—what have you been doing, and why did you let me think you had been drowned?" Her voice went down into despairing depths.

"Did you?"

"Yes—in the *Alice Arden*. And there was an S.O.S. about a man in hospital at Elston who had lost his memory, and I went to see if it was you, and they said—Jim, they said that he had just been fetched away by his wife. That wasn't you?"

"Yes."

"How could it be you?"

"It was."

"How could it be?"

Caroline felt as if everything had begun to shake a little, like a reflection in water when someone throws a stone into it. Everything that had been so safe and steady had become no more than a shaken picture in troubled water.

Jim was silent. He did not know of any answer to her question.

She went on in a trembling voice.

"I went to Ledlington. The sister said you had my letter—a bit of it—the bit with my name—with Caroline—so I went. But it wasn't you, Jim—it wasn't you."

"You went to Ledlington?"

"I found her. She dropped a bill, and the sister gave it to me, so I found her. Her name was Riddell—Mrs Riddell. She was the most horrible woman. But it was her husband who was in the hospital at Elston—it wasn't you."

Jim did not speak. He looked through the moonlight to the dark trees. Caroline gazed at him with wide, frightened eyes.

"It was her husband," she said in a whisper. "It couldn't be you—you're not her husband."

He spoke then in a loud, harsh voice.

"She says I am."

Caroline felt the words strike her like stones, like sharp, heavy stones. They hurt so much and weighed so heavily that she could not get her breath. *Jim* had hurt her like that. It was like the most dreadful nightmare. She tried to speak, and could not make any sound. And then all at once she heard Jim's voice, sharp with alarm.

"Caroline—don't look like that!"

Caroline got her breath with a gasp.

"Why did you say it? You oughtn't—you mustn't! Jim darling!"

He caught her wrists and held them in a hard, heavy grip.

"Pull yourself together! Do you hear? Oh yes, you can if you like. You're just making it more difficult for us both."

She had been straining away from him, her voice broken and her whole body shaking, but at his last words she went quiet and limp. He let go of her, and she drooped forward. It was just as if some spring had failed. She said in a little lifeless voice,

"Tell me."

A vapour, that was hardly cloud, had passed across the moon. The air was dark between them; he could not see her face. She leaned her head on her hand and waited. Her silence made her seem a long way off.

He began to speak in a strained, level voice.

"I'm going to tell you—but it isn't easy, because I don't know where I am. You see, the last thing I remember is landing at Liverpool on the first of July. I remember getting into the train for London, and after that there's a gap until I woke up in Ledlington."

"*What*?" said Caroline. All the droop went out of her. She sat bolt upright and stared at him through the dusk.

"I was told I'd been rescued from the *Alice Arden*—found on a ledge on the cliffs after she broke up, and taken to the Elston cottage hospital. I was told that my wife had fetched me away."

"Who told you?"

"She did."

"That Riddell woman?"

"Yes."

"But why?"

"She showed me a marriage certificate."

"Yours?"

"She said so."

"And you believed her?"

"I suppose I did—yes, of course I did. I didn't know who I was or how I'd got there—I didn't know anything except what she told me. She said my name was Jim Riddell, and that hers was Nesta Riddell. Her brother and sister-in-law said the same thing. She said we'd been married at the Grove Road registry office. She showed me the certificate. Of course I believed her."

"But it isn't *true*!" said Caroline in a warm, indignant voice.

He was silent.

"Jim—it *isn't* true!"

He said, "I can't remember anything after the first of July."

"Not anything?"

She saw him wince. He said,

"Bit of things broken up. . . . . It's worse than not remembering at all—much worse."

"You wrote to me on the seventh of July," said Caroline quickly.

"Where from?"

"London. But you didn't give any address—you said to write to your bank."

"And you wrote?"

"I wrote, and Aunt Grace wrote. I was staying with her at Craigellachie. She asked you to come up, and you didn't answer for three whole days—and then you didn't write to me, only to Aunt Grace."

"What did I say?"

"You said you might be able to come later on. And then you didn't write again till a fortnight ago, and you said you might be able to get off on the seventh if Aunt Grace could have you, and you would take a steamer up the coast. And then—and then—you never came."

"That was the last you heard?"

"Yes. Don't you remember anything about it?"

"No."

"You said you remembered—bits."

He shook his head impatiently.

"I don't remember writing to you at all. The things I remember—" He broke off. Vividly before his mind there appeared, like the broken bits of kaleidoscope, the things that he remembered—a decanter and two glasses; a syphon with the light striking through it; Elmer Van Berg lifting his glass; the bubbles rising in it—tiny bubbles racing upwards to the brim. That was one sharply coloured piece.

The sweat came out on his forehead. He said, quick and uneven,

"I remember drinking with Elmer Van Berg."

XIV

THE VAPOUR PASSED FROM BEFORE THE MOON, AND HE SAW Caroline like her own ghost, looking at him with wide, startled eyes. She could not have told why the words startled her so—"I remember drinking with Elmer Van Berg." Why shouldn't he remember it? What was there to startle her in that?

He went on speaking.

"There wasn't anything about that in the papers—I read them all this morning. But the tray and the glasses must have been there."

A light nervous shudder passed over Caroline.

"The papers?" she said.

He nodded.

"I read them all. The tray and the glasses must have been there when they found Elmer."

"Jim! What are you saying?"

He said, "I wonder if they've got my finger-prints."

Caroline flung herself towards him and caught his hand.

"Jim—I'm frightened. What are you saying?"

"I'm telling you what you wanted to know. That's one of the bits I remember—drinking with Elmer Van Berg the night he was shot. Do you want to hear any more?"

Caroline's hand clung to his.

"Yes," she said.

He laughed.

"You won't like it. You'd better go home."

"Tell me."

She felt his hand twitch. His voice changed.

"It's not like remembering really—it's like seeing a lot of little pictures—broken. There's one of a fog. And I can hear someone talking—I don't know whether it's me or someone else. It's beastly. The voice keeps saying, 'Like a kid's green beads—no one knows but me—no one knows where they are—a kid's green beads—' " He stopped. She felt the muscles rise as he clenched his hand.

She came nearer, pressing against him as if she could protect him from this something which threatened. Whatever it was, he was Jim, and hers. She had a passionate conviction that she could keep him safe whatever happened.

"There's another bit about the emeralds. I can see them under the light. I can't see Elmer—only his hand under the light, and the emeralds hanging from it—eight of them, with little pearl chains between them—'like a kid's green beads.' "

Caroline put her arms around him.

"Don't, darling!"

"Do you think I shot him?"

"No!" said Caroline, in a quick, fierce voice.

"She said I did—to get the emeralds."

"That woman?"

"Yes, Nesta. She said Jim Riddell shot him and took the emeralds. She was in it too. And he hid the emeralds and went off up to Glasgow by the *Alice Arden*—only he never got there, because she was wrecked."

"What has that got to do with you?" said Caroline, still in that new fierce voice.

"She says I'm Jim Riddell."

"You're *not*! Why should you be?"

"I don't know—Caroline, I don't *know*." She felt a shudder pass over him. "If I could remember—but I can't remember."

"You will."

He was silent. Her words went echoing through the empty spaces of his mind: "Remember—remember—you will remember." They repeated themselves endlessly and died away. Suppose he didn't remember. There was a six weeks gap in his life. Suppose he never remembered what had happened in those six weeks. Suppose he did remember. Suppose he had really shot Elmer Van Berg. . . . . .

"You *didn't*!" said Caroline. She pressed against him and laid her cheek to his. "Jim—*darling*—don't go all away by yourself. Talk to me. We'll find a way out."

He put her arms away from him.

"Suppose there's no way out. Suppose I did it."

Caroline sat back a little. She put her hands in her lap and lifted her face to the sky. She had a clear, untroubled look that was very comforting. She spoke softly and steadily, as if she were reasoning with a child.

"Why *should* you have shot him, darling?"

"I don't know—I was there—I remember drinking with him—"

"You wouldn't have shot him without a reason. You don't just go about shooting people for nothing—nobody does."

"The emeralds are not exactly nothing."

"That's rubbish!" The words were touched with a light scorn.

"Is it?"

"Yes, it is—you know it is, really, Jim. Do you remember anything at all about the Nesta woman?"

"No."

"Well, wouldn't you have, if you had married her?"

"I don't know." His voice sounded hopeless.

"She didn't touch a chord? I mean, sometimes you meet a total stranger and you don't know where they come from or who they are, but something goes click inside you and you feel as if you knew them. You didn't feel anything like that?"

He laughed grimly.

"I loathed her," he said.

"So did I," said Caroline happily. "Well, there you are—if you loathed her, you wouldn't have married her."

There was rather a horrid pause. Then he said,

"Perhaps I loathed her *because* I married her."

Caroline cried out quickly.

"Oh, you didn't!"

The silence fell again. She had to break it herself.

"Jim, listen—I've got an idea. You can look up your signature in that registry office. No, it's *not* your signature—it *can't* be! It's Jim Riddell's signature. You can look it up, and then you'll know that it isn't yours."

"Or that it is."

"It *isn't*! You can take the first train to-morrow—"

"That's just what I can't do."

"Why can't you?"

"Because I gather that the police are looking for me."

"*You*?"

"Jim Riddell—or Jim Randal—I don't know which. I saw a poster as I left Ledlington. 'Van Berg Case—Important Clue—Man Wanted by Police.'"

"Why should it be you?" said Caroline.

"My dear, I was there—we've got to face that. I was there, and I saw the emeralds. I don't think I'm in a position to walk into that registry office and ask to see the entry of Jim Riddell's marriage."

"I could," said Caroline quickly.

"You mustn't get mixed up in it."

"There won't be anything to mix me—the registrar won't know me from Adam."

He put his head in his hands for a minute, trying to get through the dull fatigue which clogged his thoughts.

"I don't want you to have anything to do with it. I'm too tired to think properly—but you're not to get mixed up with this—you oughtn't to be here."

She put her arms around him again.

"You'll come home with me—I'll make you a lovely bed on the sofa."

"No—I can't."

"Because of us, or because of you?"

"Both. I'll get in here somehow. I shall be all right."

Caroline laughed.

"The back door key is under a loose stone in the yard—Mrs Ledger always puts it there. She comes up once a week to light fires and air the house. Robert said she'd better when he heard you were coming home. She says the key is too 'dratted heavy to traipse up and down with.' This was one of her days, so the kitchen will be nice and warm.''

Jim felt a curious thrill of anticipation as they skirted the house and came into the dark yard behind it. There was no moonlight here. The shadow of the house lay across it like a fold of black cloth.

Caroline caught his hand and drew him lightly on.

Presently she was feeling with her foot. A stone tilted. She stooped, and came up with the key. She put it in his hand, cold and heavy, and he opened the door.

Whatever else he had forgotten, he had not forgotten the ways of the house in which he had grown up. He took Caroline by the arm and walked along the pitchdark passage to the kitchen without so much as a false step.

Caroline found matches and lit a candle end. Mrs Ledger had stuck it into one of the old brass candlesticks. The yellow light showed the brass turned bronze with streaks of verdigris. The kitchen was warm and pleasant. There was ash still hot in the range, and a line full of blankets had been wound up on a pulley and hung just clear of their heads.

"They look like ghosts," said Caroline under her breath— "sheeted ghosts. I don't think I like them very much."

But Jim was pulling them down.

"They'll make a good bed," he said.

Caroline gave a faint shriek.

"I saw two cockroaches! You can't sleep here!"

"I'll go into the study."

"There's nothing for you to eat. I'll run home and get you something."

"I bought things in Ledlington. I've got plenty left."

"Oh—" said Caroline. She stood a minute; then she said, speaking rather fast, "Could you get along till tomorrow evening?"

"Oh yes."

"Because I don't think I'd better come up in the daytime— someone might see me. People have most awfully sharp eyes when you don't want them to. Will you be all right till then?"

"Of course I shall."

"All right, then I'd better go." She came up to him and

leaned towards him across the blankets. "Jim—you'll be here? You won't go away—will you? Swear?"

"All right."

"You won't go without seeing me? You won't just vanish? Because I couldn't bear it. You *won't*?"

He shook his head.

Caroline flung her arms around his neck, held him for a moment in a tingling clasp, and ran out of the kitchen and along the black passage. Her footsteps rang on the stone, and the door shut.

XV

CAROLINE CAUGHT THE SEVEN-THIRTY TO LONDON. ALL the time she and Jim were getting into Hale Place, whilst he was pulling down the blankets and she was saying someone might see her if she came back by day, she was concocting a secret plan. In the end she ran away because she was afraid that he would guess what she meant to do. She thought he would have guessed if he hadn't been stupid with fatigue. She thought he was like a man half drugged. His mind moved slowly; he had to push it to make it move at all. That was why he hadn't guessed; and it was lucky for her, because if he had guessed, he would have tried to stop her, and she meant to go.

It was past two o'clock when she came back to the cottage. The gate was unlatched and the door stood wide open as she had left it. If Pansy Ann had only known! To Pansy there was always a burglar round the next corner.

Caroline undressed and lay down under her great-grandmother's embroidered quilt, but she did not sleep. She was too flooded with joy to sleep. Her hands still kept the touch of Jim's hands; her ears still rang with all the sounds of his voice. She had no time to fall asleep.

At six she dressed, went tiptoe down the stairs, made tea, and boiled herself an egg. Then she wrote on the slate, "Gone to town," and propped it up against the bowl of fruit in the middle of the gate-leg table; after which she set out to walk four miles across the fields to Hinton, where she caught the train.

She had the carriage to herself as far as Ledlington, where it filled up. She wondered what she would do if Nesta Riddell were to get in. How dare she say Jim was her husband? It was the most unbelievable, impudent thing. Caroline tripped up over her own words. Unbelievable meant not to be believed. But you couldn't believe that a woman would claim a man for her husband when he wasn't her husband. If you just couldn't believe it . . . . . What had Nesta Riddell done? She had gone to the hospital and taken Jim away. She had said he was her husband. This wasn't unbelievable, because she had done it. The unbelievable thing was that she should claim a stranger. But she *had* claimed a stranger. Had she? If it was unbelievable, then Caroline didn't believe it. Then he wasn't a stranger. Where did this take her. She had a terrified sense of having betrayed herself and Jim.

She pushed the word that had tripped her right out of her mind and shut the door on it. She hadn't got to account for what Nesta Riddell had done. She had only to go to the Grove Road registry office and see James Riddell's name in a stranger's writing. That would prove that Nesta was lying, and that Jim was free. It was the easiest thing in the world, and she felt that she couldn't bear to see Jim again until she had the proof that it was not he who had signed the register as Nesta Riddell's husband.

The train jogged along. It stopped at every station, but after Ledlington the carriage was too full to take in any more passengers. There was an old woman with a string bag full of vegetables and an enormous sheaf of cottage flowers—crimson phlox, red and yellow single dahlias, full-blown cabbage roses, and clove carnations which scented the whole compartment. She had a crushed black straw hat on the back of her head, a black Cashmere dress, and a thick black cloth coat. Her face was broad and red under scanty wisps of grey hair. She was very hot, because she lived two miles out of Ledlington and had hurried to catch the train. She fanned herself with a cabbage leaf, and as soon as she had got her breath she began to talk, first about the weather, and then about the Van Berg case. Three girls on the opposite seat, flimsily dressed slips of things with salmon-coloured stockings, berets, and magenta lips went on whispering and giggling together whilst she told them how the snails were over-running her garden from one end to the other, and how she had set a slug trap—" And if I was to tell you what I caught, you wouldn't believe me."

A shy young man who was fidgeting with an unlighted cigarette looked out of the window. The Miss Borings, who kept a genteel wool-shop in Mickleham Street, sat primly side by side in their neat, dowdy blue serge coats and skirts. They were identical tucked muslin blouses with high collars and rolled gold collar-supporters, and twin hats of dark blue straw with plain black ribbons. The schoolboy next to them was immersed in the last Edgar Wallace. The old gentleman with the beard went on filling his pipe. And the young married couple opposite Caroline continued to hold one another's hands.

Snails have no charm to unite a carriage full of strangers in a common bond of interest. But no sooner had the stout woman pronounced the name Van Berg than everyone had something to say.

"It's a queer thing they don't seem to catch the man that shot Mr Van Berg," she said, and the schoolboy emerged from his thriller with a jerk.

"They say they've got a clue," he began.

"That doesn't mean very much," said the old man. He tapped his pipe. "The sort of thing they say to keep the public quiet—like throwing a bone to a dog."

The girl with the large blue eyes rolled them at the shy young man and giggled.

The stout woman fanned herself.

"I was up at the Hall yesterday—"

"Packham Hall?" said both Miss Borings together.

The stout woman nodded.

"Cook's my brother's second wife's cousin-in-law, and I took her over a couple of pots of honey. The shop stuff's that watered down she don't relish it, so I took her some of mine—never been before where they didn't keep their own bees, and don't like it. And then to have a murder, or next door to it, well, she don't think she'll stay—such an upset, and not what she's used to. Why, when she heard the shot, she come over that queer she couldn't have got out of bed, not if it had been the house of fire. 'Mrs Rodgers,' she says—that being my name—'Mrs Rodgers, I give you my solemn identical word, I just pulled the clothes over my head and waited to see if I was going to be murdered in my bed.' She don't look her right colour yet."

"I don't know how I should feel if I was to hear someone being shot in the middle of the night," said the young married woman.

"I know what you'd *do*," said her husband—"pinch me, same as you're doing now."

The girl giggled, and the Miss Borings coughed.

"Ah!" said Mrs Rodgers. "It isn't everyone that's got someone to pinch. I'm a widow meself, and so's Mrs Henry that I've been telling you about. Her 'usband was a p'liceman, so it doesn't put her about having the police in and out and all over the place, as you might say—and maybe she's got told a thing or two as she wouldn't have got told if it weren't for her 'usband's official position."

Everyone leaned forward a little. The shy young man burst into speech.

"Did she tell you who they suspected?"

Mrs Rodgers shook her head.

"Were there any finger-prints?" said the schoolboy. "They'll get him if there were."

"Ah!" said Mrs Rodgers darkly. "Well, I don't know as I ought to say, but seeing as we're all friends here—" She paused, fanning herself.

Caroline caught the inside of her lips between her teeth. Her hands held each other hard. A general murmur encouraged Mrs Rodgers to proceed.

"Well, it's something as hasn't got into the papers—I can tell you that—and everyone in the house told not to say a word. They'd have kep' them from knowing if so be they could, but when there's a tray and glasses took for finger-prints, there's going to be talk in the servants' hall whether or no."

"Ah—" said the old man with the beard.

Caroline's grip relaxed a little. She knew this already; it was what Jim had told her. But then it meant—it meant he had remembered right.

Mrs Rodgers sunk her voice to a sepulchral whisper.

"There was a tray with whisky and soda and two glasses in Mr Van Berg's study, and the police took 'em for finger-prints. And Mrs Henry says to me, 'That wasn't no plain straightforward burglar,' she says. 'If a burglar comes in on a gentleman in the middle of the night, they don't sit down and have drinks together—not much they don't,' she says."

"Were the glasses full or empty?" said the shy young man.

"Empty down to the last drop," said the Mrs Rodgers. "And what's more—but there, p'raps I didn't ought to repeat that."

"I'm sure none of us will let it go any further," said the elder Miss Boring.

"Well, I don't know as I'd better, seeing as Mrs Henry wouldn't ha' told me if it hadn't been for me overhearing what passed between her and Mrs Van Berg's maid."

Caroline's heart began to beat hard and fast. What was she going to hear? She felt as if at any moment this fat good-natured woman might say something that couldn't ever be unsaid again—something dangerous, something that might hurt Jim. It was just as if she could see the shadow of something dreadful coming round the corner.

Everyone was begging Mrs Rodgers to go on.

"Well, I don't know as I ought. That's the worst of talking—you run on, and then you can't take it back again.

A sister's niece of mine lost her young man that way—said something she was sorry for next moment, and off he went and married the barmaid at The Lion. And a nice life she led him—more temper in her little finger than poor Lizzie'd got in her whole body. Lor bless me if we haven't got to Meade already!—and perhaps just as well, or I might have said more than I ought. Now, I wonder if anyone 'ud be good enough to hand my basket out after me. It's a deal easier to get out backwards when you come to me size.''

The train jerked and clanked to a standstill. The shy young man opened the door. Mrs Rodgers backed out, took her basket, and bade the carriage at large an affable farewell.

Without having thought of it beforehand, Caroline found herself saying, "Please may I pass?" She had to say that because the schoolboy was standing right in the doorway. He moved as the guard came along to shut the door.

Caroline said in a soft breathless voice, "I'm getting out," and jumped down on to the platform just as the train began to move. She didn't wait for the guard to scold her.

Mrs Rodgers was already giving her ticket. Caroline ran after her and caught her up just outside the station where Meade Hill runs steeply up between hedges full of bramble and elder.

Mrs Rodgers stared at her in astonishment, and Caroline realized that she had no idea what she was going to say. How could she when she hadn't even known that she was going to get out of the train? One minute she had just been sitting there, and the next minute she was saying, "Please, may I pass?" and jumping down from the moving train. It must have come over her suddenly that she simply couldn't let Mrs Rodgers go, and now that she had caught her up she didn't know what to say. She said the first thing that came into her head.

"Can I help you with your basket?"

Mrs Rodgers looked her up and down.

"What's a young lady like you want to carry my basket for?"

"I'm going your way."

"And how do you know what way I'm going, miss?"

Caroline looked rather as if she had been caught stealing jam. Her lips trembled into a smile.

"I r-ran after you," she said.

Mrs Rodgers set down her basket in the road and nodded.

"Honesty's the best policy. What brought you after me? For by the look of you you hadn't any thoughts of getting out here."

"No," said Caroline. "I should truly like to carry your basket." She picked it up, and they began to mount the hill.

"And that's what you came after me for, I'll be bound!"

"No—I came after you because I wanted to talk to you."

"That's straight anyway. And what have you got to say?"

"I didn't want to say anything. I wanted you to tell me what Mrs Henry told you."

Mrs Rodgers swung her ample black skirts in silence. They just cleared the dust of the road. Her colour deepened as she climbed.

Caroline wished that the road was flat. She wished Mrs Rodgers would say something. She wished that she herself had said something different. In the railway carriage Mrs Rodgers had been a jolly chattering old thing; she had fairly oozed good nature and gossip. What had happened to her all of a sudden? She said, on a quick caught breath,

"Mrs Rodgers—"

Mrs Rodgers turned a streaming crimson face upon her.

"Talk on this 'ill, I can't," she panted, and Caroline had to get what comfort she could from that. It wasn't very much.

The morning was muggy, with mist hanging about, and the heat and the hill might account for Mrs Rodgers' blank face and drawn brows—or they might not.

At the top of the hill there was a stile, and on the step of the stile Mrs Rodgers seated herself and proceeded to get her breath. Caroline stood before her with the basket and felt her courage slip and slip away.

"Well?" said Mrs Rodgers at last.

Caroline looked at her imploringly.

Mrs Rodgers fanned herself.

"Well, since we're 'ere, we'd best have it out."

Caroline spoke before all her courage left her.

"Will you please tell me what Mrs Henry said?"

"And why?"

There was something portentous in the slow, heavy voice. Not a jolly voice, not a good-natured voice; more like the voice a judge might use when he asked whether you had anything to say before sentence was passed.

"I thought I'd like to know," said Caroline rather faintly.

"And why?" said Mrs Rodgers in an even slower and more portentous manner.

To her horror, Caroline felt as if she was going to cry. How awful to cry in a public lane at eight o'clock in the morning, with a fat woman in black cashmere looking at you!

She began to speak quickly.

"You were telling us as the train stopped, and I—I wanted to know. You were telling everyone in the carriage."

Mrs Rodgers nodded.

"What's taken light can be told light. 'Twasn't nothing to them, no more than it wasn't to me. Stands to reason everybody'll talk about a murder—and this is as good as one by all accounts."

"Then won't you tell me?"

"I dunno," said Mrs Rodgers. She pursed her lips together and cast an odd look at Caroline. "Do you know where I'm going?" she said with apparent irrelevance. "No, I don't suppose you do. Well, I'm walking across the fields by this here footpath to Stowbury to spend the day with my sister, Harriet Brown, that used to be Harriet Welsh."

Caroline's colour changed sharply. She had the horrible sensation of having walked into a trap. That she should have followed her old nurse's sister was a piece of the most devastating bad luck. Perhaps she didn't know her—*perhaps*—

Mrs Rodgers nodded again.

"I knew you at once, miss, though I could see as you didn't know me. You haven't changed a mite since Harty 'ud bring you in for a cup of tea and some of my mint honey. I've put on a bit since those days, so I made sure you didn't know me. But I knew you. 'That's Miss Caroline Leigh,' I says to myself, and when you come running after me I got a turn, and all the way up the 'ill I been trying to make up my mind what I was going to say."

"Mrs Rodgers—"

"I'm a-going to tell you what Mrs Henry told me, and I'm not a-going to ask you why you want to know, because maybe I know already and maybe I don't—and anyway least said, soonest mended."

"Yes?" said Caroline in a whisper.

"What I said in the train is neither here nor there. There isn't a servant up at the Hall as don't know there was a tray and glasses in the study the night Mr Van Berg was shot, and the housemaid see with her own eyes how the police took the finger-prints—a clapper-tongued woman if there ever was one—so there ain't no secrets there. No—it was the butler told Mrs Henry what I'm a-telling you. They're keeping company, and going to be married come Christmas, and he told her and she told me, being, as I said, my brother Jim's second wife's cousin-in-law through her late 'usband, Albert Henry, being Maria's cousin, and one way and another I've know her, girl and woman, the last forty years."

"What did she tell you?"

"When they had finished taking the finger-prints and all the rest of it, the inspector he sees all the servants separate, and then he has the butler back and he says, 'I understand,' he says, 'as Mr Van Berg kep' a book with all his friends' finger-prints in it,' he says. 'That's right,' says Jackson— that's the butler's name. 'Well,' says the inspector, 'I wants to see that book.' And Jackson, he says, 'It's always a-laying on Mr Van Berg's table, and whenever he has a visitor he gets him to make his mark and sign his name.' And the inspector laughs and says, 'Very handy for us, Mr Jackson'—they being on friendly terms along of Mrs Henry— Albert Henry 'aving been a police sergeant, like I said."

Caroline's eyes widened.

"And then it wasn't so handy after all," said Mrs Rodgers— "for lo and be'old the book wasn't nowheres to be seen."

The blood came back into Caroline's cheeks with a rush. She said,

"Oh!"

Mrs Rodgers waved her hand as one who commands silence.

"And where was it?" she demanded.

Caroline caught her breath.

"Pushed right down be'ind all the books at the back of the bookshelf. They went on looking till they'd found it. And then what do you think?"

"I don't know," said Caroline, trembling. Mrs Rodgers looked at her with a kind of awful pity.

"There was a page tore out," she said.

Perhaps it was because she had been awake all night, perhaps it was because she had had a dreadful picture in her own mind of a finger-print with Jim's name signed underneath it, but at these words, she saw the stile with Mrs Rodgers sitting on it tilt at the strangest angle; the hedge swung across the road and back again. You can't stand up straight when things begin to slip and tilt and slide like that. Caroline felt the grit of the road against her knees and the palms of her hands. And then Mrs Rodgers was shaking her by the shoulder and saying something. But Caroline never knew what it was, because she had fainted.

XVI

SHE WAS REALLY ONLY UNCONSCIOUS FOR ABOUT A MINUTE, but it was long enough for Mrs Rodgers to have laid her down flat. She had got a new cabbage-leaf out of the basket and was fanning her with it. She looked hotter than ever, her face like a very red sun coming up in a fog.

Caroline opened her eyes wide. There seemed to be a good deal of fog, but it was getting less. She got up on her elbow, and was relieved to find that things had stopped tilting. Then she remembered why she had fainted—she had been so horribly afraid that Mrs Rodgers was going to say that the police had found Jim's finger-prints. Jim would have been sure to have made his mark in Mrs Van Berg's book. A page had been torn out. Was it that page? Who had torn it out?

"Better keep laying down a bit," said Mrs Rodgers.

"No—I'm all right—I am really." She sat up and leaned against the stile.

Mrs Rodgers was kneeling on the stubbly grass. She sat back on her heels, fanning herself now instead of Caroline.

"Who tore out the page?" said Caroline. She didn't feel as if she could wait a single moment before she asked that question.

"Who do you suppose?" said Mrs Rodgers.

"I don't know."

"Who would tear it out, if it wasn't the one who shot Mr Van Berg? It stands to reason he wouldn't go away and leave his finger-prints there all ready for the police, and his name signed to them—would he? That's what I said to Mrs Henry. And Jackson, he says, 'There's only Mr Van Berg's friends in that book.' Quite shocked he was. 'Then,' I says, 'it was one of his friends as shot him, Mr Jackson?' You're not feeling faint again, are you, miss?"

Caroline bit her lip. There was something wrong about the way Mrs Rodgers was arguing, but she couldn't quite get hold of it—only there was something wrong. She thought of Jim, and she said with a rush,

"Oh, he *wouldn't*! A friend *wouldn't*!"

Mrs Rodgers shook her head.

"Nobody can't say that. Folks get quarrelling, and you can't say what'll happen. But Mrs Henry, she says, and she holds to it very strong, 'What 'ud be the good of his tearing the finger-prints out of the book and leaving the glass he'd drunk out of fairly plastered with 'em? It wouldn't 'ave took 'em 'arf a minute to 'ave wiped them off,' she says—and there's something in that." She got up and dusted her knees with the cabbage leaf. "I can't sit on my 'eels like I could when I was a gel. Fourteen stone's fourteen stone—and I shouldn't wonder if it wasn't fifteen now." She sat down on the stile again.

A little colour came back into Caroline's cheeks. That was it—that was what she had been trying to get hold of. If it had been Jim who had torn the page out of the book, then why hadn't he wiped his glass? Everyone knows about finger-prints nowadays. He hadn't wiped his glass because he hadn't anything to hide. He hadn't shot Elmer Van Berg.

She knelt up by Mrs Rodgers and laid a hand on her knee.

"In the train you said—"

Mrs Rodgers looked glum.

"And I'd better have held my tongue. No need to tell me that."

"Oh, I didn't mean that—I didn't truly. Oh, dear Mrs Rodgers—I didn't mean anything like that."

Mrs Rodgers relaxed a little.

"In for a penny, in for a pound. What did I say?"

"Something about Mrs Van Berg's maid."

"A French 'ussy!" said Mrs Rodgers. "And if Mrs Van Berg 'ad 'arf an idea of the things that 'ussy's been 'inting—because 'ints is 'er line, and as Mrs Henry says to me, 'If there's one thing despisabler than another, it's an 'inting woman. Say what you've got to say and 'ave done with it,' Mrs Henry says, 'and then you know where you are—but when it comes to 'inting and prying and listening at doors and reading other people's letters, there's no one don't know where they are. Not that it's only foreigners that's given to it, for that there Miss Bussell that's housekeeper at the Hall she's the worse of the two, and the dear knows how Mrs Henry's stood it, for I wouldn't.' "

Caroline patted Mrs Rodgers' knee.

"What did the maid say?"

"Miss Louise, they call her. Well, she don't *say* nothing. That's just her aggravatingness—she'll 'int and 'int until you're sick, sore and sorry, and then she'll slip out of the whole thing and pretend she never said nothing."

"What does she hint?"

Mrs Rodgers gave a kind of snort.

"*'Int*? She's as good as said it wasn't no secret to her what name was tore out, and then went back on it."

Caroline looked up into Mrs Rodgers' red face with the look of a frightened child.

"How could she know what name had been torn out?"

"There isn't much goes on in the house as she *don't* know—picking, and prying, and 'inting! 'Orrid, I call it! Letting on she knows things about Mrs Van Berg too!"

"What sort of things?"

"She's a wicked 'ussy," said Mrs Rodgers, "and I wouldn't repeat what she says, if it weren't for a warning. You might know someone as wanted warning, or you mightn't. If you don't, there's no harm done, and if you do—well you was Harty's baby, and I took to you myself when you came to tea and thanked me so pretty for the honeycomb."

"It was lovely honey," said Caroline. "You were very, very kind. *Please*, Mrs Rodgers, tell me as much as you can."

Mrs Rodgers nodded.

"You'd a pretty coaxing way, and you've got it yet. I'll tell you what I can. Now, my dear—whether the police have got wind of it or not, I can't say, but what that 'ussy keeps 'inting is just this, that her mistress, Mrs Van Berg, knows a sight more than she lets on. It's all 'ints and no plain speech, but that's what it comes to—that Mr Van Berg found out something that he wasn't meant to find out, and that's why he was shot. 'The emeralds—' she says in her 'inting way, 'can't they be 'idden? Can't they be a fine excuse?' she says. 'Oh 'eavens!' she says. 'You make me laugh, with your emeralds!' she says. 'A gentleman quarrels with another gentleman about a lady and shoots him—what a good idea to hide the emeralds and say a thief has done it!' she says. And when Mrs Henry and me presses her, she says she is talking about a story she has been reading in a magazine—and how I kep' my hands off her, I don't know and I can't say. And she laughs and goes out of the room, and Mrs Henry says to me, 'Mrs Rodgers,' she says, 'if that's not an evil-speaking, lying, slandering 'ussy, then I never learned my catechism,' she says."

Caroline got up a little uncertainly. She held to the

cross-bar of the stile and leaned against it. She wanted to get away from Mrs Rodgers before she said anything more. Mrs Rodgers had said too much already. If she said any more, Caroline was afraid she might cry out—say Jim's name—say that it wasn't true—that it couldn't be true. Jim wasn't in love with Susie Van Berg—it couldn't be true that he was, or that he had quarrelled with Elmer Van Berg and shot him, and hidden away the emeralds to make it look like a burglary. It simply couldn't be true. She must get away quickly before she began most passionately to deny it.

She said, "There'll be another train—I must catch it."

Mrs Rodgers got up too.

"To be sure! There's the eight fifty-seven—but you'll have to hurry."

Caroline took her hand and squeezed it.

"You've been so kind! I do thank you so much. You'll give Nanna my love—won't you?"

Mrs Rodgers nodded. She watched Caroline turn away and begin to go down the hill. Then she took a step towards the stile, but almost in the act of taking it she swung about like a boat when the current catches it. She called,

"Miss Caroline! Miss Caroline!"

And Caroline came back. She didn't want to come back, but she came.

"I mustn't miss my train," she said.

"There's time," said Mrs Rodgers, and took her by the sleeve.

Caroline turned cold with dread of what she was going to hear.

"Miss Caroline—" said Mrs Rodgers.

Caroline's eyes besought her.

"My dear, you'd best know and ha' done with it. That torn out page—"

"Oh, no!" said Caroline. "*No!*"

"You'd best know it, my dear. Mrs Henry's no 'inter, and it's what she seen with her own eyes. She took pertickler notice, because there wasn't no name signed on that page."

"No name?"

"No name, my dear—nothing but the finger-prints and

two great big initials getting on for a couple of inches high. She took pertickler notice, and when the book was found pushed down behind the book-case like I told you, she took a look at it, and that there identical page was gone. I s'pose I didn't ought to tell you what the initials was, but what's the good of baking the bread if you don't take it out of the oven?''

Caroline tried to pull her sleeve away, but she couldn't. She tried to say, ''Don't tell me,'' but she couldn't speak. Mrs Rodgers' voice boomed in her ears.

''Mrs Henry won't talk unless she's asked, and it's not for me to say whether she'll be asked or no, but if so be she is, she's bound to tell the truth—not that she or anyone else around these parts 'ud want to get a young gentleman that was well liked, and his family respected, into trouble, but there's a name that 'as been mentioned, and Mrs Henry's own nephew—Willie Bowman, that's been his caddy at golf many and many a time afore he went off to foreign parts— Willie seen him in the drive getting on for midnight, and hasn't told no one, only his aunt and me. 'And what were you doing Willie?' she says, and of course he hadn't got a word to say, she knowing same as everyone else that he's carrying on with that flighty piece, Gladys Garrett, down at the Cricketer's Arms.''

Caroline's head swam. Through a jumbled whirl of irrelevant anecdote something horrible advanced upon her. She wanted to run away, but she couldn't.

Mrs Rodgers dropped her voice to a penetrating whisper.

''It was Jim Randal as Willie seen—and the initials on the tore out page was J.R.''

Caroline's mouth made a soundless ''Oh!'' There was no sound, because she did not seem to have any breath. She pulled away from Mrs Rodgers and ran down the hill, as if by running she could get away from Jim's name.

XVII

THE CLOCK OF ST MARY MAGDALENE'S CHURCH STRUCK half past twelve as Caroline turned into Grove Road. The things that Mrs Rodgers had told her were all locked away in a dark secret cupboard at the back of her mind. She wasn't going to let herself look at them or think about them until she and Jim could look at them together. What she had got to do now was to be sensible and practical and business-like. She had to prove from the entry in the register that it wasn't Jim who had married that horrible Nesta woman on July 25th. It stood to reason that it wasn't Jim, but she had got to prove it. Well, one glance at the register would do that, because she would know Jim's writing anywhere, and she was quite sure that the entry wouldn't be in Jim's writing.

She found the office quite easily. Why did anyone ever get married in a registry office? It was the most depressing place, with linoleum on the floor, a bench against the wall, and an air of gloom. A faint but distinct smell of disinfect-ant was the last depressing touch.

An elderly clerk inquired Caroline's business. He had a pale plump face, and reminded her of one of those fish which slap slowly to and fro behind the plate glass of an aquarium. The light in the office was almost as opaque as water, and he had the pale unwinking stare of a fish. Caroline thought that if a fish had hair, it would have just such thin, smarmed hair, breaking into little colourless tufts over the ears. She was so fascinated by this thought that he had to repeat his question. He had a voice that matched the hair, high and weak.

Caroline remembered why she had come. The burden had lifted for a moment; now she remembered again.

"Please may I see an entry in the register? It's a marriage—on the twenty-fifth of July."

"Last?"

Caroline did not take his meaning. She looked at him with bewildered eyes.

"The twenty-fifth ultimo?"

Caroline remembered to have seen *ult* and *prox* occurring in conjunction with dates in business communications from Robert Arbuthnot. They conveyed nothing to her. She said,

"Please may I see the register of marriages for the twenty-fifth of July?"

"Last July?"

"Yes—oh yes."

She stood and waited. She wasn't afraid; she kept insisting on that. There was nothing to be afraid about—there couldn't be. She was going to see Jim Riddell's signature, and it would be the signature of a stranger. There wasn't the very slightest possible doubt about that.

She saw the clerk turn the pages of the register—big, stiff pages thick with the names of men and women who had gone adventuring into marriage through this drab back door. Perhaps if you loved someone very much, you wouldn't notice the linoleum and the smell of disinfectant.

The clerk turned another page, and a window flew open in Caroline's mind. A very bright clear light shone in, and she knew that if she had come here to marry Jim, this ugly room would be a happy, holy place all golden with romance. The light shone in her mind and went out. The window closed.

"Here you are," said the clerk in his high weak voice. He stood aside and pointed at the left-hand page of the open book.

Caroline, a little dazed with the light that had come and gone, looked down at the names. She saw Nesta's name first—"Nesta Williams, spinster." And then—"James Riddell, bachelor." It wasn't Jim's writing—*of course it wasn't.*

What odd writing it was—like a child's. No, it wasn't. A child wrote round hand. This was more like shaky print.

She looked up with a puzzled frown.

"What funny writing!"

"What?" said the clerk. "Oh, that? Written with his left hand, that was, on account of having his right arm in a sling—motor-bicycle accident, I think he said."

Caroline's heart jumped; she didn't quite know why. Jim hadn't got his arm in a sling. Jim hadn't had an accident. Jim hadn't written that signature. Why didn't she feel all happy and triumphant? Why didn't she even feel relief? Why did she feel as if there was something horrid just round the next corner?

The clerk was speaking, and she tried to give him her attention.

"If you want a certified copy, it will be five shillings."

Caroline flamed. A copy of this abominable lie! She made her voice gentle and polite with a terrible effort.

"No, thank you."

"You don't want a copy?"

"No, thank you."

The flame died down. she felt businesslike and rather tired. Jim Riddell's address was given as 14 Saracen Row. Nesta Williams' as 3 Grove Road. His father's name was James Riddell too; her father's name was Thomas Williams. She wrote down both the addresses and asked to be directed to Saracen Row.

"Third to the left, second to the right, and third to the left again," said the clerk.

Caroline turned back at the door.

"Do you remember this Mr Riddell—could you describe him?"

The clerk's pale, prominent eyes looked at her without intelligence.

"He had his arm in a sling."

"Oh, can't you tell me what he looked like?"

"Why," said the clerk, "we get them coming in all day. I shouldn't remember about his arm if it wasn't for the writing—said he'd never signed his name with his left hand before, and you can see what an awkward job he made of it. If it wasn't for that, I wouldn't remember him.''

"You can't remember at all? Not whether he was dark or fair, or short or tall?''

"No, miss, I can't—and you might take that to mean that there wasn't anything very much to remember. You take my meaning? I might have remembered red hair, or a squint, or bandy legs, or anything over six foot or under five, so you may take it he was just one of the average lot—and, as I said before, they keep on coming in. What with births, marriages, and deaths, they keep coming in all day, and after a bit you stop taking notice.''

Caroline went out feeling very much discouraged.

She turned to the left, and she turned to the right; then she turned to the left again and arrived at Saracen Row. It was a narrow street of prim, decent houses. No 14 was about half way down on the right-hand side.

She rang the bell, and presently the door was opened by a thin middle-aged woman in a lilac overall. Her drab hair was curled across her forehead under a net. She looked as if she had been interrupted in the middle of her cooking, for her face was flushed and damp, and there was a dab of flour on her sleeve.

"I'm so sorry to trouble you," said Caroline, "but was a Mr James Riddell living here in July?''

"You've made a mistake," said the thin woman, and moved to shut the door. The smell of cabbage came up behind her.

Caroline took a quick step forward. With one part of her mind she wondered why people who lived in small houses nearly always had cabbage for lunch; with another part she was thinking, "I mustn't let her shut the door.''

"Oh *please*," she said—"won't you try and help me?''

"I don't take gentlemen lodgers." She had a tight voice and a polite accent.

"He gave this address," said Caroline. "You don't know the name at all?''

"Sorry I don't," said the thin woman, and made such a decided movement to shut the door that Caroline stepped back and next moment found herself looking at the shabby letter-box. The cabbage was shut in, and she was shut out.

Whoever Jim Riddell might be, it seemed pretty clear that he had given a false address. She wondered what had made him pitch on this one. Perhaps the name had stuck in his mind. Saracen Row—it was the sort of name that might stick. And as for the number, 14 was as good as any other.

She went back to Grove Road and rang the bell of No 3.

Here was quite a different type of landlady—a stout rolling person with a bibulous eye and an easy, jolly tongue. Of course she remembered Miss Williams—"Why, she was married from here—and a pity she couldn't have a proper wedding with white satin and orange blossom, and a good heartening glass of champagne to make things go, same as I had meself. After all, you can't get married that way only once, with a wreath and a veil, and white satin slippers. A small four was what I took, though you wouldn't think it now—but that's being on me feet all day, and once you've given in to elastic-sided shoes you're done as far as looks is concerned. But a four it was, and a small one at that, and me waist a bare eighteen inches. Stays were stays in those days, and when I'd got mine laced, I'd as good a bust and as smart a waist as any of your society beauties."

"Oh, *yes*," said Caroline. "And about Miss Williams?"

"Ah! She's in the handsome, haughty style. I was more clinging—a way with me, if you understand what I mean—a bit on the playful side. It goes down with the gentlemen—especially if they're in the strong silent way themselves. It's the little fellows that fall for the big upstanding girls."

Caroline's heart jumped. She said quickly and breathlessly.

"The man Miss Williams married—was he small?"

"Never set eyes on him. Yes, you may well look surprised. Now thirty years ago she might have been afraid I'd cut her out." She laughed, a broad chuckling laugh. "Well, it wouldn't be that now, and I'm the first to admit it! 'The mystery man,' I called him, and fine and angry she was—'And what do you mean by that, Mrs Hawkins?' 'Why,' I said, 'when a young lady keeps her young gentleman as dark as you do yours—meeting him round the corner and not so much as letting him see you home—well, she must expect remarks to be passed, and whether she expects it or not, passed they will be.' Really, you know, she'd a violent temper, for I'd hardly got the words out of my lips, when she was through the door and banged it so hard that my first-floor-front came out on the landing to know what was up. 'Tempers,' I said. 'And mystery or no mystery, I'm sorry for the man that marries her, for she's one of those that'll have the upper hand or bust herself.''

"Was she here long?" said Caroline.

"Took the room for three weeks and came and went. You've got to live three weeks in a district before you can get married there, so she left a bag, and she'd be here for a day and gone for a week—and I'm not saying I wasn't just as pleased, because the opinion I got of her was that if she'd been here the whole three weeks, she'd have been running the show, and me doing odd jobs and cleaning the boots and knives.''

Caroline felt an affection for the bibulous lady. She felt that way about Nesta herself. She was a little cheered; but at the same time she didn't really seem to be making any progress.

"And you never saw the man she married?"

"No one in this house so much as set eyes on him," said the fat woman regretfully.

XVIII

IT WAS AFTER SIX WHEN CAROLINE GOT BACK TO THE cottage. She found Pansy Ann sitting pensively on the hearthrug. She had a thimble on the middle finger of her right hand, and some blue velvet, a needle-case, a reel of silk, and two pairs of scissors in her lap. But she was not sewing; she did not seem even to have got as far as threading one of the needles. When the door opened, she was gazing into the fire, which was on the point of going out. Without turning her head, she said,

"Is that you? Have you had tea?"

Caroline had expected to be assailed with fussy questions. Pansy Ann was a most dreadful fusser. She had armed herself against a torrent of questions. To be asked only one, and that in a decidedly absent tone, was odd and a little damping. She said,

"I had a cup of tea at Ledlington. I had to change there and wait ten minutes."

Even then Pansy didn't say, "Where have you been?" Instead, she spread out the bright blue velvet on her lap, turning it this way and that.

"Three-cornered pieces are so difficult to do anything with—but I thought I might get one of those new tight caps out of it. Do you think it would matter if there was a join? I thought perhaps piped with that silver ribbon Bessie Holmes gave me—I've never been able to use it for anything yet. What do you think?"

Caroline sat down on the bottom step of the stairs. She did not know how tired she was until she sat down; then she felt as if it was going to be too much trouble ever to get up again. Why not just spend the rest of one's life sitting peacefully on the bottom step and letting everything happen just as it liked? She felt as if she had been trying to stop the heavy wheels of the world. But why try—why not just let them go on? A voice in her mind said, "Juggernaut." And then the queer minute passed, and there was Pansy Ann, frightfully peeved at not being attended to.

"I think you might *answer* when I ask you a question."

"Sorry, darling—I wasn't there. Say it again."

Pansy said it again.

"You see what I mean about the piping—round the edge and along the join, so that it would look as if it was *meant*."

Caroline shuddered.

"Darling, you *can't*! Make it into pin-cushions for the deserving poor—you know, the sort you stuff with bran and stick into a shell. I know someone who'd love one." She thought of Mrs Rodgers, and her voice stopped.

Pansy had twisted round and was looking at her across the bright blue velvet. Her colour was high and her glance a little evasive.

"Robert Arbuthnot has been here," she said in a casual way.

"My poor thing! What's gone wrong now?"

"I don't see why anything should have gone wrong."

"Robert doesn't generally come unless it has. Why, it's only about a month since he dropped in to say your Beet Sugar bonds had passed their dividend. What is it this time?"

Pansy was pleating the bright folds of the velvet.

"Robert came to lunch."

"He always does—and breaks the glad news over the coffee."

Pansy's head came up suddenly.

"Why do you always make fun of Robert? I think it's very *wrong* of you! I'm sure it's very good of him to take so much trouble over our affairs."

"Good gracious, Pansy Ann!"

Miss Arbuthnot's already high colour was now considerably higher.

"I suppose it's never occurred to you that he *needn't*! I suppose it's never occurred to you that it would be much easier for him to write—much easier and much *pleasanter*, if it wasn't—if it wasn't that he *wanted* to come!"

"Golly!" said Caroline to herself. If she hadn't been so tired, it would have said itself out loud. Was it possible that Robert had an Ulterior Object? Caroline dwelt with joy on Robert under the Influence of a Tender Passion, of Robert Pursuing a Courtship, of Robert Proposing and Being Accepted. She forgot that she was going to sit on a bottom step and let the world go by. Her eyes sparkled. She swooped down upon the hearth-rug beside Pansy.

"Pansy Ann—what have you been up to? What has

Robert been up to? How could you be so indiscreet as to have him to lunch in the absence of your chaperon? A gay young man like that! Tell your Aunt Caroline all!''

Pansy began to cry. Her face worked. Tears came rolling down her cheeks. She sniffed loudly between angry sobs.

"You've never done him justice! I've had to put up with your making fun of him *always*! I didn't say anything—because it wouldn't have been any *use* saying anything! You only think about your own affairs—you don't confide in me—you never have! I'm sure if you'd been *engaged* to Jim, you couldn't have shut me up more—when I asked the simplest and most natural questions—though if I'd *chosen*—'' She stopped and dabbed her eyes with the blue velvet. She was not quite prepared to claim Jim as a lover. She plunged hastily back into the original grievance. "You always make fun of Robert! If you were older, you'd appreciate him as *I* do. He has a very *high* sense of duty and a *pure* Roman nose. It isn't you he wants to marry, so it doesn't matter *what* you think of him!''

Caroline was appalled.

"Pansy darling—*don't*! I never, never, never meant to hurt your feelings. Darling, you know how one laughs at all sorts of things one respects most frightfully—like bishops—and the Bank of England—and—and Parliament.''

Pansy continued to sob.

"Robert isn't an—institution!''

That was exactly what he was. But never, never, never again must Caroline say so. She hugged the weeping Pansy.

"Darling, I respect him most *frightfully*. He's as safe as the Bank of England and as good as a bishop. Are you going to marry him? Has he asked you? Have you said yes? Here's my hanky—you're simply ruining that blue velvet.''

Pansy blew her nose on the proffered handkerchief.

"There's nothing settled,'' she said in a muffled voice—"nothing at all. Only he said—he did say—his mother thought—he ought to marry. He's such a good son—and he said he would like to please her—and did I think forty-seven was too old—and when I said no, it was just the *prime* of life, he said he was very glad I thought so—because he valued my opinion very much. He said that twice—and then he asked me—whether I had any views about—cousins marrying—and I said I didn't think it mattered so long as they weren't very near."

"Darling! That was practically a proposal!"

Pansy gave a final sob.

"I—thought—it was—because he got up and looked out of the window—and then he said, 'Your great-grandfather was second cousin once removed to my grandfather.' And then he said he must be going—and then—just at the end—he pressed my hand—and said, 'You will hear from me in confirmation of this interview.' "

Caroline sprang up hastily. If she laughed, Pansy would never forgive her. She went quickly towards the stair, saying,

"I'll just take my things off and come down again."

"You *do* think he meant something?"

"It sounds like it." Caroline was gathering up her bag and gloves.

"Of course he *said* he'd come down to ask us about Jim."

With her foot on the bottom step, Caroline stood rigid. What had Robert Arbuthnot wanted to find out? She made an effort and said,

"About Jim?"

"Yes. Someone has told him about that broadcast, but they'd forgotten the name of the hospital. He wanted to know whether we had any reason to suppose that Jim was on the *Alice Arden*."

"And you said?"

"I said you thought he might have been. I told him it was the Elston cottage hospital, and that you had been over and found the man wasn't Jim. I told him the name wasn't Randal at all—it was a man called Riddell, and his wife had fetched him away."

"He was quite satisfied?"

"He went on asking questions. He's so thorough. I think it's wonderful to be so thorough and conscientious."

Caroline leaned on the old oak balustrade. The cottage

had been there for three hundred years, and for three hundred years the hands of men, and women, and little children had been rubbing the baluster smooth. Caroline's hands slipped on it now. She came down a step and stood against the newel. What sort of questions had Robert been asking, and what sort of answers had Pansy given him?

"What did he want to know?" she said.

"When you heard from Jim last—and what his plans were—and whether we'd seen him since he landed.... Oh, and most particularly, whether we'd heard from him, or about him, since the wreck of the *Alice Arden*. And of course I said no, we hadn't. And then he said a most awfully curious thing."

"What did he say?"

"It wasn't so much what he said as the way he said it. He coughed and cleared his throat, and poked the fire, and then he asked me whether we'd heard any *rumours*. What *do* you suppose he meant?"

"What did you say?"

"Well, I *hadn't* heard anything really, so I said I never listened to gossip. And he said, 'Quite right—quite right,' and blew his nose and wouldn't say anything more except vague things like not getting drawn into any scandal, and remembering that we were two women living alone. And of course, after saying that about not listening to gossip, I didn't like to ask what he meant—he mightn't have thought it quite nice of me. You know, he thinks women ought to be protected from contact with the sordid side of life. He said so at lunch. He said their place was the home, and that a really nice woman asked for no higher or wider sphere. He said—"

"*Why?*"

"That's the sort of woman he admires."

"I don't mean that. Why did he say all that about a scandal?"

"I don't know. It sounded—well, it *sounded* as if Jim—"

Caroline stamped her foot.

"*Pansy Ann!*"

"Well, it did sound like that—and of course when Mrs

Smith was scrubbing out the kitchen yesterday she did say—you know her sister-in-law's eldest girl is kitchen-maid at Packham Hall—she did tell me—''

"Well?" said Caroline.

"You know how she talks—I wouldn't ask her anything, but you can't help listening—well, she says there used to be a photograph of Jim in Mrs Van Berg's sitting-room—a big one like yours—'' She paused.

Caroline did not speak; she looked instead—proudly and a little contemptuously.

Pansy's colour rose.

"It's no use your looking at me like that! And you didn't let me finish. Mrs Van Berg might have fifty photographs of Jim if she liked, and if her husband didn't mind. Even Mrs Smith didn't mind her *having* the photograph.''

"What did she mind?" said Caroline in a deep, angry voice.

"Well, it isn't there now," said Pansy.

"Why should it be?"

"It isn't. But it *was*—it was there the very day Mr Van Berg was shot, and it's never been there since—and, as Mrs Smith says, things like that are bound to make people talk.''

Caroline turned round and went up the stair. Her door shut sharply.

XIX

TRY HOW SHE WOULD, CAROLINE COULD SEE NO WAY OF getting to Hale Place before Pansy Ann and the village were in bed and asleep. People in villages have terribly sharp eyes and a superhuman faculty for putting two and two together even when they don't really exist. As for Pansy Ann, she had got over being peeved and was affectionate, clinging and conversational to the last degree. She sat up till eleven o'clock talking about Robert. This was the main theme, but it proved to be prolific in side shoots, such as, would it be tactful to insist upon new curtains and chair-covers in the drawing-room—the existing ones having been installed by Robert's mother at a period when maroon plush was considered the last word in elegance. The contemporary chair-covers had, fortunately, disintegrated, but Robert had replaced them by an indestructible olive-green tapestry.

"Of *course*," said Pansy earnestly, "I couldn't possibly say anything until he has really proposed. But what do you think about it? Could I say something *afterwards*? Something on the lines of one's room being a form of self-expression."

Caroline shook her head.

"I shouldn't talk about self-expression to Robert. Be Victorian. Cling—whisper in his ear that it's been the dream of your life to make a happy home for Someone, with rose-coloured curtains and a foxglove chintz."

"I thought of *blue*," said Pansy with a rapt expression—"powder-blue, and a delphinium cretonne, and pink and purple cushions. And would you have a plain blue carpet? They show every mark."

"It's a case of what Robert will have," said Caroline.

They passed presently to the wedding. Pansy had set her heart on a veil and orange-blossoms, and a white velvet dress with a court train, and Caroline for a bridesmaid, also in white, carrying lilies.

Caroline had a feeling that Robert would be a little out of the picture. To be sure, he was a fine figure of a man, well featured and neither bald nor grey, *but*—as far as Caroline was concerned there would always be a but.

She discussed the decorations of the church with a feeling that, to be really appropriate, they should be, not floral, but vegetable—piles of neatly scrubbed potatoes, festoons of Brussels sprouts, and good bold clumps of cabbages and marrows. There was so much solid worth about Robert; and of course solid worth was an excellent thing, and Pansy Ann would probably live happily ever after.

They passed to the trousseau and the burning question of whether it was worth while to put hand embroidery into things which might fade, if not in the first, at any rate in the third or fourth wash.

When they said good-night, Pansy became suddenly tearful.

"Perhaps I've just imagined the whole thing—perhaps he doesn't care for me at all like that—perhaps it's someone else altogether, and he was just trying to tell me about her. Why did you let me talk about my trousseau? I'm sure it's horribly unlucky!"

Caroline felt unhappy. Pansy Ann did jump to conclusions. There was no saying—She cast about for something to say.

"If he really cares—"

"If!" said Pansy with a sob. Then, with pitiful humility, "Why should he?"

"Why shouldn't he?" Caroline kissed her. "Don't let's talk about it any more to-night. If he means anything he'll write to you."

"He *said* he'd write," said Pansy, and went to bed comforted.

Before falling asleep she had decided on names for two children, a boy and a girl, to be called respectively Robert Lancelot and Pansy Elaine. In spite of the fact that she and Robert were dark, both these children were to have golden curls and eyes of forget-me-not blue. In her dreams they hovered, smiling.

Caroline passed through the village and up the drive to Hale Place in the pitch dark. There was no moon to-night; a thick haze covered the whole sky, and the air was heavy with damp. If she had not known every step of the way, she might have lost herself a dozen times. She came round the house and felt her way through the yard to the back door. She did not mind the dark loneliness of the drive, but as she came near the house, its silence and its emptiness came to meet her. She felt cold and rather frightened.

She turned the handle of the back door and pushed it

open. The darkness of the passage lay before her like the darkness of a cave. She stood on the threshold and called into the darkness softly.

"Jim—"

There wasn't any answer. What was she going to do if he didn't answer? He might be somewhere deep in the old house—he might be asleep—he might have gone away. . . . . No, he wouldn't have gone away, because he had promised.

She called again, and heard the silence smother his name. The really dreadful thought that she might have to wander through the dark house looking for him turned her perfectly cold. There were cockroaches. There were probably mice. There might easily be spiders. It was a grim business. A furry thing might run across one's foot. One might tread on something that squelched.

She called once more, and no one answered her. She was a most perfect fool not to have brought a torch. There was nothing for it but to go on.

She felt her way to the kitchen, set down the basket she was carrying, and went on until her outstretched hands touched the green baize door that shut off the servants' wing. On the other side of it, she stood listening and searching the darkness. She was in the hall, with the staircase going up on her right, and beyond it a door leading into the drawing-room. On this side two doors, one into the dining-room and the other into the library. Both of these doors were locked on the outside. Between them the huge old-fashioned hearth with a chimney as large as a room.

She crossed the hall and tried the drawing-room door. That too was locked.

She had her foot on the bottom step of the stairs, when suddenly away above her in the darkness a door banged. There was the momentary flash of a torch, just a sharp stab of light, and then the sound of someone running.

Caroline shrank back against the newel. The distant door that had banged was wrenched open. Jim called out. The running feet came down the stair and passed her. There was a sound of panting breath. The torch stabbed again. She made out the black outline of a man's head and arm, and a vague something that was head and shoulders. Then he was gone through the baize door, and with a rush of air and a swishing sound Jim had slid the banisters, jumped clear, and was after him. It all rather took her breath away. Spiders, cockroaches and mice she had been prepared for, but not a game of devil-in-the-dark.

She sat down on the stairs and waited for Jim to come back. She had to wait for what seemed like a long time. The silence settled round her. The darkness was like a thick impenetrable curtain. The air of the house was cold and dead. Caroline couldn't make up her mind which would be worse, to hear some terrifying sound, or to go on hearing nothing. After a little she began to think she would rather hear something—anything. The silence seemed to be stopping her ears, and the black dark pressing against her eyeballs.

Then after a long time she heard Jim coming back—footsteps in the passage and the swing of the baize door. Then he was crossing the hall, walking quickly and firmly like a man who knows his way. He was actually passing her before she stood up and said,

"Jim—"

His startled "Caroline!" came from less than a yard away. Then his hand touched her face, and she gave an odd little cry. It *was* just like a game of devil-in-the-dark.

"Caroline! Where did you spring from?"

She caught him by the arm, holding him tight.

"Why didn't you wait for me? It's the horridest thing I've ever done in my life, coming into an empty, pitchy house like this."

"It wasn't empty," said Jim a little grimly.

"That made it *worse*." Her voice reached tragic depths. "I sort of strung myself up to bear spiders and cockroaches and things, but I didn't bargain for people *plunging* down the stairs at me in the dark."

"Were you there?"

"I was here—and he nearly knocked me down," declared Caroline quite untruthfully.

Jim spoke quickly.

"You didn't see him when he put the torch on?"

"Only his hand. Jim—who was it?"

"I wish I knew. Look here, come upstairs—we needn't talk in the dark—I've found some candles."

"I've brought you some—and things to eat. The basket's in the kitchen."

They fetched it, and came back through the hall and up the stairs. Jim put his arm round her at the top and guided her along the right-hand corridor; then to the left, two steps down, a little way along, and three steps up. A door stood open.

Jim let go of Caroline, struck a match, and lighted a candle in a tall white candlestick. The light fell yellow and soft upon a queer room panelled with oak. It had five tall, narrow windows and a deep alcove which contained an old four-post bed with a heavy valance of blue damask. The windows were shuttered and had curtains of the same damask as the bed-hangings. The fireplace was on the right of the door. It had a deep brick hearth. On the shelf above it stood the candle.

Jim shut the door.

"Come and sit down. I've locked the back door, so we shan't have any more visitors."

There were no chairs in the room. They sat side by side on the bed and looked at one another.

Moonlight can only show a ghostly image. It is like memory; it sets one aching for reality. In the candle light Caroline looked warm, and soft, and young. Her eyes were bright and her cheeks like damask roses. Jim could have kissed her for being so sweetly alive. She began to speak with a rush of words.

"Who was he? Why did he come? Tell me all about it."

"He came in through the back door. I'd left it open for you, and I'd gone down to the kitchen to wait for you. Well, I heard the door, and of course I thought it was you, but before I had time to call out he switched on his torch and the light just caught his hand. I got back behind the kitchen door in a hurry, and he went on down the passage and into the hall. He obviously hadn't seen me. Well, then I thought

I'd find out what he was up to, so I went after him—and the light was half way up the stairs. I let him get to the top and go off to the right, and then I followed him. He turned off again and came down here. When I got to the door, he was shining his torch all round the room. I thought I'd rather like to know what he was after. I—it was rather odd—I felt as if I did know. He put down the torch, pulled out a box of matches, and struck a match. He was just going to light the candle on the mantelpiece, when I walked into the room. I ought to have waited, but the heavy householder got the better of me—there was something so damned riling about the way he struck that match!'' He gave a short laugh. ''I said, 'What the something are you doing here?' and he dropped the match, grabbed his torch, charged right into the middle of me, and banged the door in my face before I got my breath back. It makes me sound like a stiff, but he was most uncommon nippy. It was like trying to get hold of a cat. I wish I'd seen his face.''

''You didn't—when he struck the match?''

''No. He had his back to me. The whole thing didn't take half a minute. As I stepped into the room, he dropped the match and butted me. I hoped you'd seen him.''

''What did he want?'' said Caroline.

Jim looked past her with a strained expression in his eyes.

''I—I don't know—'' There was a pause. He made a movement as if shaking something off. ''He may have been a burglar—or just a common or garden tramp.''

''Yes,'' said Caroline. Why did he look like that? She came a little nearer. ''Jim—what's the matter?''

He was frowning in a puzzled way.

''I dreamt about this room—it's just come back to me.''

''There isn't anything odd about that. Why shouldn't you dream about it? I often dream about places I know.''

''There *was* something odd about it. A round room, with five windows like slits—that's the way I dreamt about it. Why? We've always called it the Blue Room. Why didn't I dream of it like that? I mean''—his frown deepened—''why should I make up a perfectly new description of it and dream of that?''

"I don't know," said Caroline. "You can do anything in a dream—they're quite mad." She slipped her hand through his arm. "Jim, I've got simply heaps to tell you."

Her eyes were as eager as a child's. The things that she wanted to tell Jim crowded together in her mind, jostling and pushing one another for first place. The last comer had it.

"Jim, I've been to London," she said, and pinched his arm quite hard.

"What for?"

"To see whether it was you who signed that old register. I thought if I went and looked we should know."

He had a moment of sickening suspense. He said, "Well?" quietly enough.

"I know it wasn't you—but—"

"But what?" There was the giddy feeling of being uncertain where the next step was to take him.

"It wasn't a proper signature—just a sort of higgledy-piggledy printing. And the clerk remembered that it was because Jim Riddell had his right arm in a sling."

The feeling of giddiness increased.

"But you haven't had anything wrong with your arm, Jim. You haven't—have you? And that proves that it wasn't you."

He was looking across at the shuttered window opposite—the narrow window with the blue curtains, the window that was like a slit. He was silent. She was getting frightened, when he said,

"I'm afraid that doesn't prove anything. A crook might have very good reasons for not giving away a specimen of his handwriting. You didn't get hold of anyone who could describe him?"

"I tried," said Caroline. "I did try, Jim. But the woman at the address he gave said she never took men lodgers, so he must have given a false address. Then I tried Nesta Williams' place. Her landlady was terribly chatty and all that, but as she never set eyes on Nesta's young man, it wasn't much good."

Jim sat leaning forward on the bed, his elbows on his

knees and rather a blank look on his face. It was as if he had put up his shutters and behind them were setting out Caroline's puzzle pieces. They fitted into the bits that Nesta had given him and the bits which he himself had been able to produce. Up to the time of his landing his memory was perfectly clear. There was a six weeks' gap. The pieces fitted into the gap. He had landed on the first of July. He might have married Nesta Williams on the twenty-fifth. If between the first and the twenty-fifth he had run off the rails and conceived the crazy idea of robbing Elmer Van Berg, he would probably have taken steps to cover his tracks. Why, even if crazy, he should have married Nesta Williams was beyond him. He reckoned it as a form of suicidal mania and left it at that.

XX

"I've got heaps more to tell you, Jim," said Caroline. She began to pour out the story of her interview with Mrs Rodgers. "I didn't know that I was going to follow her, but when she got out of the train, something just yanked me out of my seat and pushed me on to the platform, and the next thing I knew, we were climbing Meade Hill practically hand in hand, and I was imploring her to tell me all."

"What did she tell you?"

"I don't believe she'd have told me anything if she hadn't turned out to be Nanna's sister. I didn't recognize her, because she used to be thin like Nanna, and now she's exactly like a feather-bed. But she knew me at once—she said I hadn't changed a bit."

"No—you haven't," said Jim.

And that was the last moment that he could have said it, because, in the very middle of saying it, Caroline stopped being the dearly familiar child, half playmate and half sister, whom he had teased, petted and adored from the time she had first clutched at his hair with her baby fingers. Something happened, and she was a new Caroline—a Caroline whom he knew, and did not know, whose hand on his arm sent a tremor all over him. It was horribly disconcerting and embarrassing. He lost the thread of what she was saying, because there was a pounding noise in his ears. And then, there was Caroline sitting well away from him on the extreme corner of the bed and saying, in that odd deep voice of hers,

"Of course you needn't tell me if you don't *want* to."

He said haltingly, "I'm sorry—I didn't get that."

"You didn't what?"

"I didn't hear what you said—I was thinking about something else."

A bright carnation bloomed in Caroline's cheeks.

"You mustn't think about anything else—you must listen."

He looked at her, and then looked quickly away. She was a new, enchanted Caroline, who took his breath with her warmth and beauty—enchanted, and enchanting.

"Jim, you're being stupid. I thought, if *that's* what they're saying, you—you ought to know. But you needn't—you needn't tell me anything you don't want to."

Jim took hold of himself.

"I didn't hear what you said. I'll tell you anything I can."

He looked no higher than the dust-sheet which covered the bed, but he knew that she was looking at him. He hadn't the faintest idea what she had said, or what she was going to say. It came like a bomb-shell.

"They think you were in love with Mrs Van Berg."

He looked up then with a sharply interrogative jerk of the head.

"With *Susie*?"

"Yes." Her eyes were very bright. "Were you? You needn't say if you don't want to."

"Well, I wasn't. What put it into anyone's head that I was?"

"That's what I was telling you," said Caroline earnestly. "Mrs Rodgers had just been up at Packham Hall. She's a friend of the cook's, and the cook is friends with the police because her husband was a policeman, so Mrs Rodgers had been having a lovely time and simply lapping up gossip, and that's one of the things she lapped up. You see, Mrs Van Berg's maid is going about saying that Mr Van Berg was shot because he found out something he wasn't meant to—that's to say, she doesn't say it right out, she just drops hints. Mrs Rodgers calls her an ' 'inting' ussy.' And she says—she says perhaps the emeralds weren't stolen at all, only hidden to make it look as if there had been a burglary."

"What damned nonsense!"

"Jim, you didn't think I believed her! It was only—I thought—you might have—cared for her—and there might have been—a quarrel."

"Well, I didn't!"

He got up and began to walk about the room. It was more than he could do to sit within a yard of Caroline and hear her ask him whether he was in love with another woman.

She sat where she was, bareheaded, her old brown coat open over a cream shirt and shabby tweed skirt. Her eyes followed him.

"There wasn't any quarrel?"

"How do I know?"

It was damnable, but he didn't know.

"Jim—you don't mind my telling you? The hussy says Mrs Van Berg used to have a photograph of you. She says it was always out until that night. She says it has never been out since."

He stood in the middle of the room frowning intently.

"I gave her a photograph—they'd been awfully good to me. She may have had half a dozen reasons for putting it away." He said it without conviction. Why should she have put his photograph away like that? You'd think a woman whose husband had just been shot would have something better to do. You wouldn't expect her to be fiddling with photographs. It wasn't like Susie either. She panicked easily—he would have expected her to be having a nerve-storm, with her maid dabbing eau-de-cologne on her forehead in a darkened room.

He began to wonder whether Susie Van Berg knew that he had been with Elmer that night.

"I was there," he said. "Elmer and I had drinks together. I wonder if Susie knew that. In her statement she said that she came down to get a book and heard voices in the study. She may have heard more than she said—she may have recognized my voice."

"Wouldn't she have said?"

"I don't know—we were pretty good friends—she'd know I wouldn't—" He broke off sharp.

Suppose by any horrible chance he and Elmer had had a row. Suppose Susie had heard them quarreling. And then Elmer Van Berg had been found shot. Would Susie have kept his photograph out after that? Or would she have pushed it out of sight with nervous, shaking hands?

He lost a bit of what Caroline was saying—something about finger-prints. Then he got it. She was talking about Elmer's finger-print book.

"There was a page torn out," said Caroline.

He felt the shock of that as she had felt it.

"When?"

"Oh afterwards—when the police found it. You see, you were right about the drinks. There was a tray and glasses, and the police took the finger-prints. And then the butler told them about Mr Van Berg's book. He told them it was on the table, but when they looked for it, it wasn't there. They found it stuffed down behind the book-case. And there was a page torn out."

"A page torn out!" Then, sharply, "How did they know?"

Caroline felt frightened; she didn't know why. She had to tell him these things, but it hurt. She hadn't known that it was going to hurt as much as this. She leaned against the dark carved bed-post and pushed her hands deep down into the pockets of the old brown coat.

"The cook says she remembers the page. She hasn't told

the police yet. Mrs Rodgers says she won't unless she is asked, but they might ask her at any minute. She says she remembers because there wasn't any name on that page, only initials. I suppose she takes an interest in finger-prints because of her husband being a policeman. I suppose—''

"What were the initials?''

Caroline looked at him piteously. It hurt too much. Her carnation colour was all gone. Her voice was a whisper as she said,

"J.R.''

Jim laughed. His laughter had a hard edge to it.

"We're putting the rope round my neck all right—'' he said.

"Jim!''

"They were my finger-prints—I remember making them and putting my initials there. But I'll swear—'' He stopped short.

"What?'' said Caroline quickly.

He laughed again.

"I was going to say I could swear I hadn't torn the page out, but I can't—I can't swear to anything. Go on. Are there any more damning bits of evidence?''

Caroline clenched her hands.

"The cook's nephew saw you in the drive. He used to caddy for you—a boy called Willie Bowman.''

"Willie? He knew me?''

"Yes, he did. He told his aunt—he said it was about midnight.''

"That's a bit of bad luck, but it can't be helped. I don't seem to have covered my tracks very well—do I?''

He began to walk up and down in the room with a turn at one of the narrow windows and another turn at the fireplace. There were two spent matches lying on the hearth, one that he had struck himself, and one that had been struck by the burglar. His mind became obsessed by the burglar. Why start operations on this room, when a drawing-room, a dining-room, a library, and all the more important bedrooms lay between him and it? He had passed them by and come straight to this bare, unlikely spot.

He turned again and saw the mantelpiece with its two plain china candlesticks. One of them had had the top broken off and lacked a candle. They were the only ornaments in the room. You can't walk off with a four-post bed or linen-fold panelling—and there was nothing else in the room except a square of Brussels carpet which had once been blue, but was now worn and faded to a dreary shade of grey.

He turned again, and saw Caroline looking at him with loving, anxious eyes. The candle light was bright on her ruffled hair. He looked away from her and spoke from where he stood with his back to the hearth.

"I've got to make up my mind what I'm going to do."

"Yes."

He squared his shoulders.

"What I should like to do is to open up the house, get in servants, and go about my affairs as I've a perfect right to do."

"Yes," said Caroline. Her eyes brightened. Jim at Hale Place—Jim quite near! It was like the most lovely dream. But she knew quite well that it was a dream.

"That's what I'd like to do. What I expect I ought to do is go up to town and see Robert Arbuthnot—" He paused. The pause lasted a long time. . . . . "What I'm going to do is what will look most horribly damning if things go wrong and it comes to a trial. I'm going to mark time." He began to pace the room again with a certain restless energy. "You see, if I come out into the open, everyone will ask me questions, and every time it's a question I can't answer, I'll be making things worse. Where have I been—and what have I been doing—and was I on the *Alice Arden*, and why—and when did I see Elmer Van Berg last, and were those my finger-prints on the glass in his study—and what was I doing in the drive when Willie Bowman saw me—and so on. And if I go and see Robert, he'll ask questions too—all those and a lot more. Then there's Nesta Riddell. If she sticks to it that I'm her husband, I can't prove that I'm not—till my memory comes back. If I could remember, I could stand up to the questions, but as things are at present, they'll defeat their own ends. The minute I'm asked a question my head goes muzzy. You know how it is when you've forgotten something—the more effort you make, the less you can remember; but if you stop trying, it comes back to you. You see what I mean—I want a breathing space, I want to be able to let myself alone. Sometimes I'm on the edge of remembering. When I wake up it feels as if it was all there, and then before I can get hold of it it's gone again. If Robert were to start cross examining me, it might go altogether. I want to give myself a chance—stay here—keep quiet—"

Caroline interrupted him with a frightened,

"Here?"

"Why not? You said Mrs Ledger only came once a week. If she was here yesterday, that gives me five clear days. If I can't remember things by then, I shall send for Robert and put myself in his hands." He stopped in the middle of the floor. "And now you must go."

Caroline got up.

"Have you got enough blankets? Are they aired?"

He laughed—a real laugh this time.

"Who do you think's been airing my bedclothes for the last seven years?"

"I don't know," said Caroline. "And you needn't laugh—it's nice of me to want you to have dry blankets. Don't you think so?"

She came up close and stood on tiptoe, putting up her face.

"Good-night—darling ungrateful Jim!"

He said,

"I'm not ungrateful."

In the middle of the short sentence his voice changed. He would have stepped back, but she held him with a hand on either arm.

"Perhaps you'll be grateful when you see what a nice supper I've brought you. I bought the things in town. Good-night!"

She kissed him as if it were seven years ago, and she a child and he her all but brother. But all of a sudden her heart beat quick and hard. When she had kissed Jim last her heart had not beaten like this. She stepped back, too confused and troubled by her own feelings to be aware of his. She wanted to be out of the room and out of the house.

She went to the door and opened it. The dark passage lay before her. She stepped out into it with her thoughts still in great confusion. Why should it make her feel like this to touch Jim's cheek with her lips? She had always kissed him. What was there to make this kiss any different from all the other kisses?

His rigid silence escaped her. She was scarcely aware that he had taken up the candle and was following. They walked along the corridor and down the stair without a spoken word. Words unspoken clamoured in them both.

He walked with her down the dark drive and through the sleeping village. At the cottage gate he broke the long silence.

"You mustn't come again."

"I must," said Caroline.

"No, you mustn't."

"I shall come to-morrow," said Caroline, and was gone before he could answer.

XXI

THE FIRST POST IN THE MORNING BROUGHT A PROPOSAL IN due form from Robert Arbuthnot. Pansy Ann glowed and blushed over it as if it had been the most ardent of love-letters. She read it aloud in snatches, with agitated and enthusiastic comments. It began:

My dear Pansy,

You may perhaps be surprised at receiving a letter from me which does not concern your business affairs or my position as your trustee—

"I don't think I'd better say I'm not surprised. Do you? Robert might think I oughtn't to have *guessed*. Do you think it would be deceitful if I didn't tell him? He does think such a lot of people being truthful."

Caroline gave her deep gurgling laugh.

"What a horrible problem! Are you always going to tell Robert everything?"

"I *hope* so."

"Golly!"

Pansy went back to the letter.

This is an entirely personal and private letter, and one which has cost me much thought—

"It's rather wonderful, isn't it, to think he has been thinking of me like that—*Robert*!"

She turned a crackling page. Robert employed the stiffest and most legal looking blue paper for his private correspondence. It was neatly typed, and upon one side only.

I am well aware that you have been accustomed to think of me as a relative, no longer young, who has stood towards you for many years in a position of trust. I am writing to ask you whether you could bring yourself to think of me in another and, may I say, a more intimate capacity—

"I think he puts it *beautifully*! Don't you? And as to *trusting* him, I'm sure anyone would trust Robert with *anything*."

With her feet on the firmest of firm ground, Caroline agreed. Robert was undoubtedly the most trustworthy of men.

Pansy went on reading, her eyes full of happy tears.

* * *

I have, for some time, been considering the question of matrimony. I hope you know me well enough to be sure that I should give such a subject the most serious consideration before taking what I regard as an irrevocable step. From the tenor of your conversation yesterday I gather that you would not consider a distant degree of relationship, such as subsists between yourself and me, as an insuperable bar to marriage. May I therefore ask whether you could entertain the idea of accepting me as your husband?

Pansy broke off and dabbed her eyes.

"He makes it sound so solemn—doesn't he? I think it's a *wonderful* letter. Don't you?"

I know I need not urge upon you the serious nature of the step. I would only urge my own deep affection, and hope, my dear Pansy, that you may find it worthy of your acceptance.

The usual signature followed in an upright formal hand— "Robert Arbuthnot."

Pansy dabbed her eyes again.

"I don't know how to answer it. I can't write a beautiful letter like that."

"I shouldn't try," said Caroline. "That's Robert's sort of letter. You write your own sort, and perhaps he'll sit down at the other end and wonder how you did it."

"Do you think so? Do you think I could just say that he's made me very happy—would that do?"

"Beautifully," said Caroline.

As she said it, the telephone bell began to ring. A scarlet Pansy caught up the receiver.

"Caroline—if it's him—what shall I say?"

Then as Caroline, laughing and shaking her head, was about to run out of the room, there was a change in voice and manner. A puzzled look came over Pansy's face; her colour receded, and her voice took on a tone of disappointment.

"Oh . . . Yes, she's here. Who shall I say? . . . Oh . . . Very well, I'll call her."

She turned from the instrument, which was fastened to the wall at the foot of the stair.

"Caroline—someone wants you. She won't give any name."

Caroline took the receiver with some impatience. It was so stupid of people not to give their names. If you were cut off, you never knew who had been calling you. She simply hated that.

There came to her along the wire an almost inaudible voice.

"Is that Caroline Leigh?"

"Who is speaking?"

"Is that Caroline Leigh?"

"Yes. Who is speaking?"

"Will you come and see me? I want to see you very badly."

"But who are you? I didn't hear—"

"I didn't say. I want to see you—about—Jim." There was a faint desperate catch in the voice before the name came out.

It took Caroline a moment to get her own voice steady.

"Are you—no, you're not—Nesta?"

"Who is Nesta? No, never mind. I'm Susie. You know now, don't you? Will you come and see me?"

Caroline's heart leapt. Susie Van Berg wanted to see her. Why? Of all things in the world, she wanted most to see Susie Van Berg. She wanted it so much that she was afraid to say yes. Could she go—might she go? Was there any possible hurt to Jim in her going? She couldn't see any.

Susie Van Berg spoke again, a little louder, a little more insistently.

"Are you there? Will you come?"

"Yes," said Caroline, and had the feeling, like Robert, that she was taking an irrevocable step.

"How will you come?" said Susie Van Berg. "I would send the car—but then the servants would talk—"

"They'll do that anyhow," said Caroline with the ghost of a laugh. "But you needn't bother—I've got my own little car. When shall I come?"

The voice said, "At once."

Caroline's thoughts moved rapidly. She said,

"Not if you don't want to make talk. It isn't as if I knew you very well. It would be better if I came in the afternoon—anyone can come in the afternoon."

"What time?" The voice fluttered.

"Between five and six," said Caroline. "Will that do?"

The voice said, "Yes." The click of the receiver put a full stop to the word.

Susie Van Berg turned from the telephone, clutching with both hands at the pale blue satin wrap she was wearing. She had locked both doors before she rang up Caroline Leigh—the bedroom door, and the door of the big dressing-room which she had turned into a sitting-room for herself. The communicating door stood open between the two rooms. The telephone was in the sitting-room. She had hung up the receiver because she had heard someone try the handle of the bedroom door.

She stood for a moment, listening in a strained position, the light of the grey rainy morning falling cold upon her pallor. She had the type of looks which needs the sun. Her hair was so pale as to be almost silver, her eyes a forget-me-not blue, her skin as white as privet, with no more than a faint rose to tinge the cheeks, and deepen to the colour of pink hawthorn in the lips. These faint delicious tints were all blurred and faded now. Her face was waxy white, and much weeping had washed the shading from her lashes, leaving them as pale as her hair. She wore a diaphanous night-gown under the satin wrap. Her feet were bare in their pink embroidered mules.

She stood there listening, and heard the handle tried again. In an instant she had stepped out of her slippers and, picking them up, she crossed the floor and went through the communicating door, moving without a sound. The bedroom blinds were down, and the curtains drawn. The only light came from the sitting-room.

Susie Van Berg slipped into the turned-down bed and, leaning over the edge, set her slippers down beneath it.

Then, pulling the clothes about her, she reached out her hand and rang the bell.

XXII

As Caroline followed a tall young footman up the imposing staircase of Packham Hall, she looked about her with interest. She had not been in the house since she was a little girl. Mrs Entwhistle had given a wonderful children's fancy dress ball to celebrate the Armistice. A year later she died, and the house opened its doors no more. Little Caroline had taken off her coat and shawl in one of the big bedrooms upstairs and then walked down the wide, shallow steps proudly and shyly in a flounced Kate Greenaway dress of buttercup yellow, with a tight posy of buttercups and daisies in her hand and a daisy chain on her bright brown curls.

The picture slipped through her mind. She saw the empty hall below her, full of children. She saw Pansy Ann, quite grown up of course, in a blue and silver eastern dress, and Jim as Haroun al Raschid, with his eyebrows corked and a fierce real scimitar at his side.

The picture broke. The footman was handing her over to Mrs Van Berg's maid. Caroline came back to the present with a jerk and took a good look at the " 'inting 'ussy." She saw a middle-sized person of very discreet appearance with a manner nicely attuned to what might at any moment become a house of mourning.

As they turned into a long corridor, one of Elmer Van Berg's nurses passed them, going in the direction of the stairs, a pretty, rather hard-featured girl with bright blue eyes.

"Ah—the poor monsieur!" said Louise under her breath when the nurse had turned the corner.

"Isn't he any better?" said Caroline.

Louise threw up her hands.

"He does not speak—he does not move! It is terrible!" She paused, cast a sideways glance at Caroline, and added, "*Pauvre Madame!*"

"How is Mrs Van Berg?" said Caroline.

"*Bien souffrante.* What would you? A so terrible shock! It is enough to kill, is it not?"

They had turned again. Louise opened a door and announced "Miss Leigh—"

Caroline passed into the small sitting-room and heard the door softly closed behind her.

The room was very warm; that was Caroline's first impression. It was like coming into a hot-house. There was a fire on the hearth and a scent of pastilles in the air. Though it was not yet six o'clock, the cold, wet daylight had been shut out. Two lamps with pale blue shades filled the room with a light that was rather like moonlight. Susie Van Berg must have imported both the shades and the blue brocaded curtains which covered the windows. Quiet, melancholy Mr Entwhistle could scarcely have been responsible for them.

The room was most unmistakably that of a pretty, spoilt woman.

Susie Van Berg herself lay on a couch in front of the fire, banked up with cushions. There was a silver cushion under her head, a pale pink pouffe behind her shoulders, and a three-cornered violet cushion just slipping to the floor as she made a startled movement.

Caroline was startled too. She didn't know what she had expected, but not this. The setting was so elaborate, so artificial. Susie Van Berg herself looked like someone in a play. She wore one of those garments which one sees in catalogues. Caroline had always wondered whether anyone ever really wore them. Susie Van Berg was wearing one now—frilled, beflowered, embroidered georgette pyjamas in pale blue shading to green, with a satin coat to match. But the eyes which she fixed on Caroline as she made that movement to rise were the eyes of a frightened child. A dry, hot hand clung to hers, and the voice that she had heard on the telephone said,

"Caroline Leigh?"

Caroline nodded.

"Won't you sit down? Where will you sit? Come here beside me on the sofa so we needn't talk loud." She slipped her feet off the couch as she spoke, pulling herself into a sitting position.

Caroline took off her tweed coat and sat down.

"It was very good of you to come," said Susie Van Berg. She spoke as if she had not quite enough breath for what she wanted to say.

Caroline saw her with compassion. It was obvious that she had wept bitterly during the last few days; her eyes had a drowned and faded look. Her hands kept plucking at one another, and from time to time a nervous tremor shook her. Yet her nails were carefully henna'd, her pale hair immaculately set, and her lips made up in an artificial curve. She had a lost, tormented look.

Caroline's soft heart was a good deal moved. She put her hand on the twisting, plucking fingers and said,

"What can I do for you, Mrs Van Berg?"

For a moment the restless movement ceased.

"Your hand is so cool," said Susie Van Berg in a little, surprised voice.

"I've been driving in the rain. I had the screen open because the rain beat on it so. My screen-wiper's out or order and I couldn't see. I can't drive in gloves."

"Is it raining?"

"Drenching."

Susie Van Berg drew her hands away.

"It doesn't matter—nothing matters. Why did you come?"

"You wanted to see me."

"Yes—it was good of you. But it's no use—nothing's any use."

There was a pause whilst Caroline tried to think of something to say. What could she say to unhappiness like this? She didn't know.

She said nothing.

Susie Van Berg flung round with outstretched hands.

"What shall I do if Elmer dies?"

"Perhaps he won't."

"But if he does—if he *does*!"

She jumped up with a sudden-surprising energy, ran to the door and opened it. For a moment she stood looking out into the corridor. Then she came back, her blue wrap trailing, her hand at her side, and a faint tinge of natural colour in her face.

"There's no one there," she said, and sank back into the sofa corner again. After a moment she said, "Louise listens," and then, "There isn't anyone there."

She bent and picked up the violet cushion and put it behind her. All her movements were nervous and uncertain. She leaned back and looked at Caroline.

"Louise listens—I think she talks—I suppose they all talk. You said so—didn't you? It's dreadful! I can't stop them talking. It's dreadful to know they're doing it. It's dreadful to have to be careful all the time—to be afraid to speak. I am afraid to speak, you know. There are the doctors and the nurses, and the servants, and the police. I'm afraid all the time of saying something—something—"

"Why?" said Caroline. She looked straight into Susie Van Berg's frightened eyes; her voice was steady and deep.

Susie went on speaking in a desperate, fluttered voice.

"It's awful to be afraid to speak. It's awful not to have anyone to speak to. That's why I asked you to come."

"Did Jim talk to you about me?"

Susie nodded.

"He talked about you a lot—he thought the world of you—he wanted us to meet. Men are funny like that—if two women are fond of them, they can't see why they won't be fond of each other. Elmer's like that too. He had a sister who kept house for him before we were married, and he thought it real unnatural when she didn't love me. Considering I was turning her out after she'd made up her mind that Elmer wasn't going to get married, it was expecting a good deal—but he can't see why to this day.'' A little animation had come to her as she talked, but with the last word a nervous shudder took her again.

"What is it?'' said Caroline gently.

"I felt I'd go mad if I hadn't someone to speak to. I thought you would be safe because, whatever I told you, you wouldn't want to hurt Jim.''

A moment before, Caroline had been too hot. She had wondered how anyone could bear the heat of the room. Now she knew, because, like Susie, she was afraid—so much afraid that her feet were cold and heavy in her country shoes, and her hands heavy and cold on the brown tweed that covered her knees. She didn't know that she was going to speak, but she said,

"Jim—''

Susie looked at her out of panic-stricken eyes and whispered, "I've killed Elmer.''

Caroline straightened herself.

She said, "Nonsense!'' and her own voice comforted her and made her feel sure that what Susie had just said could not possibly be true.

Susie shook her head.

"You don't know. He was jealous—I made him jealous— of Jim. It was only nonsense. You said nonsense, didn't you? That was all it was. One oughtn't to be punished like this just for a bit of nonsense—it isn't *fair*. Elmer wouldn't want me to be punished like this.''

"What did you do?'' said Caroline.

"I must tell someone. It just goes on and on in my head all the time. I don't sleep, you know.''

"You can tell me—I'm safe.'' And then as soon as she had said it she had a revulsion of feeling. "No, don't tell me—don't! Don't tell me anything! Because if you did it, and they thought it was Jim, I should have to tell them.''

Susie shook her head again.

"It wasn't like that. What did you think? I didn't shoot Elmer—I didn't mean that. Did you think I did?''

"I don't know. I didn't want you to tell me anything you'd feel sorry about afterwards."

"I must tell someone," said Susie piteously. "I've just got to the place where I'm bound to tell someone. If I don't I'll go crazy. Why, I've been afraid I'd get up in the night and run down the corridor screaming out that I'd killed Elmer." She broke off with a start. "Look out of that door and see there's no one listening!"

Caroline opened the door and looked out. There was no one in sight. The contrast between the room and the passage was extreme. The air was cold. Against an uncurtained window about three yards away the rain was beating. An inky cloud hung like a curtain across the sky. It was so dark that the sun might have set already.

She turned back into the lighted room. The blue shades made everything look as if they were under water. She went back to the sofa and sat down.

"There's no one there."

And at once, without any preliminaries, Susie Van Berg said,

"Jim shot Elmer."

"*No!*" said Caroline. *No!*"

"Jim shot him. It was my fault—I made Elmer jealous. You know I can't help flirting—I'm made that way. What did Elmer marry me for if he didn't like it? It made him mad, and—you know the way it is—I liked making him mad. But he ought to have known there was nothing in it."

Caroline heard her voice, harsh and unfamiliar.

"Wasn't there anything in it?"

"Only nonsense—and he wouldn't even play up to that. He thought a lot of Elmer. There was an invention they both thought a lot of. That's what Jim came to see him about that night. Did you know he was here the night Elmer was shot?"

Caroline nodded.

"Elmer didn't tell me Jim was coming. If he had, I wouldn't have worked him up like I did. I only wanted to make him mad, and then kiss and be friends. I didn't know he'd got a date with Jim—I wouldn't have done it if I'd known.''

"What happened?"

"Did you read what I told the police? I didn't tell any lies, but I didn't tell all the truth. They'd have arrested Jim straight away if I had.''

"What didn't you tell?"

"I told them I went downstairs to get a book, and heard voices in the study. I didn't tell them that it was Jim's voice I heard.''

"You're sure?"

"Of course I'm sure—I went right up to the door and listened.''

"Did you hear anything?"

"Yes, I did.''

"What did you hear?"

"They were quarrelling—that's why I listened. I heard Elmer say, 'I'm through with you!' And I heard Jim say, 'I'm damned if I'll be spoken to like that!' ''

"Was that all?"

"No, it wasn't. Jim said, 'You take that back!' And then Elmer got up—I heard his chair scrape along the floor and he came towards the door, and I thought how mad he'd be if he found me there and I ran away.''

"Is that all you heard?" Caroline was conscious of relief.

"Yes. I was too frightened to stop another minute.''

"Jim never shot Mr Van Berg,'' said Caroline. "Jim isn't a thief. The person who shot Mr Van Berg is the person who stole the emeralds.''

Susie Van Berg put her hand to her head. She spoke in a weak, extinguished voice.

"I don't mind about the emeralds—he shot Elmer. And I tore the page with his finger-prints out of Elmer's book. I knew if the police found it they would arrest him, so I tore it out.'' She sat bolt upright, her hands locked upon her knee. "I tore it out, but I didn't tear it up. Do you know where he is? If you do, will you tell him that?''

"That you tore it out?"

Susie had a small hard spot of colour on either cheek; her

eyes were bright and hard, her voice louder than it had been.

"Tell him I tore it out, but I didn't tear it up. If Elmer gets better, I'll tear it up, but if he doesn't—" Her locked hands strained one against the other; a line of livid pallor showed beyond the painted line of her lips. "If he doesn't— if he dies—I'm going to give those finger-prints to the police, and I'm going to swear that I heard his voice and that I heard him threaten Elmer."

XXIII

CAROLINE FOUGHT THE SHARPEST FEAR SHE HAD EVER known. What had really happened in the library that night? Jim had quarrelled with Elmer Van Berg on the other side of that door at which Susie had listened. Why hadn't she opened it and gone in? Would things have turned out differently if she had. . . . . It was no good asking that now. She had gone away upstairs to her room—to this very room in which they were—and in the morning Elmer Van Berg had been found shot. Jim had quarrelled with him. Was it possible that Jim had shot him? Everything in Caroline's heart said "No"; but in her mind a faint terrible whisper said "Perhaps." It rustled there like dry leaves and would not be still.

She steadied herself. Only a moment had passed really. Susie Van Berg had not moved. The patch of colour on either cheek had spread a little, as a stain spreads in milk.

Caroline said, "Why?" Then as Susie went on staring at her she made a quick movement. "I don't understand. Why did you tear the page out?"

"To help Jim—because it was my fault."

"You won't have helped him very much if you mean to tell the police in the end."

"Only if Elmer dies," said Susie with dry lips. Her eyes stared past Caroline at a picture of Elmer dead.

Caroline spoke again.

"Jim didn't shoot him."

Susie shook her head.

"Yes—he did. If Elmer gets well, he'll tell me what to do. That's why I tore out the page, and why I didn't tell the police. I was waiting for Elmer to tell me what to do, but if he doesn't get well, I shall say that Jim shot him, and that it was my fault. I can't go on like this." There was a dreadful finality about the way she said it.

Caroline had a feeling that if they were to go on talking for hours, they would never get beyond this point. If Elmer Van Berg died, then Susie would say that they had quarrelled on her account, and that Jim had shot him. She prayed with all her might that Elmer should not die. There was nothing else that she could do or say.

She got up and put on her coat.

"Are you going?"

"Yes," said Caroline.

Susie drew a long sighing breath and turned her head.

"Is it still raining?"

"I expect so—it looked very black."

For a moment, they were both silent, as if neither of them were able to put an end to this strange meeting. Through the silence came the sound of the rain and a deep roll of thunder.

Susie shuddered and stood up.

"There's a storm. You can't go if there's a storm."

"I'll get home before it breaks," said Caroline.

Now that she was on her feet, she wanted to be gone. Her head burned with the heat of the room, and her knees were trembling. Outside, in the wind and the rain, it might be easier to feel sure about Jim. She said "Good-bye," and went out without touching Susie's hand.

As soon as she had shut the door she began to run. She

wanted to get right away, and she had a feeling that Susie might call her back. She turned the corner, and then turned again. The passages were very dark. She stopped running and wondered if she had taken the wrong turning. The house was old and rambling. She had a bewildered feeling of having lost her sense of direction. A sudden flare of lightning gave a blinding picture of two corridors meeting at the foot of a narrow stair. Darkness followed immediately, and one of those peals of thunder which sound like giant girders being thrown down upon an iron roof. The noise was deafening. Caroline shrank instinctively away from the window, and found herself six or seven steps up the stair, holding to the narrow baluster and waiting for the horrible noise to stop.

The stair was enclosed on either side—a little winding stair running up between two walls. Another stabbing flash sent Caroline round the turn. She put her fingers in her ears and leaned against the wall. There could be no question of going out into a storm like this. The whole house seemed to shake as the thunder pealed overhead.

She felt that she was shaking too. She had never minded a thunderstorm before; now, for the first time in her life, she knew herself to be upon the edge of panic. She shut her eyes and tried to steady herself. The noise diminished. The wall against which she leaned began to feel solid again. She told herself that the storm had passed overhead and was going down the river. She let her hands drop and moved away from the wall.

When she opened her eyes, she saw above her a very faint streak of light. There was a door a few steps up, and the light came from under it. It was just a thin pale streak, but it meant that there was someone in the room. Caroline had a feeling that someone else's company would be pleasant. She could say that she had lost her way in the passages.

She went up to the level of the door, and as she lifted her hand to knock, the light of another flash flared up from behind her and below, and a crash more violent than either of the others followed. Urged by a blind instinct for shelter, Caroline opened the door.

She was inside the door and leaning against the jamb with the door shut behind her before the second crack of thunder came. She could not have moved to save her life. The shock, the impact, the mere sound, was beyond anything she could have imagined. After a little while she was able to take her breath and gather her bewildered thoughts. She was inside the room from which the light had come, but there was so little light that she wondered why she had seen it. She was in the room, but she could not see it at all, because a four-leafed screen covered the door, one panel being flat against the wall on her left, whilst the other three zigzagged out from it at an angle.

Caroline took her hand from the door and moved forward, following the line of the screen. It was tall and solidly made, a heavy old-fashioned piece of furniture covered with dark crimson rep. She had taken about three steps, when, in the room on the other side of the screen, someone spoke.

"Do you think it's going over?"

Caroline stood still just where she was. She had only heard that voice once before, but she would have known it anywhere. It was Nesta Riddell who had spoken. Beyond any possibility of doubt it was Nesta Riddell.

Someone answered her.

"Yes, it's going over. It'll draw down river now."

Caroline had never heard this voice before, or any quite like it. It reminded her of a fly in treacle, or a voice heard in a thick muffling fog. It had a peculiar soft tonelessness that blurred the words, and the pitch never varied.

"Then we'd better get on with it," said Nesta. "That last crash put me right off—but I shall have a train to catch presently, and I've got to know about Jim before I go."

Caroline had taken another step, but these words halted her. She had not meant to listen, but when Nesta said, "I've got to know about Jim," she knew that she was going to listen. If there was anything to know about Jim, she was going to know it. She heard the soft sound of someone moving, and the gurgle of water or some other liquid. The smooth toneless voice said,

"Look into the pool."

"What shall I see? Suppose I don't see anything." This was Nesta.

"I don't say you'll see, nor what you'll see—there's no saying. If you don't see nothing, there's no harm done. Look in the pool."

Silence fell on the room—a curious silence, enclosed by the sound of restless, hurrying wind and distant thunder. It was like the still place at the centre of the storm. Caroline edged forward and looked round the screen.

The room was full of a half light except for one bright patch—a Victorian room, with a round walnut table between the windows, crimson rep curtains closely drawn, a faded carpet with moribund rose wreaths on a mustard ground, a mantel-drapery of crimson plush with an edging of little silk balls, and photographs everywhere. There was a fire on the hearth banked down with coal dust. In front of it on a black wool hearth-rug stood a reading-lamp with a piece of black velvet draped round its shade. The light was directed downwards upon a bowl of dark blue glass which appeared to be full of ink. It was about the size of a hyacinth bowl, and it stood on a stool with a worked cross-stitch top. On one side of this stool Nesta Riddell was kneeling, and on the other, in a low armless chair sat a plump elderly woman. This must be the other Caroline—Caroline Bussell, Nesta Riddell's cousin, the housekeeper at Packham Hall. She wore a dark stiff dress buttoned up to the throat, where a collar of hand-made crochet was fastened by one of those large old-fashioned brooches which contain quite a substantial quantity of hair. She had a pale flat face, pale and plump, and a tight curled fringe of faded hair controlled by a net. Her hands lay in her lap. She leaned forward over them, watching Nesta.

Nesta Riddell had taken off her coat. Her rose-coloured jumper caught the light as she bent over the bowl of ink. Her hard handsome face had a look of frowning intensity. Caroline had the feeling that she and Caroline Bussell were a long way off. She stopped being afraid that they would see her or notice her presence. They were enclosed in that odd concentrated silence.

There was no sound in the room at all, and the sound of the wind and the thunder was drowned in a steady downrush of rain. Time did not seem to pass; it stood still. Caroline stood still, with her hand on the edge of the screen. She looked at Nesta, and Nesta looked into the bowl of ink.

All at once the silence broke. Nesta said in her hard voice,

"I can't see anything but fog."

"Sometimes the fog comes first," said Caroline Bussell. "Maybe it'll clear away."

Nesta had lifted her head a little. She bent it again and stared into the ink. The air in the room felt heavy and hot. The dark curtains hung straight at the two low windows. On the other side of the glass hung the heavy curtain of the rain.

"There's nothing but fog!" Nesta's voice was fretful. She jerked back suddenly on to her heels. "There's nothing but fog going up and down like waves—it makes me giddy. I'm not going to look any more. I didn't come all the way here to do the thing myself either."

Caroline Bussell spoke in her smooth voice.

"You've not got the patience—it needs patience. And you mustn't have your thoughts all churned up neither—you might as well go stirring up the mud in a pond and then expect to see clear to the bottom."

"Do it yourself!" said Nesta sulkily. "That's what I came here for. If I could do it, I'd have done it at home, and no need to come all this way."

Caroline Bussell leaned down and took up the bowl of ink. She set it in the hollow of her lap and drew the lamp so that the light shown upon it. All her movements were slow, smooth, and noiseless. Caroline thought of a snake's coils moving without seeming to move—a smooth brown snake. The light from the lamp shone down on the bowl of ink and on two pale, plump hands and a fold of smooth brown skirt. Nesta Riddell was just a shadow now.

Caroline began to feel afraid. She didn't like Nesta, but she wasn't afraid of her. It was Caroline Bussell who was making her afraid, sitting there in her respectable Victorian clothes practising some secret art. The time seemed endless before she spoke, swaying forward a little.

"Ask—the fog is lifting."

Nesta knelt up. The movement brought her almost to the edge of the light again.

"Where's Jim? That's what I want to know. Where is he?"

Caroline Bussell began to speak slowly and monotonously.

"I see the fog lifting—waves breaking—a ledge on a cliff—he is on the ledge—"

"What's the good of that? That's the part I know! I don't need you to tell me what I know already! I want to know about Jim!"

Caroline Bussell put up one of her plump hands.

"You have broken the picture. Perhaps it was not what you think—perhaps there was something you did not know."

"What?"

"You did not give me time to see. You broke the picture, and it will not come again."

Nesta made an impatient movement.

"Come down to present day! Where is he now?"

Caroline Bussell put up her hand again. Then she leaned over the bowl of ink. Her brooch caught the light. It had a rim of pale plaited gold. The stranded hair within it was pale—old pale hair, in a pale gold rim. She spoke again.

"Windows—blue—windows—up to the ceiling and down to the floor—no, that's curtain—blue—narrow—like slits—windows like slits—narrow—one, two, three, four—I'm in the middle of the room—I must turn round—one, two, three, four, five—five narrow windows like slits—"

Caroline felt cold water run down her spine. Caroline Bussell wasn't looking into the ink pool now. The bowl was in her lap, but her hands had fallen; they hung straight down at her side like pale, heavy weights. She had lifted her head, and sat stiffly upright with her eyes fixed on some point above Nesta's head. The light that struck upwards showed her eyes pale and set. Her lips hardly moved as she spoke.

"Five windows—like slits—"

That was the Blue Room at Hale Place. She had said

blue. How did she know? Cold drops kept running down Caroline's back.

"Is he there? Can you see him?" Nesta's voice was low but insistent.

"No—not there."

"What room is it? Why do you see it if he's not there?"

"He has been there—I can feel him there—I am in the room—I am turning in the room—I am counting the windows— one, two, three, four, five—five windows—like slits—and blue curtains—now the fireplace—deep hearth—china candlesticks—one of them is broken—I think he broke it—now the door—I am still turning—he came through the door—fear jumped out at him and he ran away—I am turning again—there is a bed set back in the wall—headpiece, footpieces, and four posts—the bed draws him—if he reaches it—no, not yet—not now—because of the other—"

Nesta leaned closer.

"What room is it? Where is it? Why do you keep on describing it? Where is it?"

Caroline Bussell sat silent.

"Can't you see where it is? You haven't told me anything at all."

"Eight—green—stones—" said Caroline Bussell.

Nesta made an abrupt movement.

"Where are they? In that room? Are they in that room?"

"Eight—green—" She swayed a little, stiffly like a figure carved in wood. "Eight—green—stones—five windows— like slits—I am counting the windows—"

"You've counted them!" said Nesta angrily. "You don't need to start all that again! Get back to the stones! Where are the eight green stones?"

Caroline Bussell swayed from side to side. The white of her eyes showed all round the iris. Her voice dragged.

"Five windows—blue—count—one, two, three, four, five—hearth—door—bed—"

"*Where are the emeralds?*" said Nesta in a furious whisper.

Caroline Bussell gave a violent start. She said in a loud, heavy voice, "He's alive," and the bowl of ink tilted over.

The ink ran down over her brown skirt, soaking into it. The bowl slipped off her lap and broke.

Nesta jumped up with an angry exclamation, but after that one violent start Caroline Bussell sat quite still, blinking her eyes. She did not seem to notice the ink that was soaking into her dress. After a moment she said in a bewildered voice,

"Did you know that he was alive?"

Caroline took three steps backwards and opened the door. The dark winding stair was before her. She went down half a dozen steps on tiptoe, holding her breath, and then ran as if there were wolves behind her.

XXIV

It was more than an hour past midnight when Caroline came to Hale Place again. Instead of going to bed at ten o'clock, or, if she had a very exciting book, at a quarter past, Pansy Ann had broken all records by staying up till nearly twelve. For nearly five hours she had talked about Robert—his looks; his character, temperament and disposition; anecdotes of his infancy and youth, as provided by old Mrs Arbuthnot; his school prizes; his industry, his perseverance, his steadiness, his filial piety; the designing females who had wished to marry him, and the firmness with which he had repelled their advances; his house, his servants, his favourite dishes; his drawing-room carpet, and whether a new one could be substituted, with excursions into furnishing in general and Pansy Ann's own preferences in particular. It was an avalanche of Robert, a Robertian landslide. When at eleven o'clock Caroline, exhausted, had managed to say good-night and reach her bedroom, she found it not a refuge but a trap, for after a bare ten minutes Pansy knocked at the door and, wrapped in a dressing-gown, sat down on Caroline's bed and devoted another hour to Robert.

Out in the dark, with the damp air blowing in her face and the trees of the avenue making a soft swishing sound overhead, Caroline had her first chance of thinking over the events of the afternoon. The more she thought about them, the more they frightened her. If Elmer Van Berg died and Susie went to the police with her story of Jim's finger-prints.... Caroline simply couldn't force her thought any farther. It encountered an icy wall of fear and shuddered back.

She passed to the scene in Caroline Bussell's room. The woman terrified her with her smooth voice, and her hints, and her pool of ink. But she hadn't looked into the pool while she described the Blue Room. She had looked straight past Nesta's head with fixed eyes, and what she saw was not her own plush-draped mantelpiece with its photographs and its china vases, but the Blue Room at Hale Place. Nesta had asked about Jim, and Caroline Bussell had described the Blue Room at Hale Place. She hadn't seen Jim in it; she had just described the room. And Nesta had asked about the emeralds—Susie Van Berg's emeralds—eight green stones; and again Caroline Bussell had described the Blue Room. Caroline wondered, shivering, whether she knew what room it was, and where. She felt sure that Nesta didn't know.

How could Susie Van Berg's emeralds be at Hale Place? How could they be in the Blue Room? Caroline Bussell had never said that they were there, but she had described the room. She had described the room, and she had begun to describe the bed..... *Was it possible?* Nesta had stopped her. If she had only known..... "No, it's silly to feel so frightened. She doesn't know—she *doesn't*! Suppose Caroline Bussell tells her. ... She mustn't—oh, she *mustn't*! Hurry, hurry, hurry—hurry and tell Jim!" She ran the last part of the way and came breathless to the back door.

It was open; not just unlatched, but wide, stark, staring open, and that halted Caroline. She had brought a torch with her this time, and she sent the little bright ray questing ahead of her before she entered. Where was Jim? She had thought that she might find the door shut against her—he had forbidden her to come again. He might have locked her out. He might be sleeping in one of the rooms upstairs. He might be in the Blue Room asleep in the four-post bed. But if he did not expect her, why was the door wide open? And if he expected her, why was he not here?

All at once she felt the ray of her torch was a danger. Suppose yesterday's burglar had returned. Suppose Jim were not here. . . . She did not wait to suppose any more, but turned off her torch and went through the hall and up the stair in the dark. The house had an empty, friendly feeling. It did not frighten her to be alone in it. Generations of her own people had gone up and down these same stairs, had been born and married and had died in the dark rooms on either hand.

She came to the door of the Blue Room and, feeling before her, found it open too. She knew that the room was empty even before she crossed the threshold. She stood in the middle of the floor and switched on her torch again. This was what Caroline Bussell had seen with those pale, fixed eyes—five narrow windows like slits, with the blue curtains drawn across them and hanging to the floor. "I am in the middle of the room—I am turning—" That was what Caroline Bussell had said. Caroline Leigh stood in the middle of the floor and turned slowly, counting the windows as Caroline Bussell had counted them—one, two, three, four, five narrow windows like slits. Then the fireplace— two candlesticks on the shelf, one of them broken, with the candle lying beside it.

She went on turning. Caroline Bussell had said, "I am still turning." The door came next, then a space of wall, and then the recess that held the bed. The torch shone on the wall and flickered over the bed foot and the two carved pillars.

Caroline went on turning. In a moment she would have made the circle of the room. Caroline Bussell had not made the circle, because Nesta had broken the picture. Caroline sent the ray of her torch straight to the head of the bed, a piece of massive carving supported by pillars. The pattern of the carving was an apple-tree with Adam and Eve on either side of it, and in the middle of the tree a shield with the arms of Ralph de Burgh, whose heiress had married a Randal and brought this bed with her. The arms should have been there, a castle and three spear-heads, but—Caroline caught her breath. The beam wavered in her shaking hand. With both hands on the torch to steady it, she came up to the bed.

The shield stood out at an angle like a door and showed a dark cavity behind it. Caroline knew the trick of it well enough. Jim had showed it to her when she was fourteen. You twisted the third apple from the bottom, and it turned the latch which held the shield in place.

She kneeled on the bed and focused the torch upon the cavity. It was a little cupboard with a shelf across it. In the bottom of it was a pencil and a button. Caroline remembered them quite well; she had put them there ages and ages ago. They were part of a terribly secret game. The pencil was Jim's; his initials were on it in an ink-smeared scrawl. The button was an old-fashioned waistcoat button of dark blue enamel with a paste centre.

There was nothing else at all in the little secret cupboard.

A sort of numbness came on Caroline. She couldn't move, and she couldn't think. She kneeled on the edge of the bed and stared along the ray of her torch at the empty space behind Ralph de Burgh's shield. Presently the numbness passed. She got up and closed the shield. You had to turn the apple again to do this. Half a turn to the right lifted the latch; then, when the door was shut, you turned the apple back again and the latch fell down and held it fast.

Only someone who knew the trick could open the shield.

Who had opened the shield?

Caroline went to the door and looked down the passage. It was empty. The secret place behind the shield was empty. Had it been empty this afternoon when Caroline Bussell looked into the ink pool? Nesta had said, ''Where are the emeralds?'' and Caroline Bussell had begun to describe this room and this bed. Was the place behind the shield empty then? Or were the emeralds there? If they were there, who had put them there? If they were there then, where were they now? Who had left the secret door standing open? Who had left the outer door standing wide?

Where was Jim?

Caroline had no answer to any of these questions. They were like great stones that she couldn't move. They blocked her path on every side. It was like a horrible dream. She couldn't move them and she couldn't get by them.

She came out of the Blue Room and passed along the passage to where it joined the main corridor. She had been sure for some time that she was alone in the house. Jim wasn't here. Yet she forced herself to make sure. It was strange to be alone in the house which had always been so full. She went all over it, opening door after door and throwing the light of the torch round the empty rooms. This was the nursery, and this the schoolroom. This was Jim's room, and this long bare attic playroom and muddle-room. This was Aunt Margaret's own little room. The delicate, gracious presence rose again as Caroline stood on the threshold. It was Aunt Margaret who had gathered the orphan children of three families under her sheltering care—Jim, Pansy, and little Caroline. Here was Uncle James' study—he was only a cousin really. Poor old Uncle James—so lost when Aunt Margaret went. Aunt Margaret would never have allowed the quarrel with Jim to go on.

Caroline came slowly downstairs into the hall. The house wasn't empty now. It was full of all the people she had known when she was a child—Mrs Crofts, the very fat cook who made such frightfully good spongecakes; Miss Milton, the jolly young governess who had only stayed six months because Major Palmer fell in love with her and whisked her off to Egypt; Aunt Margaret's maid, Halliday, frightfully grim; Nanna, who spoiled them all; and a succession of parlour-maids, house-maids, and between-maids, with one or two standing out from the rest—that very pretty Cissie Jones who married the milkman, good-natured Maggie, who had to be called by her surname, because her Christian name was the same as Aunt Margaret's, and Emily, whom nobody liked. There had been a little mystery about Emily— she just went without any notice. That wasn't like Aunt Margaret. Looking back, Caroline wondered what Emily had done. A prying girl—Nanna's word—with a fib always ready if she was blamed.

Caroline had looked into the drawing-room and library. It was whilst she was opening the dining-room door that she remembered Emily's surname. It came to her in one of those quick irrelevant flashes which sometimes show one things which have been forgotten for years. A moment before, she might have said that she had never known it; but as she opened the dining-room door, there it was in her mind, clear and distinct—Emily Rudd.

The dining-room was quite empty.

She came to the back door again. The house was empty behind her. Jim wasn't there. The key was on the inside of the door. She hesitated, and then left it there. Jim might come back. Something stabbed at her heart. She didn't think that Jim would come back. She thought that he was gone. Something had happened, and he was gone. She felt very tired.

She switched off her torch and stepped out into the dark yard, closing the door of the house behind her.

XXV

JIM RANDAL HAD TOLD CAROLINE THAT SHE WAS NOT TO come again to Hale Place, but he did not really expect that she would obey him—she had in fact immediately announced that she would not. When, therefore, he returned from a walk across his own dark fields at a little after ten o'clock, he did not lock the back door behind him, but left it just ajar. Caroline, if she came, would not be here very much before eleven, since she must wait till Pansy was safely asleep.

He went into the kitchen and sat on the edge of the table. He had spent the day in trying to remember, and had gained nothing but a horrid sense of strain. He made up his mind not to try any more. What had come back to him already had come without effort.

He began to feel drowsy in the dark, and lighted one of the candles which Caroline had brought. The windows were shuttered, so it was safe enough to have a light. As he struck the match, he had a sudden vivid recollection of the man whom he had followed into the Blue Room the night before. What on earth did the fellow want? He had walked in and struck a match as if the place belonged to him. Jim cursed himself for a fool for not having waited to see what he was after.

He blew out the match and stepped back, and then and there a voice spoke aloud in his mind: "Eight green stones—five windows like slits—no one knows where they are but me." He stood just where he was, and the words said themselves again. Then the voice stopped. He was left staring at the candle flame with a most frightful feeling of apprehension. The words were horribly familiar. He knew them by heart. They said themselves without effort. They linked Elmer Van Berg's emeralds with the Blue Room.

The shock of the thought was tremendous. If the emeralds were here at Hale Place in the Blue Room........How could they have come here? There was only one answer. If they were here, he must have brought them. If they were here, then he had shot Elmer Van Berg.

They couldn't be here.

A little mocking devil began to turn catherine-wheels in his mind. It cocked snooks and dared him—"Couldn't be here, couldn't they? Yah! Go and see! You daren't—yah! And why? Because they're there, and you know it!" A devil with the lowest gutter manners. Jim pitched him out of his mind and banged the door. "You daren't!" shrieked the devil through the keyhole. "Yah to you!"

Jim took the candle end which he had lighted and went upstairs to the Blue Room. If the emeralds were here, if he had brought them here, there was just one place where they would be. They weren't there—they couldn't possibly be there—but he was bound to satisfy himself that the impossible hadn't happened.

He went up to the four-post bed and threw the candlelight upon the headpiece with its carving of the Tree of Knowledge. It was a very set, symmetrical Tree, with Adam and Eve on either side, rather prematurely dressed in fig-leaves. The Serpent trailed his length across the whole panel and doubled back to coil about the Tree. There were four apples on one side and four apples on the other, and right in the middle of the Tree, just over the Serpent's head, the shield of Ralph de Burgh, bearing a crenellated castle and three spear-heads.

Jim set the candle end down upon the bed and twisted the bottom apple on the right-hand side; at the same time he pulled on the shield. It opened like a door. He remembered how thrilled Caroline had been when he showed her the trick of it. He bent forward and dropped his left hand, because the shadow of it was dark across the hole behind the shield. His hand fell, and the yellow candlelight shone into the cavity.

Jim took hold of the bed-post to steady himself. He had one knee on the bed, and for a moment he was in danger of losing his balance; he had the feeling that the bed with its pillars and its massive head and foot-pieces had heaved beneath him. His hand clenched on the bed-post and he stared at the cavity. It had a partition across it like a shelf, and all the space above the shelf was a dazzle of gold, and white, and green—links of fine wrought gold strung with pearls, and a twist and more pearls, and a great green stone wedged sideways that drank the light like water.

Jim stayed, staring. Here were the emeralds—here, in this secret place. He tried to stir his mind to thought, but nothing moved. The emeralds were here—that was a fact.

You can't get away from a fact. The emeralds were in the secret place behind Ralph de Burgh's shield.

His thoughts began to move again, but slowly and stiffly. He couldn't remember putting the emeralds here. He ought to be able to remember. He remembered Elmer Van Berg's hand under the light, and the eight green stones with the fine gold chains in between, and the pearls. And he remembered the piece about the Blue Room—"five narrow windows like slits." But he couldn't remember anything about the shield, and he couldn't remember hiding the emeralds.

Without altering his position, he put out a hand, took hold of the gold chain, and pulled it out of the cupboard. It swung as he had seen it swing from Elmer Van Berg's hand—eight square green stones with pearls between them—"like a kid's green beads." He checked the swing of the chain with a jerk of his lifted hand. Ridiculous! They weren't in the least like beads! Beads were pierced; but these square stones were set in heavy gold. It kept coming back—"like a kid's green beads."

"I didn't say that. Who said it?"

He had got as far as that, when the first sound reached him. As he half stood, half kneeled at the bedside with the candle end burnt to its last inch on the white coverlet, he was in full view, not only of the door, but of the whole length of the passage between the door and the main corridor.

The man who had turned the corner a moment before had first started back and then come cautiously on. He could see the lighted panel of the door, and beyond it the bed head with the right hand pillar, and Jim half turned away, a knee upon the bed and his left hand just out of the picture. Another yard, and the hand was in view—the hand and what it was holding—the eight green stones, rimmed with gold and dripping with pearls. The low candle made black shadows everywhere.

The man came soft-foot to the door, as soundless as might be. Yet there must have been a sound, for Jim let go of the post and made to turn. At his first movement the man charged him, snatching at the hand which held the chain. They came down together across the bed. The darkness came down too. As he fell, Jim struck the jutting shield with his head. The chain was wrenched out of his grasp. He had the man by the shoulder with an awkward left-hand grip—a hard, wiry fellow with a twist on him like an eel. He was twisting all the time. If Jim could not get a better hold, he would lose him. He tried to roll over, to get his right arm free, but the soft bed gave no purchase. He was a little dazed with the suddenness and the blow to his head. The smothered candle smelled to heaven. With a violent effort he heaved over, and as he did so, the man wrenched aside and got his teeth into his left wrist. He bit deep, jerked backwards, and with a rip of cloth he was free. He must have been as quick on his feet as a cat, for in the same moment he was across the room and through the door.

Jim stumbled up, heard the sound of running feet in the passage, and gave chase. He had cut his forehead and the blood ran down into his eyes and bothered him. The man had the start of him, and this time Jim was not sufficiently sure of himself to slide the banisters. As he came to the foot of the stairs, he heard the dull thud of the baize door which led to the kitchen wing. When he reached it, the wind was blowing to meet him down the long stone passage.

He dashed his hand across his eyes and ran at top speed down the passage and out of the open door.

XXVI

THE HEAD-LONG INSTINCT OF PURSUIT CARRIED JIM ACROSS the yard and out of the gate. There his mind checked him.

He stood still and listened. It was no use just blundering on in the dark. He'd got to listen, and he'd got to think. If the thief was a local man, he would take some side path or cut across the garden. If he was a stranger, he would probably stick to the drive.

Jim caught the sound of crushed gravel and began to run again. The fellow was sticking to the drive. That looked like a stranger. He wondered how he had got here. If he had a car or a motor-bike, he was as good as gone already. If he was on his flat feet, he might be come up with. The dark was very hampering. Only a novice would go on running away when every hedge and bush offered a hiding place. Remembering the wriggle-and-twist brand of fight the thief had put up, Jim didn't think he had to do with a novice.

He had almost reached the gate, when he stopped suddenly and ran back again past the house along a gravel path which wound between shrubberies. He had taken a sudden decision and was going nap on it. To catch a lighter, faster man with a twenty yard start and the darkness to help him offered no chances. In a rapid survey of the possibilities he had seen only one real chance.

There are three ways out of Hazelbury West—the main north road, to take which the thief would have had to turn right-handed as soon as he passed the gate; the Ledlington road, for which he would have to turn left; and the path across the fields to Hinton which was the nearest railway station. If you walked to the station, you took the field path, and the distance was four miles. If you drove, you followed the Ledlington road, and it was six.

The path along which Jim was running came out upon the field path to Hinton, cutting the corner. If the thief was making for Hinton with the idea of catching the last train there, Jim had a reasonable chance of intercepting him. He hadn't gone north; Jim had heard those running footsteps go off to the left before he himself turned back. Of course, even setting aside the possibilities of a car or bicycle, the fellow might take the high road to Hinton and then leave it by the Packham fork, but somehow it didn't seem so very likely. If he was a chance-come thief, yes; but if he knew that he had snatched the Van Berg emeralds, then Packham would be about the last place on earth that he would be heading for. No, if he knew what he had got, he would make for Ledlington, and later perhaps for London.

As he ran, Jim wondered whether they had altered all the trains. Seven years is a long time to be away. There used to be a crawling local train that stopped at Hinton—the twelve-twenty-five—and fetched up at Ledlington about one. It didn't go any farther.

Jim kept a steady pace across the fields. The farther he went, the more of a wild goose chase did the whole thing appear. He had had a hunch, and he had followed it. Sometimes hunches turned out all right; sometimes they let you down. He began to feel gloomily certain that he was going to be let down flat.

He wasn't in training for running four miles; besides there was plenty of time. He ran a bit and walked a bit. The heavy rain had made the path rather soggy. He wondered if the other man was before him or behind. He might be either. If he had been very nippy, he might have got past the Hale Place back gate before Jim emerged from it. On the other hand, if he had slacked off a bit, he was probably behind—*probably*, with a query. He was probably a mile or two away on some perfectly different tack. All the same, Jim was going to Hinton.

His pace admitted of thought, and he had plenty to think about. He had to think about the emeralds. How had they come to be where he had found them? As far as he knew, only two people now living knew of the secret hiding-place behind Ralph de Burgh's shield. Uncle James and Aunt Margaret had known, and Uncle James had told him with a good deal of humming and hawing and some heavy business on the lines of, "Family heirloom—family secret—future head of the family, my boy"; and, "It will all be yours some day." He remembered saying, "I hope it won't—not for ages, I mean." And Uncle James, a good deal embarrassed, pulling at his walrus moustache, and saying, "I hope not—I hope not—but you never can tell." Well, that was eight years ago, and he had told Caroline to console her before he went away. And of course Caroline might have told anyone. No, she wouldn't—she had promised. Rubbish! A child's promise! She had probably told all her bosom friends. No—not Caroline. He felt ashamed of having had the thought. He could hear her funny deep voice now: "Jim, I faithfully promise." No—Caroline wouldn't have told after that.

He frowned impatiently. Any number of people might know about the thing. But if they didn't—if only he and Caroline knew—then it was he who had put the emeralds there. It was a damned bad show. How could he have put the emeralds there? How had they got there if he hadn't put them there? And why had he been haunted by snatches of memory in which the emeralds and the five narrow windows of the Blue Room came and went?

An obstinate denial rose in him. He might have shot Elmer Van Berg, but he couldn't have taken the emeralds. He said that he might have shot Elmer. He began to turn that over. He wouldn't have gone to see Elmer with a gun on him—not in England. But if they had had a violent quarrel and Elmer had drawn on him, there might have been a struggle in which Elmer was shot. But in that case what had happened to the weapon? There wasn't anything about a weapon in the newspaper stories. He wondered if that was one of the things the police were lying low about. . . . .

Well, say he and Elmer had quarrelled. What would they have quarrelled about? It would have to be something that made Elmer suddenly see red. Well then, it would have to be something about Susie. Susie liked to play him up and make him jealous. If Elmer was jealous, he'd be formidable— he'd be liable to forget where he was and pull a gun. But then Jim had a perfectly clear memory of drinking with Elmer. They weren't quarrelling then. He could see that one moment of their interview perfectly clearly—his own hand lifting his drink, and Elmer's hand under the light holding up the emeralds. He came to a puzzled obstinate certainty. He might have shot Elmer, though he couldn't think why. He couldn't have taken the emeralds and hidden them at Hale Place.

He crossed a stile, and came in sight of the lights of Hinton station. As he did so, the church clock of Hinton St Margaret chimed out the hour of twelve. If the train had not been altered, he had a quarter of an hour in hand, and a couple of hundred yards between him and the main road.

The field path ended in a gap with posts across it. Jim emerged, crossed the road, and began to walk down the incline which led to the station. It is a long incline. He had only just begun the descent, when it was borne in upon him that the time-table had certainly been altered. The clock had only just struck twelve, but the train was coming in. It might now be anything from the eleven-fifty-five to the twelve-five, but it couldn't any longer be the twelve-fifteen.

He started to run, and as he did so, something black began to bob up and down ahead of him. It was another man, also running, and presumably with the same object. Jim put on all the pace he could, gained a little, and then saw the black figure draw away. They would hold him at the wicket. If they held him, he'd be likely to miss the train. Would they hold him? No, he was through, with a hand thrust out as if he were showing a ticket. That was it—he'd come down by train, and he'd got his return ticket. He was across the platform and into one of the rear carriages as the train began to move. Jim flung himself against the wicket, and saw the red tail-light slide off into the dark. He had shot his bolt. That was the last train, and even if he felt like walking into Ledlington, which he didn't, it wouldn't be of the least use. The fellow would have had several hours in which to get off the map. He turned round and walked back up the incline.

Well, he had lost the train. Had he gained anything? He had seen the man's back for a moment as he ran across the platform. The light was poor, and he certainly hadn't seen anything that he could be sure of recognizing—medium height—medium build—some sort of cap on the head—a suit, not an overcoat. That was all, except just for one thing, and that he couldn't have sworn to. He thought there was something odd about the man's right shoulder as he ran—his shoulder, or his sleeve. There was something that might be a shadow, or a stain, or a tear; and he remembered his own left-hand grip, that last wrench when the man bit him and pulled free, and the sound of tearing cloth.

He passed between the posts and took the path across the fields again. He was angry and fagged, he had a bump on his head, and a bitten wrist. He had had the emeralds in his grasp and had lost them. But gradually, as he walked, it came to him that the alteration in the local time-table which had turned the twelve-fifteen into the twelve-three or something of that sort had saved him from plunging into the devil of a mess. If he had come up with his burglar, what was he going to have done about it? Chasing him was all right, but what happened if you caught him? That was where the fun began. He sketched out some snappy dialogue as he walked:

"I charge this man with breaking into my house at Hazelbury West and committing an assault by biting me on the wrist."

"What is the name of your house?"

"Hale Place."

"What is your name?"

"James Randal."

"Do you charge the prisoner with theft?"

"Yes—I charge him with the theft of the Van Berg emeralds."

"And may we inquire what the Van Berg emeralds were doing in your possession, Mr Randal?"

After that the dialogue broke up in disorder, to the accompaniment of a heavy hand on his shoulder and a stolid voice informing him that he was under arrest for the murder of Elmer Van Berg, and that anything he said would be liable to be used in evidence against him. He began to feel a good deal of gratitude to the person responsible for the altered time-table.

That lasted for a bit, and then something else loomed up. Suppose the thief didn't know what he'd got. Suppose he just went blundering off with the emeralds to his usual fence. It was a hundred to one he'd be nabbed. And if he was nabbed, it was about ten thousand to one that he'd give the whole show away—he would be bound to if he didn't want to be charged with the murder, or the attempted murder, of Elmer Van Berg. He would save his neck by owning up to having burgled Hale Place.

The dialogue began again.

"And who does Hale Place belong to?"

"It belongs to me."

"Now, Mr Randal—can you offer any explanation as to how these emeralds, the property of Mr Van Berg—or would it be the late Mr Van Berg—can you offer any explanation as to how these emeralds came to be concealed in your house?"

"No, I can't."

"Evidence has been given that they were in a hiding-place the secret of which was known only to yourself. Do you deny this?"

"No, I don't."

"I put it to you that you stole the emeralds and placed them in this receptacle."

It was a nightmare—the deadliest, beastliest kind of nightmare; because it was all perfectly logical, possible, and probable. His mind began to sort out the facts and array its conclusions.

He couldn't go to the police, because, quite definitely, he couldn't afford to charge his burglar.

On the other hand—

He must do everything in his power to trace the man and get the emeralds away from him. If he didn't succeed in doing this, he would probably find himself in the dock for the theft of the emeralds and the murder of Elmer Van Berg.

He had no idea how he was going to trace the man. He had no clue to his identity except that of a torn coat sleeve. A torn coat may be changed or mended. Exit the torn coat.

The man had got into a train which went to Ledlington and didn't go any farther. Going to Ledlington doesn't necessarily mean staying in Ledlington. Still, it was some sort of a clue to the man's whereabouts.

A torn coat and a Ledlington train were all he had to go upon. They did not provide him with very much encouragement.

He came back to Hale Place dog-tired, missing Caroline by a bare five minutes. He had left the door wide open, and he found it closed. So Caroline had come. He thought she might be there still. He called her name. When there was no reply, he went forward into the kitchen and groped for and lit another of the candles she had brought him. He wanted to wash the blood from his face, and to bathe his bitten wrist.

At the scullery sink he let the tap run and put his head under it. Then he took a look at his wrist. It was a good deal bruised, but the skin was only broken in one place. As he held it under the tap and the smear of blood ran off, he gave a start and caught up the candle in his other hand. The mark of the bite showed plain on both sides of the wrist. On the under side were six indentations, all close together. But on the top of the wrist there were only four—two on one side and two on the the other, and a widish gap between.

Here at last was a real clue. The man who had bitten him had lost the two front teeth in the middle of his upper jaw.

XXVII

IF YOU CANNOT GO BACK OR GO FORWARD, YOU MUST JUST make the best of it and go whatever way you can.

Jim walked back across the fields in the early hours of the morning and took the milk train into Ledlington. It used to leave Hinton at six-thirty. He discovered that it now left at six-thirty-one. It reached Ledlington at ten minutes to seven, which is a cold, uncomfortable hour to arrive anywhere, but especially when you have no fixed destination and very little money.

He had a cup of tea and a sandwich, and put in time in

the waiting-room until he could buy a paper. He chose one of the more dramatic dailies, and was immediately confronted by a large picture of Packham Hall and a photograph, described as unique, of Susie Van Berg with the emeralds all across the front of her dress. It wasn't a very good photograph of Susie, but it was a speaking likeness of the emeralds. Jim wondered whether the burglar would see it, and what he would do if he did see it. If he had a grain of sense, he'd chuck the chain away into the nearest ditch and make himself scarce. That was assuming that he didn't already know what he had got. But didn't he? *Didn't he?* What had brought him to Hale Place *twice*? Would he have come back a second time, and come back to a room which appeared to contain nothing stealable if he hadn't got wind of the emeralds? It was taking a risk to come back. There must have been a strong motive. The emeralds would provide the motive. A room containing nothing but panelling, two china candlesticks, and an immovable four-post bed frankly would not. It became most urgently necessary to find the burglar.

Jim had a pleasant picture of himself asking the forty thousand odd adult inhabitants of Ledlington to show him their front teeth. There didn't seem to be any other way of identifying the burglar.

He read all that his paper had to say about the Van Berg case. There was a lot of it, but it didn't amount to anything at all. He gathered that Elmer was about the same, that Susie was refusing to be interviewed—the journalistic euphemism for this is, "absolutely prostrated"—and that the police were sitting tight. He thought that he would go and have another look at the back numbers as soon as the free library opened. There were several points on which he felt he could do with a little more information.

He left the station at half past eight and walked in the direction of the library. It would not be open until nine o'clock, so he walked down the High Street, through Poulter's Row, and round the Market Square.

The library is upon the east side of the square. It was presented to Ledlington by the late Sir Albert Dawnish in recognition of the fact that it was in Ledlington that the first of Dawnish's Quick Cash Stores had had its birth. Sir Albert himself, three times life size, stands in the middle of the square attired in the strange garments peculiar to statuary. There are the trousers that would break any man's leg, the negligent tie, the flapping collar, and the cloak. It was a very expensive statue. Ledlington regards it with pride.

Jim was passing the statue a second time, when a girl who had just come down Market Street with a basket on her arm stopped short not a yard away and said "Oh!" in a tone of so much surprise that his attention was arrested. A moment before, he had not known that there was a girl there, but when she said "Oh!" he saw Min Williams staring at him and recognized her at once. She had on a blue serge coat and skirt and a very neat little dark blue hat which threw up the gold of her hair and the blue of her eyes.

She said "Oh!" again, and her cheeks turned bright pink. It was an embarrassing encounter. There was nothing for it but to make it as ordinary as possible.

He said good morning, asked her why she was out so early, and was about to pass on, when she stopped him.

"Are you in a hurry?" It was said timidly, hesitatingly. Her colour came and went. Only a very hard-hearted person could have admitted to being in a hurry.

Jim said, "Not at all."

"Then if we could just walk round the square—"

They began to walk. He wondered what she wanted to say to him. Apparently nothing, for she remained perfectly silent. When they reached the colonnade which embellishes the west side of the square, however, she turned to him with a look of embarrassed appeal.

"Aren't you coming back?" She was brightly flushed. The effort to speak had brought tears into her eyes.

Jim was rather touched.

"I don't think so, Min."

The colonnade was quite empty. She stood still and looked at him earnestly.

"I'm not one to interfere—but she's very unhappy."

"Nesta?"

She nodded.

"I don't think it's on my account."

She nodded again, blinking away a tear.

"What makes you think so?" he said.

Min's eyes reproached him.

"You've not been married a month."

He looked hard at her.

"I'm not admitting I'm married at all."

She backed away from him.

"You haven't remembered?"

"I haven't remembered marrying Nesta."

"Don't you want to remember?"

He gave a short laugh.

"Not *that*!"

"It's dreadful for her," she said in a soft, distressed way. "It seems as if that would be a thing you couldn't help remembering—it seems as if it would be too dreadful if anyone could forget that they were married. I'm so sorry for Nesta I don't know what to do."

"What makes you think she minds, Min?"

"She's so cross," said Min ingenuously. "There isn't nothing right from morning till night."

He got a kind of hard amusement out of that. He wanted Min to go on talking, so he said,

"You think she really minds?"

"If it was *Tom*—" said Min, and turned quite pale.

"Tom's a very lucky young man, and I expect he knows it."

He wanted her to talk, because an idea was shaping itself in his mind. When he had waked up in her house, it was Min who told him he was Jim Riddell. How did she know? What was she going on when she said that? He thought he could size up a liar, and he didn't believe that Min was a liar; he thought she was just what she seemed to be—a nice, simple girl, rather pathetically fond of Tom, who didn't strike him as being nearly good enough for her. Now if Min had known him—really known him—as Jim Riddell, and as Nesta's husband before the wreck of the *Alice Arden*, he wouldn't have to believe her, but he would certainly have to take her evidence very seriously into account.

Min blushed.

"Oh, I don't know about that," she said.

Someone had turned into the colonnade from Poulter's Row. The last thing that Jim wanted was to attract attention. He said, "We'd better walk." And then, as they moved, "Min—I don't know about anything. For instance, I haven't any idea of where I first met you."

Min said "Oh!" in a startled way.

"If I'm Nesta's husband, I'm your brother-in-law."

"That's right."

"Then I suppose we're old acquaintances—you've known me for a long time."

If she wasn't truthful, she'd say yes to that and land with both feet in his trap. The gap in his memory only covered the last six weeks. On the farther side of it were the seven years he had spent overseas. He felt an odd relief when she shook her head and said,

"Oh no."

"We're not old friends?"

"Oh no," said Min again.

"Min—when did you meet me first?"

He got a round blue stare.

"Oh, you *know*."

"I'm afraid I don't. Shall we turn and walk back again? I don't suppose anyone knows us, but you never can tell. And now—when *did* you meet me first?"

"Oh, but you do know that—you can't have forgotten so soon!"

"So soon?"

"It's not a week," said Min. "You can't have forgotten!"

Jim felt a rising excitement. He was aware that he changed colour; he hoped not too noticeably.

"Not a week? Do you mean you never saw me before Nesta fetched me from that hospital at Elston?"

"No, never." She looked up at him with an air of childlike candour.

"Then it was Nesta who told you I was Jim Riddell?"

"Oh yes."

"So when I said I didn't know who I was, and you said I was Jim Riddell, you were only saying what Nesta told you to say?"

Min coloured up to the roots of her fair hair. There was distress and bewilderment in her voice as she protested,

"But she couldn't have made a mistake. She must have known—her own husband—"

Jim thought he would let it go at that. But he wanted to know about Tom. Where did Tom stand? He felt a little chary of accepting Tom as a guileless innocent. He asked abruptly,

"Hadn't Tom met me either?"

"Oh no."

So that was that. Jim felt as if a heavy paving-stone had been lifted off his back. He still carried one or two more, but this particular one was gone. If it was only Nesta who identified him as Jim Riddell, he was prepared to lay very long odds that he wasn't Jim Riddell, and never had been Jim Riddell. At the same time his opinion of Nesta as an adversary went up. It had been nothing short of a stroke of genius to put up Min to answer his bewildered questions. Simple good faith is more effective than the cleverest of lies.

They reached the end of the colonnade once more.

"I mustn't keep you," he said.

Min blushed again.

"Oh, won't you please come back with me and just see her? You don't know what mayn't come of it if you go on staying away. Won't you please come back?" She spoke with what was obviously a great effort. Her hands, in their neat thread gloves, were twisting the straps of the shopping basket.

That very delicate extra sense which sometimes warns, and sometimes discerns things of which we have no evidence, became suddenly active in Jim. He had owed his life to it before now. It prompted him to go on talking to Min. Instead of saying good-bye he turned and began to walk slowly back along the colonnade.

Min, flushed and encouraged, moved beside him with small quick steps, two or three to his one. It would be so lovely if she could bring them together again. Married people oughtn't to live separate; it always led to trouble. Mother always said. . . . . She found she was saying this out loud:

"Mother always says—"

And then Jim discomposed her by turning a most attentive look upon her.

"Yes—what does your mother say?"

"If you won't think I'm saying anything I shouldn't—"

"I promise you I won't, Min."

She didn't feel quite so flustered after that. He had a real kind look in his eyes when he spoke her name. His voice was kind too, and if he didn't take it amiss, there was no saying what good she mightn't do if she could only get the courage to speak out.

"Well?" said Jim. That odd unclassified sense was alert and waiting, but he felt free to be amused and a little charmed by Min's hesitancies.

"I don't hardly like to."

"Oh come—you were going to tell me what your mother says. I'm sure you can manage that."

Min looked up and then down again. Her eyes were really most uncommonly blue, and her lashes dark enough to set them off. He smiled encouragingly.

"Out with it, Min!"

"Mother always says married folk should stick close, because if they don't—"

"Yes—if they don't?"

"There's room for a third between them."

"So there is," said Jim.

"So you *will* come back?"

Jim got a hunch.

"My dear Min, are you trying to warn me?"

They had reached the corner again. Min stopped and faced him, nodding.

"You are!"

She nodded again solemnly.

The hunch got stronger.

"You're warning me that if I don't come back, I may find that Nesta has given me the chuck?"

Min nodded for the third time.

He would have liked to laugh, but refrained.

"All right, we'd better take another turn, and you shall tell me about it. Who's the man?"

"I don't know," said Min in a low reluctant voice.

"Unknown Rival Alienates Wife's Affections—is that it?"

Min looked up with brimming eyes.

"It isn't a thing to talk light of!"

His voice changed.

"My dear, I'm most horribly in earnest. Won't you tell me what you mean?"

Min took a handkerchief out of her pocket and dabbed her eyes.

"I don't know if I ought."

Jim didn't know either. He only knew that he was bound to get it out of her if he could. He said gravely,

"You've got to tell me."

She twisted the handle of her basket.

"I've never been a tale-tatler, nor a mischief-maker."

"You won't be making mischief."

Min's voice became what she herself would have called all trembly.

"I'm not saying there's anything in it, and I'm not one to think harm where no harm's meant, and if it had been a matter of coming home late after the pictures or anything like that, I'd not have thought anything about it—though 'tis different when you're married, and I wouldn't go to the pictures with anyone but Tom, not if it was ever so—"

Jim gathered that Nesta had fewer prejudices.

"So Nesta's been going to the pictures?"

"Oh *no*!" said Min. "I wouldn't mind if it was only the pictures, or if it was a friend of Tom's or anyone we knew."

"Well, what was it if it wasn't the pictures?"

"I don't know what I ought to say," said Min in a shrinking voice.

Min Williams was a dear little thing, and a pretty little thing, and a good little thing, but Jim wondered if he wouldn't end by shaking her.

"You've said too much not to go on."

She gave him a frightened glance curiously mingled with virtuous pride.

"Throwing stones up at her window, and long past midnight!" she said.

An extraordinary sense of anticipation quickened his pulses.

"Last night?" he said.

"And long past midnight!" said Min with a wide scandalized gaze fixed on his face.

Jim's thoughts began to march to a triumphant band. There was a lot of blaring brass in it. He saluted his hunch. He saluted the extra sense which had set him off on this tack.

He turned at the top of the colonnade and proceeded to the question direct.

"A man threw stones up at Nesta's window last night?"

Min gulped and nodded again.

"What happened? Did she come down?"

Min nodded.

"You saw her?"

"I heard the pebbles against the glass. I dreamt it was hailing, and I got up and went to the window, and it was quite fine. And I was just going back to bed again, when he threw some more, and I saw him under the other window— Nesta's. And then she looked out—I could just see her face. And he said her name—just Nesta, not Mrs Riddell at all. And then he said, 'Come down.' "

"What did she say?"

"She didn't say anything, not that I could hear. She went back from the window, and I was wondering about waking Tom, because it didn't seem right—one o'clock in the morning, and him calling her Nesta—only it came into my head that maybe it was you, and I didn't want to stand in the way of your making it up together."

"I see. Then what happened?"

"She went down. I never heard her come out of her room, but the third stair from the bottom will creak, no matter what you do—and I'm sure Tom's tried all ways."

"Nesta went out?"

Min nodded.

"And I dursn't go to bed with the door on the latch, so I put a blanket round me and waited for her to come in."

"Yes?"

"I hoped it was you, and that you were making it up. Married people didn't ought to quarrel. Mother says it's easier begun with than done with." The blue eyes looked up pleadingly.

"When did you find out that it wasn't me?"

"When she came back. She opened the door and came in, and I was just going to get into bed, when I heard that stair again. I went back to the window, and he was outside the gate."

"She went in and came out again? What did she do? Was it light enough to see anything?"

"It was beginning to get light—sort of betwixt and between. It must have been getting on for three by the look of it, and I could see enough to know that it wasn't you."

"What happened?" said Jim.

"She went to the gate and gave him something."

"She gave him something? You're sure it wasn't the other way about?"

"I think it was money," said Min.

"What makes you think that?"

She hesitated.

"I think it was."

"But why?"

He was wondering whether it was the Van Berg emeralds that had changed hands over the gate of Happicot at three o'clock in the morning. For this was what he thought his hunch had done for him—he thought it had brought him hot on the track of his burglar. The twelve-three or whatever it was, which he had missed and last night's burglar had caught, would have reached Ledlington in very nice time to allow of Nesta being serenaded with a handful of pebbles.

But in that case the man who had taken the emeralds must have known exactly what it was that he had snatched in the Blue Room. And he hadn't come there blind. He had come there to get the emeralds. There were a good many ifs in the affair.

He said, "But why?" and looked at Min, who didn't look at him.

"I could see it wasn't you," she said—"and I was frightened. Mother always said I could hear a mouse move his whiskers in the dark."

"You heard something?"

Min nodded.

"Nesta said, 'It's all I've got'—and something about keeping money in the house."

"Is that all you heard?"

She shook her head.

"No—he said—at least he said a lot more than what I'm telling you—but all mumbly like as if he'd got something in his mouth."

Jim restrained himself.

"What *did* you hear, Min?"

"It didn't amount to anything."

"Have you ever been sworn at in Spanish?" said Jim.

She stared at him, and the corners of his mouth twitched.

"Well, my dear, it's a copious language, and if you don't want it loosed on you, you'll get down to brass tacks and tell me exactly what Nesta's friend did say."

She looked at him in alarm.

"Maybe he didn't mean anything."

"What did he say?"

"He said, 'Don't be late,'" said Min with a gasp.

Don't be late. . . . Well, don't be late for what—and when—and where?. . . . . And he spoke as if he had something in his mouth. . . . . Perhaps it was a gap in his upper jaw—perhaps it wasn't. Jim's head whirled with possibilities.

"Anything more?" he asked.

She shook her head.

"He went off, and she came in."

"Which way did he go?"

"Ledlington way."

He walked beside her in silence for a moment.

"You could see that it wasn't me? Now Min, how much could you see? Would you know him again?"

"Oh no."

"Then how did you know it wasn't me?"

"He wasn't so tall."

"A small man?"

"Not to say small."

"Wasn't there anything you noticed particularly?"

She shook her head helplessly.

"I could just see the shape of him like."

He got no more out of her than that.

At the lower end of the colonnade they parted.

He crossed the square and went into the library.

XXVIII

As Jim Randal entered the free library in Ledlington, a car stopped at Miss Pansy Arbuthnot's wicket gate and a small dapper man got out. He slammed the door of the car behind him, clicked open the gate, marched up the path to the front door, and delivered a smart rat-tat. His hair and moustache were white, the former thick and the latter bristling, and his face so tanned that strangers learned with surprise that it was ten years since he had set foot outside the British Isles. He wore an air of military impatience, and after the briefest of intervals his knock was repeated, and so loudly as to bring Pansy Ann out of the scullery without waiting to dry her hands. Her consternation was considerable at finding the Chief Constable on the doorstep at such an hour—the breakfast things not cleared away; her feet—Pansy was proud of her feet—in her oldest shoes; and her hands and arms dripping with the geranium dye in which she had just immersed an aged pink sports coat. It was all very agitating, and if she hadn't thought it might be the post and a letter from Robert, she wouldn't have gone near the door—and what on earth Major Anderson was doing here at half past nine, heaven alone knew.

Her colour rose. She put up a hand to her hair, left a gruesome stain on her temple, and said in an agitated voice, "Oh good morning, Major Anderson—I'm dyeing."

Major Anderson when at school had recited Macauley's *Lays of Ancient Rome*. He was reminded of one of them now. He had a martinetish sense of humour which he kept under strict control. Macauley's words bobbed up and tickled it.

> *On the right side went Romulus*
> *With arms to the shoulder red—*

Was it shoulder, or elbow? Tut tut! He couldn't be sure, but the bit about Remus was really more appropriate.

> *On the left side went Remus*
> *With wrists and fingers red—*

Hang it all, the girl looked as if she had been killing a pig.

With all this in the back of his mind, he removed his hat and said, "Good morning."

"I'm afraid I'm an early visitor," he proceeded, "but I've come on a matter of business. Perhaps I might see Miss Leigh."

Pansy made a heroic effort to conceal her anguish. If she left her coat in the dye, unstirred and unprodded, it would certainly come out streaky, and if she took it out now, it would be only half done. She indicated a chair, apologised for the breakfast things, and ran upstairs in despair to inform Caroline.

"Major Anderson is downstairs, and my coat's only half done—and just look at me!"

Caroline was dusting her dressing-table. She straightened up with her back to Pansy.

"Major Anderson?"

"Yes—the Chief Constable—on business. What *can* he want? He asked for you. I must just get some of this stuff off my hands. Do go down."

"All right," said Caroline without moving.

She heard Pansy go into her own room.

The Chief Constable. . . . . She must go down. Her legs felt weak and shaky. She looked in the glass and saw that she was as white as a sheet. If she went down looking like that, she might just as well throw up the sponge and have done with it.

She put on a little colour and went down.

Major Anderson was looking out of the window. He might have been admiring the dahlias. He turned as she came down the stair, said, "How do you do?" and pulled a chair away from the breakfast table for her.

Caroline was glad to sit down, because her joints felt exactly as if they were made of melting wax. She bit the inside of her lip hard and waited for the Chief Constable to tell her that Jim had been arrested. Instead, he gave a funny little cough and, sitting very bolt upright in their best wheelback chair,

"Miss Leigh," he said, "I've called at what, I hope, is not a very inconvenient hour to make some inquiries about—well, about Jim Randal."

Caroline said, "Yes?" Her voice sounded deep and mournful. It did not shake; that was one comfort. It didn't matter how mournful it sounded, because, as far as Chief Constables and people like that were concerned, Jim had better be drowned. If you are feeling horribly frightened, it is quite easy to look tragic—it is, indeed, a relief.

"Now, Miss Leigh," said Major Anderson—"perhaps you wouldn't mind telling me when you last heard from Jim Randal."

"It was the beginning of August," said Caroline.

"Can you give me the date?"

"Yes—the fourth."

"Would you mind telling me what he said?"

"Oh no. It was just a few lines. I was staying with Mrs Ogilvie at Craigellachie. Jim was coming there too. He wrote to say he would take a steamer up the coast."

"Did he say what steamer?"

"No."

"Did you hear again?"

"No, we didn't."

Major Anderson leaned forward.

"Had you any reason to suppose that he was on the *Alice Arden*?" His small, sharp grey eyes fixed Caroline.

"We thought he must have been."

"Why?"

"He didn't come, and he didn't write."

"I see. . . . . You say he didn't write. You're sure of that? You're sure he hasn't communicated with you since the wreck of the *Alice Arden*?"

"Quite sure," said Caroline. She wondered whether this was a lie. What was "communicating"?

"Now, Miss Leigh—I believe you went to the Elston cottage hospital in response to a broadcast message stating that they had a man there who appeared to have lost his memory. It was believed that his name was Jim Riddell, or Randal. You went there?"

"Yes."

"You didn't see the man?"

"No—his wife had fetched him away."

"Yes, his wife—and left no address."

"She said his name was Riddell," said Caroline. She hoped she did not say it too quickly.

"You were satisfied that it could not have been Jim Randal?"

"Jim isn't married—she said it was her husband."

"And you've heard nothing from your cousin since then?"

The telephone bell rang on the other side of the room. Caroline had never been so glad to hear anything in her life. She went over to the foot of the stair and lifted the receiver.

As she did so, Pansy's door opened and Pansy's voice called to her.

"I expect that's Jenny to know whether I'm coming to the treasure hunt this evening. If it is, tell her I can't. You can easily get someone to go with you if you want to. I'm *just* coming down."

"I'm so sorry," aid Caroline over her shoulder to Major Anderson. Then she put the receiver to her ear, and heard Jim say,

"Caroline—"

It was the most paralysing shock. For one moment Caroline thought she was going to faint. The telephone was just by the stair foot. She leaned hard on the balustrade. Jim— telephoning to her—and the Chief Constable exactly three yards away, waiting for an answer to his question: "And you've heard nothing from your cousin since then?"

Jim's voice again:

"Caroline—"

Pansy was coming down the stairs.

"I'm so sorry, Major Anderson, but I was simply drenched with dye. Do forgive me for being so long. Caroline won't be a moment. Jenny Ross has got a treasure hunt this evening, and I said perhaps I'd go, but I don't think I will. I don't care for them really, and after last night—Wasn't it a frightful storm? I don't think I ever remember anything worse than that last crack of thunder. Caroline was out, and I was dreadfully nervous."

"Yes, yes," said Major Anderson—"Miss Ross' treasure hunt—I hope it will be fine. My nephew Jack is going, I believe. I hope there will be no more thunder."

Caroline spoke into the telephone.

"Yes?"

"Caroline, I've just rung up to say I've had to go off. You mustn't go there again. Good-bye, my dear."

"Wait," said Caroline. "Wait." Her lips were so stiff that she could hardly get them to move. How was she to find words that would mean nothing to Pansy and Major Anderson and yet stop Jim from going away where she couldn't find him or get into touch with him? She *had* to give him Susie Van Berg's message and to let him know the frightful danger he was in. If Elmer died, Susie would tell the police that she had heard him quarrelling with Jim, and that it was Jim who had shot him.

"I mustn't wait," said Jim. "Don't worry."

"Where are you ringing from?"

As she waited for Jim's answer, she heard Major Anderson say to Pansy,

"Then you believe that your cousin was drowned?"

Then Jim:

"Ledlington post office. I can't stop."

Caroline's head cleared suddenly. She had got to see Jim and tell him about Susie, and about Caroline Bussell and Nesta. She bent down to the mouthpiece and spoke in quite a natural voice.

"Wait a moment—you don't forget you're coming to Jenny Ross' treasure hunt, do you? They won't begin while it's light, so we'd better meet about nine."

"What are you talking about? Caroline, you've got to keep out of this."

Caroline achieved a laugh.

"I can't stop either—I've got a visitor. I'll be at the end of Nesta's road—I can't remember its name—at nine o'clock. Will that be all right?"

"Caroline, you're not to come! I can't be there."

"Very well, I'll be there at nine. . . . Yes, of course I'll come—I wouldn't miss it for anything."

She hung up the receiver and turned to face the room.

"That wasn't Jenny?" said Pansy.

"No," said Caroline.

Major Anderson rose to his feet.

"If you have any news of your cousin—" He stopped, said "H'm!" and changed the construction of his sentence. "If your cousin should communicate with either of you, will you ask him to get into touch with me as soon as possible—in his own interests—" He checked himself for the second time. It was more than probable that Jim Randal would never communicate with anyone again, since he had either been drowned or else had the very strongest motives for making himself scarce. A bad business. Much better if he's drowned—much better all round. Used to be a damn nice youngster. Well, well.

He shook hands with an air of relief and reflected that Pansy Arbuthnot talked enough for half a dozen, and that Caroline Leigh was an uncommon pretty girl—bit peaky when he first came in, but she'd cheered up after answering that telephone call—some young fellow-my-lad she was going off treasure-hunting with to-night—wouldn't have done to have asked who it was, he supposed. Well, well— let the boys and girls have their fun. But twenty years ago it wouldn't have been considered quite the thing for a girl to be running round treasure-hunting when there had just been a death in the family. Pretty girl though—uncommon pretty.

He got into his car and drove away.

XXIX

JIM RANDAL WENT INTO THE FREE LIBRARY, BUT HE DID not stay there long. He did not even ask for the file which he had come there to look at. The past and what had happened in the past was nothing like so important as the present and what was likely to happen in the immediate future.

He sat down on one of the stiff upright chairs, shut his eyes, and went over what Min had told him. It was just as if she had pushed into his hand half a dozen of those queerly shaped and coloured bits of wood which go to make up a jig-saw puzzle. Of the rest of the bits, some were in place, others set down tentatively here and there, and a great many still entirely missing. The question was, did the bits that

Min had just given him fit in with the bits he had already? He thought they did. He put them down one by one, and saw them slip smoothly into place.

Nesta had come down in the small hours at the summons of a handful of gravel thrown up against her window. She must have both known who was summoning her and have agreed with him that their interview must be a secret one. She had been away for something over an hour. That meant either an intrigue or the deuce of a lot to talk over. He dismissed the idea of an intrigue. Nesta struck him as a good deal too practical to embark on a haphazard, snatched, uncomfortable affair like this. No—Nesta's passion was for the Van Berg emeralds. If she left her comfortable bed, it was because she had some strong inducement. Well, she had gone out, stayed out for more than an hour, come back, and then immediately gone out again as far as the gate, bringing with her something, presumably money. Min had then heard her say "It's all I've got," and something about keeping money in the house; after which the man said a lot of things she didn't hear, and one that she did. She heard him say, "Don't be late."

With all the pieces in place, what he made of them was this—Nesta had given the fellow all the money she'd got in the house, and was under an agreement to meet him next day with more. He might be wrong, but that was what he made of it. If he was right, Nesta would be drawing money out of the bank some time during the day. Some time after that she would meet the fellow at a place agreed upon between them, but totally unknown to Jim. And when that meeting took place, it would be greatly to his own advantage if he could contrive to make an unobtrusive third.

The immediate result of this line of thought was the conclusion that he had no time to waste. He had got to keep an eye on Nesta Riddell's movements. He had not at the moment any idea how he was going to manage this, but he would have to think out a plan of campaign. Meanwhile he was going to risk a telephone call to Caroline. From now on she had got to keep right out of the business. She had got to be told that, and that he had left Hale Place. He didn't like to think of her going up there in the dark to find an empty house.

He crossed over to the north side of the square, went into the post office, and rang up Hazelbury West.

When Caroline's voice came to him after that long strange pause, his heart jumped. He had passed from eager anticipation to a sense that there was something wrong. Then when she said "Yes," his heart jumped and he told himself that he was a fool. He had come there to say good-bye to Caroline, and the sooner he got it over the better.

He said what he had come there to say, and heard Caroline say "Wait." She said it twice. There was no expression in her voice, not the least shade of it. Two little stiff words in an expressionless voice, and he was wild with anxiety. What was the matter? Was it because he had said good-bye that her voice was still and dead?

He said, "I mustn't wait. Don't worry."

He was a fool to have said that, because the thought of Caroline worrying filled him with an insensate desire to go to her.

"Where are you ringing up from?"

He told her. He said,

"I can't stop."

His hand made a movement to replace the receiver, when quick and warm there came to his ear a rush of quite unintelligible words. He wasn't to forget that he was coming to Jenny Ross' treasure hunt. They wouldn't begin whilst it was light—"so we'd better meet about nine."

"What are you talking about? Caroline, you've got to keep out of this."

He heard her laugh and say, "I can't stop either—I've got a visitor. I'll be at the end of Nesta's road—I can't remember its name—at nine o'clock. Will that be all right?"

There was someone there. That was why she was speaking so oddly.

Impossible to have her cutting in now that he was definitely implicated in the affair of the emeralds.

He told her not to come. He said—and even to himself his voice sounded harsh—

"I can't be there."

Caroline did not seem to notice anything. She answered gaily,

"Very well, I'll be there at nine—I wouldn't miss it for anything." And before he could say another word there was a click and she was twenty miles away.

He left the post office, reached the High Street by way of Market Street, and walked out to Ledlington End.

It was all very well to say that he had got to keep an eye on Nesta Riddell, but how was it going to be done? Sandringham Drive offered about as much cover as a parade ground. All the houses were just like Happicot—neat, small, new and fully occupied; and all the gardens were practically non-existent. There was, as far as he could remember, an incipient laburnum at Balmoral, and a rudimentary lilac or two at Mon Répos and Wyshcumtru, but not even a kitten could have lurked unseen. There was the Kosy Korner Kafé at the near end of the drive. But the bother was that the beastly road had two ends. If he waited for Nesta at one end, she'd be bound to go out by the other. It all depended where she was going to meet the fellow. If it was in Ledlington, she would pass the Kosy Korner Kafé, but if it was somewhere out in the country, she would come out on to the main road at the lower end of Sandringham Drive.

He tried to think which was the most likely, but could not arrive at any conclusion. You could argue it both ways. A man who was in hiding might lie up in a wood or on a common, or he might go to ground in one of the slums down by the river. There used to be a fairly tough lot down there seven years ago, and he didn't suppose things were very different now. A man who lived by his wits probably had a bolt-hole or two.

He passed the War Memorial, and presently the Kosy Korner Kafé. If there was a point on the main road from which he could see both ends of Sandringham Drive, things were going to be a little easier. The drive wasn't very long, so he had hopes. Another minute more and the hopes were justified. For a distance of five or six yards it was possible to see both turnings. These five or six yards covered the lower gate and part of the shrubbery of one of those large out-of-date houses which have been abandoned before the encroaching tide of bungalows and villas. Its four storeys stood up with an isolated, neglected air. The ivy had begun to cross the blank windows. The drive was green with moss, the garden a mere tangle. Between it and the road ran a low brick wall topped by an unclipped hedge. The whole place had a desolate, unvisited look.

Jim pushed open the gate with some difficulty and walked in. Nothing could have suited him better. There were half a dozen places where laurels, laurustinus, lilac and yew crowded up to the unkempt hedge, and where he could stand and see without being seen.

He had not to wait very long. In about half an hour Nesta Riddell walked briskly past the Kosy Korner and proceeded in the Ledlington direction. It was easy enough to follow her, since he guessed that she was bound for one of the three banks, of which two were in the High Street and one in Market Street. He had only to keep one turning behind her and follow on. In point of fact she never looked round, but walked briskly into the town, where she entered the London County and Westminster Bank.

The question was, what was she going to do next? She might be going to meet the fellow straight away. It wasn't likely, but it was possible. Jim went into a tobacconist's on the other side of the High Street, bought a paper, and, unfolding it, kept a watch upon the door of the bank.

After about five minutes Nesta came out. She stood for an instant on the pavement, and then gave him the fright of his life by crossing the road.

A newspaper held wide open makes a good screen. There was a moment's suspense, and then he saw from under the lower edge of his paper six inches of bright blue skirt and eight or nine inches of rather light stocking ending in flimsy imitation leather shoe go up the two worn steps of the pastry-cook's next door. He was so near that he could hear her rather strident voice asking for milk chocolate.

He moved farther down the street, and presently she came

out and walked back along the way by which she had come, and at the same brisk pace. How women managed to walk at all in the pinched, shoddy, stilt-heeled atrocities some of them wore was a mystery to him. He watched Nesta disappear round the curve of Sandringham Drive and went back to his shrubbery.

The day passed with intolerable slowness. It did not rain, but the clouds hung low and the air was full of damp. At ten o'clock Min returned with her shopping basket full. At one Tom Williams came back to his midday meal on the motorbike which shared his heart with Min. It was inconceivable that Nesta would choose a family meal-time for her assignation, so Jim went out over to the Kosy Korner and lunched on cold sausage rolls and hot coffee. Inspired by Nesta's example, he bought a packet of chocolate and put it away in his pocket. His next meal was rather problematical.

In his own mind he felt quite sure that Nesta would not meet the man until it was dark. He judged her to be the kind of person who would never take an unnecessary risk. He did not think she was deficient in courage—far from it. She would take a necessary risk however great; but an unnecessary one, never. He could have wished that they were in December instead of August, for even on a gloomy day like this it would not be dark until after nine.

And Caroline was coming here at nine o'clock. He had tried to stop her, and she wouldn't be stopped. He fell into thoughts of Caroline which were angry, impatient, tender, and passionately self-accusing. He had had no business to let her get mixed up in this affair at all. Even if he were not Nesta Riddell's husband, he was very definitely under suspicion of attempted murder, and beyond all question he had been in possession of stolen property. He didn't believe that he was Nesta Riddell's husband; he believed it less than ever since his talk with Min. But he could not prove that he was not Jim Riddell unless and until the gap in his memory closed up and gave him back the lost weeks between the first of July and the fifteenth of August. He might during those weeks have masqueraded as Jim Riddell, and, as Jim Riddell, have married Nesta Williams, but he didn't believe it. It rested on Nesta's word, and, quite frankly, he didn't think Nesta's word was worth a tinker's damn. On the other hand, the Van Berg affair in some sort corroborated Nesta's statements. That didn't depend on Nesta's words. He himself remembered drinking with Elmer on the night that he was shot. He remembered seeing the emeralds in Elmer's hand. And, most damning of all, he had found them in his own house in a secret hiding-place known only to Caroline and himself. Men had been hanged on slighter evidence than this. There were the emeralds to provide a motive. There was the opportunity—his presence could easily be proved from his finger-prints. And, if the stolen property was traced to his possession, there was the sort of case which Public Prosecutors dream of. Caroline mustn't come within a thousand miles of it.

He went on thinking about Caroline.

XXX

BY NINE O'CLOCK TWILIGHT WAS MERGING INTO DARKNESS. Jim had come out upon the high road and was getting the stiffness out of his limbs by walking up and down. A clock struck the hour from one of the Ledlington churches—he thought it would be St John the Baptist. A faint medley of other chimes followed from St Ethelbert's and the public clock in Market Place. Between them they made nine into something like nineteen. The air was very still, and the clouds low. Cars went by.

Jim frowned in the dusk. This dazzle of headlights, with its succeeding darkness, was going to make it most frightfully difficult to spot Nesta.

He turned at the end of his beat and walked in the Ledlington direction, and as he did so, an Austin Seven came slowly up behind him. It passed and drew up by the kerb. The lights of a big Daimler flashing past showed him Caroline at the wheel. She looked over her shoulder as the light swept them both, and in a flash she was out of the car and holding on to him.

"Oh, Jim darling!" she said, and was in his arms.

She put up her face, and he kissed her. They had always kissed one another, but this was a different kiss. They were both trembling. Caroline clung to him. After a moment he got hold of himself.

He said, "You mustn't!" and tried to put her away.

She pressed closer.

"Jim—do you love me—really?"

"I haven't got any right to."

A little shaky laugh came from somewhere just under his chin. Her hair rubbed against his cheek.

"I never asked you that." An arm slid round his neck. "Jim—say you love me!"

"Don't you know it?"

"Of course I do—but I want you to say it."

"My darling, I love you with all my heart and soul. . . . . I mustn't."

"*Silly!*" said Caroline. She stood on tiptoe, dragged his head down, and kissed him shamelessly. "Jim—*darling!*"

She was lifted, held so close that she could not breathe, and most passionately kissed. Then with her heart thumping and her head spinning, she was set down at arm's length and held there.

"Now you've got to go home," said Jim in an odd hard voice. "No, it's no use—you've got to. If I get out of this, we'll get married, but until I do you've got to stand clear."

"Oh!" said Caroline rather faintly. Jim's grip was hurting her. His wrists must be like iron; she couldn't move the least fraction of an inch.

He continued to hold her away from him, because when she rubbed her head against his cheek like that and said "Jim—*darling!*" he couldn't be answerable for what he might do. "Jim—*darling*!" all soft and warm against his neck—flesh and blood couldn't stand it. He held her at arms' length and breathed hard and deep.

"Caroline, you've got to go home. I'm here on a job, and you mustn't hinder me. I haven't time to tell you about it. I'm waiting to see if Nesta comes out. If she does, I've got to follow her. I think she's going to meet the man who's got the emeralds."

"Oh!" said Caroline. This was a different "Oh"—a breath of pure surprise.

"So you must go quickly. I mustn't miss her. You see, I don't know which way she will be going—I've got to watch both ends of the drive."

"And suppose she's got a bicycle—what will you do then?"

"She hasn't got one."

"Isn't there one in the house?"

"Only Tom's motor-bike."

"Suppose she takes that."

"Then I shall be dished. But it's not likely."

"Jim," said Caroline in a low eager voice. "Oh, Jim darling, do let me help! You see, if you get into the car, we can stand in a good dark place between the lamp-posts in Sandringham Drive and watch the house. Look how dark it's getting. You'll miss her if you stay here. Oh, Jim, let me help! It's not as if there was any harm in what we're doing—as if I could get into trouble over it. It's all quite simple and easy and—and legal—and if you won't do it with me, I shall just go off and do it by myself."

For a moment his grasp tightened. Then he took his hands away and said,

"All right—we'd better hurry." Then, with a short laugh, "What's the odds she's gone? I'd forgotten she existed."

Caroline was still shaking as she started the car. She dimmed the headlights and crawled round the corner into Sandringham Drive. There was a darkish patch opposite Balmoral, and she drew up there.

Happicot was across the road in a diagonal line. All the front of the house was dark. That meant they were in the kitchen. The lamp-post a yard or two from the gate cast a pale wavering light upon the solitary geranium in the front garden. The red was all gone out of it; it looked black, and so did its circle of lobelias.

Caroline had stopped trembling. She felt as light as air, and so full of happiness that it would hardly have surprised her if she and Jim and Jemima—all Caroline's possessions had names, and the car was Jemima—had floated up into the air and gone drifting away into some lovely golden place of dreams. She said in a laughing voice,

"I feel like a toy balloon—all floaty! Oh, Jim—isn't it fun?"

Jim took her by the shoulder and shook her.

"Now look here, Caroline—this is a job. You're not to talk nonsense, and you're not to snuggle, and you're not to say 'Jim darling.' "

"*Oh!*" said Caroline in a tone of outrage. "I wasn't snuggling!"

"You were. You do. You always did."

"Jim darling, don't you like it?"

"There you are—two blobs at one go! You little idiot—don't you think I want to make love to you? And don't you see that it would be damned dishonourable if I did? You may just as well face it—if Elmer Van Berg dies, I'm a great deal more likely to be hanged than not. If I made love to you, I should be a dirty cad."

Caroline sat as far away from him as she could. Two burning tears ran down her cheeks. She dug the nails of one hand into the palm of the other.

Jim went on speaking.

"Now I'll tell you what I'm doing here. You'd better be prepared for a bit of a shock. The emeralds were at Hale Place, in the Blue Room under Ralph de Burgh's shield."

Caroline's tears dried suddenly. She sat bolt upright and drew a sharply audible breath.

"I found them there," said Jim. "It knocked me endways. I was staring at them like the village idiot, when a fellow barged in and snatched them. We had a rough-and-tumble, but he got away. I went after him along the field path to Hinton, but it was no go. They've altered the time of the last train. He caught it by the skin of his teeth, and I missed it. I believe he came into Ledlington and knocked Nesta up. And I believe she's meeting him to-night. That's that. But what I want to know is—did you ever tell anyone—*anyone*, mind—about the hiding-place behind the shield?''

"No, I didn't,'' said Caroline.

"Sure?''

"Sure.''

"Then I must have put the damned things there myself.''

"You couldn't have,'' said Caroline in a deep sure voice.

"Then who did?''

"I don't know. It wasn't you. Now, Jim, listen—because I've seen Susie Van Berg, and I've got to tell you what she said. It's—it's not very good news, Jim.''

She told him about Susie. When she had finished, Jim said quietly,

"That puts the lid on—doesn't it? I suppose I did it. I can't believe it, but I suppose I did do it.''

Caroline said, "I'll *never* believe you did it!''

"My dear,'' said Jim, "if Susie goes to the police with that story of a quarrel, I shouldn't think the jury would even leave the box.''

Caroline caught her breath. She went on quickly.

"There's something else. After I left Susie I lost my way. That frightful storm was right overhead. I was in a sort of panic and blundered into someone's room. There was a screen in front of the door, so they didn't see me.''

"Who is 'they'?'' said Jim.

"Nesta and that cousin of hers who is housekeeper there—Caroline Bussell.''

He said, "Well?''

"Aren't you surprised? I was. I nearly dropped right through the floor.''

Jim gave a short laugh.

"I've stopped being surprised. Well, what were they up to?''

"I listened,'' said Caroline rather defiantly.

"Well?''

"They were doing a sort of magic with a bowl of ink."
"*What!*"

Caroline nodded.

"Like crystal-gazing. That Bussell woman is rather frightening. She made Nesta look into the ink, but she couldn't see anything except fog."

"Fog?" said Jim in a startled voice. Fog—that was what lay at the back of his own mind—fog, and waves, and a voice.

"Yes," said Caroline. "Nesta wouldn't go on. And then Caroline Bussell picked up the bowl of ink, and put it on her lap and looked into it."

"Well?"

Caroline shivered.

"I hated it! She looked like some horrid sort of waxwork. And then all of a sudden she stopped looking into the ink and began to describe the Blue Room at Hale Place. Nesta asked her where the emeralds were, and she described the Blue Room."

"Well, they were there all right," said Jim. "Did she say anything about the shield?"

"No, she didn't. She called out suddenly, 'He's alive! Did you know that he was alive?' And the bowl tilted and all the ink upset. I ran away."

He leaned forward and took her by the wrist.

"Who were they talking about?"

"I don't know."

"Hadn't they mentioned anyone?"

Caroline's hand trembled under his.

"I don't know—yes, Nesta did. She said, 'Where's Jim?'"

"Was that before or after she asked about the emeralds?"

"I can't remember." Her voice was distressed. "I think it was before."

"She asked, 'Where is Jim?' What did the Bussell woman say?"

"I can't remember—I've got it all sort of muddled. There was the thunder, and what Susie had just been saying, and that creepy waxwork woman. I don't think I've ever been so frightened in my life."

"But you're sure she said, 'He's alive'?"

"Yes—I'm sure about that. She said, 'He's alive!' in a loud startled sort of way. And she said 'Did you know he was alive?' and the ink bowl tipped over and I ran away. I don't know why she said it, because of course Nesta knew that you were alive."

Jim let go of her wrist and sat back.

"I don't think she meant me," he said in a slow controlled voice.

XXXI

ABOUT TEN MINUTES LATER JIM SUDDENLY CLUTCHED Caroline and said, "Hush!" The front door of Happicot had opened and someone was coming out. There was no light in the little passage. The door shut again.

Jim spoke under his breath.

"It's Tom—"

The light of the street-lamp showed overalls, a leather cap, and goggles.

"She's sending Tom," said Jim.

They saw him go round the house into the shadow.

"Suppose it's a blind," said Caroline.

Jim's hand tightened on her wrist. He said,

"Look!"

The light in the room over the sitting-room had gone on. Min stood there, drawing down the blinds. There were two windows. A dark blind blotted out one of them. Min came up to the other. The second blind snapped down, but just before it shut the lighted room from view they both saw a hand fall on Min's shoulder. It was a man's hand with a bit of shirt sleeve showing. Then both windows were dark, and out of the shadow beside the house came the figure in overalls, pushing Tom's motor-bike.

"It isn't Tom—Tom's up there with Min. That's Nesta! Get ready to start as soon as she's making enough noise not to notice us. What can you do?"

"Fifty," said Caroline.

The chug-chugging of the motor-bicycle filled the quiet road. A corner of the blind above was lifted. Someone was watching Nesta start. Jim thought Tom would probably hear all about that later on.

The bicycle began to move, the blind was reluctantly dropped, and the next moment Jemima was off and the chase was up. Fifty wasn't going to be very much good if Nesta was really out for speed; the motorbike could do seventy and still have something in hand. Jim thanked his stars that Nesta was on her own job. If she had sent Tom, they would probably have lost him round the first corner and never set eyes on him again. As it was, the tail-light was well in view when they came upon the main road, and it became obvious that she was not doing more than a cautious thirty-five.

Caroline kept about thirty yards behind. There was very little traffic on the road, and it was now practically dark. They ran for five miles, and then the taillight disappeared.

"Where's she gone?" said Jim in a puzzled voice.

"Sandy Lane," said Caroline.

"Is it drivable?"

"They've made a parking-ground in a field about a quarter of a mile along to the left. They get simply loads of trippers now. The road's all right as far as that, but I can get Jemima a good bit nearer the ruins. Do you think she's going there?"

They turned off, and saw the red spark again. Jim said,

"It wouldn't be a bad place to lie up in except for the trippers."

"They'll have gone hours ago—not likely to be many in this weather."

They ran on past the parking-place. Caroline switched off her lights and crawled forward over a horribly rough surface. She could just see a black line of hedge on either side. The red spark drew away and then suddenly went out.

Jim whispered, "Has she turned off?"

"Stopped, I think. We must too. I can't turn here—we shall have to back."

He opened the door and jumped out.

"Caroline—will you do just what I say? Back down to the parking-place and turn, then stay there till I come. Get as much out of the way as you can."

He did not wait for an answer, but made off up the lane. It was years since he had been here. He tried to remember where the footpath left the lane, and to fix in his mind the exact spot at which the red light had vanished. He must be getting near it now.

And then all of a sudden there was the motor-bike, jammed up against the hedge. A bare yard farther on he came on the wicket gate.

The ruin of St Leonard's Priory is one of the sights of the country. It cannot be said to be easy of access, but in summer weather it is much in favour with school treats, sketching-parties, and lovers. There are one or two graceful arches, several lengths of crumbling wall, and an ivy-grown tower. There is also a sufficiency of fallen stones to afford seats for everyone.

Jim followed the path until he could see the dark mass of the tower loom up between him and a sky which was not quite so dark. He stood still and listened. For all he knew, he was on the wrong tack, but if he were on the right one, he would be in luck if he could discover Nesta before she discovered him.

From this point onward there ceased to be a path, or else he had lost it. He had to feel before him with his foot at every step. There were blackberry trails, very thorny; there were nettles; and there was fallen masonry in every stage of decay.

At intervals he stopped to listen. His only real chance of finding Nesta lay in his unusually keen sense of hearing. If she spoke in however low a tone, he thought, on a night as still as this, that he would hear something. And then all at once he didn't hear, he saw.

He was about a dozen yards from the tower, which was really only a shell, the hollow side towards him. The winding stair, which had once led to the top, had long since fallen, but the slits which had lighted it remained, piercing the outer wall at regular intervals. What Jim saw was the lowest of these slits, and he saw it because on the other side of the tower wall someone had struck a match. The tiny flame showed the slit as a narrow, faintly illuminated panel on a black wall.

Jim crossed the intervening space as quickly and as noiselessly as possible. As he approached the slit, he heard the murmur of voices. He laid a hand on the rough, damp wall of the tower, stooped to the slit, and from the other side of it heard Nesta say,

"I want to see them."

He listened eagerly for the man's voice. All that he knew of him up to the present was the feel of his agile twisting body and the sharpness of his teeth. He had not the slightest doubt that it was his burglar to whom Nesta was speaking, and when she said, "I want to see them," he had not the slightest doubt that she was asking for the emeralds.

He listened for the man's voice. When it came, he thrust a second hand against the wall and leaned upon both hands heavily.

The voice was as familiar to him as his own—a rather soft-sounding voice, with no particular mark of age or class—a smooth, low-pitched voice. *And it had been sounding in his mind ever since the wreck of the Alice Arden.*

In the shock of this recognition he lost what was said. Nesta spoke again in a sharp undertone.

"I want to see them."

Then the voice, and this time he got the words too.

"Then want'll have to be your master."

"Will it?" said Nesta. "We'll see about that. I'm going to see them, and I'm going to have them in my hands."

"Not much, you're not! Anyway I haven't got them on me—I told you that before—not such a fool."

Nesta did not speak any louder, but her voice had the true scold's rasp in it.

"I'm to run your errands, and fetch and carry for you, and go here and go there, and be cheated out of what I've earned? You can think again!"

"Look here," said the man—"that's enough! Do you hear? You'll get your share all right when I get mine. Neither of us is going to get a penny until I'm safe out of the country. The sooner I'm out of the country the sooner you'll get your share. Stop talking like a lunatic and hand over the cash!"

"And I tell you," said Nesta, "that I won't hand over a penny if I don't see the emeralds!" Her voice broke on the word and choked.

On the other side of the wall, Jim wondered whether she was being silenced for the moment or for good and all. If she was being murdered, he would have to go to the rescue, and the prospect enraged him. Next moment however there was an indignant spluttering whisper.

"Take your filthy hand away!"

"All right—but you'll get scragged in earnest if you start mentioning names."

"Who's going to hear them?" said Nesta.

"No one," said the smooth voice very smoothly. "And shall I tell you why? Because you'll be dead before you get them out. It'll look fine on the hoardings—'Woman Found Strangled.' You'll get your photograph into the Sunday papers if that's what you want. Pity you won't be there to see them!"

"Tom knows where I've gone."

For all his dislike, Jim could admire her nerve. He wondered how much Tom did know.

"Oh—Tom knows, does he? Well, you be careful, or he'll know more than he likes. Hand over the cash!"

"Not till I've seen them!"

They were so close against the wall that Jim could hear every movement and—almost—every breath. He heard the man step sideways, and he heard Nesta take a sharp breath.

"Hand that money over!" said the man.

Nesta laughed.

"Do you think I'm such a fool as to have it on me? Keep your hands to yourself, and keep your distance!"

There was another movement. Jim thought the man stepped back.

"Where's the money?" The smoothness of his voice was broken.

"That's it," said Nesta—"where is it? I don't mind telling you, you know. It's not a hundred miles away. For the matter of that, it's not a dozen yards away. It's where I put it, and there it'll stay until I've seen what I want to see. Of course you can start looking for it if you like. You've got a box of matches—I should try if I were you. I shan't mind seeing you burn your fingers!"

There was an empty, dangerous pause. It occurred to Jim that it would be bad luck if he were to get mixed up in another murder. Some day Nesta would go too far. He wondered if the day had come. He would not himself have gambled on the self-control of the man on the other side of the wall.

The pause broke. The voice was smooth again.

"That true?"

Nesta laughed.

"Cross my heart!"

"You'll get it crossed with a knife if you're not careful!"

"Not this time," she said. "Let me see them, and you won't have to waste your matches."

There was another pause.

"Come on, or I'll think you haven't got them! And if you haven't got them, I'm off."

A match head scraped on emery, and the slit in the wall flared yellow. Jim, stooping forward on the inner side, saw, framed by the black wall, a man's hand with eight green stones dangling, just as he had seen it in his dreams. In his dreams it had been Elmer's hand, but this was a smaller, smoother hand than Elmer Van Berg's. The match was out of the picture. It was above and behind the green stones, making a transparency of them.

Jim heard Nesta exclaim, then saw her face, avid and dark, lips parted, close-set eyes intent. On the other side there came into view a man's profile—straight forehead, long nose, straight thin lips, long chin—and all in a moment was blotted out again. The match fell, trailing a spark across the darkened picture, and in the same instant Jim reached at arm's length through the slit, caught the swinging chain, and jerked it clear.

XXXII

CAROLINE SAT IN THE CAR, AND FELT THE DARKNESS AND the silence come blanketing down. She had backed into the parking-ground and run up close under the hedge, so that on one side she had a black wall of thorny twigs, and on the other the formless shadows of the field. She had switched off her lights lest by any chance she should be seen. The time went slowly.

After a bit she shut her eyes and began to think about Jim. Of course she had been thinking of him all the time, but this was a very special kind of thinking. He had kissed her differently, and he had said, "I love you with all my heart and soul." And he had said, "If I get out of this, we'll get married."

Caroline thought about these things. It was like looking out from under an angry black cloud into a heavenly sunny place. It was like looking into a dream and finding beauty and gladness beyond anything you had imagined. Caroline looked.

She was not sure how long she had been dreaming, when a light startled her broad awake. It shone red through her eyelids, and she opened them, dazzled, to meet the head-lights of a car. As she exclaimed, someone shouted. The light swung aside and a car drew up at right angles to Jemima. Instantly the doors were flung open and she was hailed by name. Two people jumped out.

"Hi, Caroline—I spotted you! You were asleep—we jolly nearly ran you down! Who are you with? Have you got your clue? Because if you have, you might just as well hand it on and save us trekking up to the Tower."

With her first words, Caroline recognized Kitty Lefroy, the daughter of the Hinton doctor. She had just left school, and was a lively tom-boy.

"Beastly unsporting!" said a boy's voice. "You've got to find your own clue. Besides, it won't be the Tower—I said so all along."

"Of course it's the Tower!" said Kitty. "It is—isn't it, Caroline? I say, you know Jock Anderson, don't you— Major Anderson's nephew? He's just taken a special prize for pig-headedness at Sandhurst, so he's rather above himself— but you needn't take any notice of him."

"Well, I say it isn't the Tower—it's too easy."

"Of course if you want to be *clever*—" said Kitty.

> " 'A finger pointing to the east
> The ointment of the royal beast.'

If that doesn't mean Leonard's Tower, what does it mean?"

"It's too easy," said Jock Anderson.

Caroline was leaning out of the window. Her one desire was to get rid of them. If Jenny Ross had fixed on St Leonard's Tower as one of the clues in her treasure hunt, about two dozen people might be here at any moment. She had told Major Anderson she was going treasure-hunting, and she was being taken at her word. It was like an Awful Warning out of the most horrid sort of Moral Tract. It was a

Judgment. It trembled on the edge of being a Disaster. She said rather breathlessly,

"I should hurry up if I were you—I think you're the first."

"Well, what price you?"

"I've given up," said Caroline. "I'm not feeling like treasure-hunting. I'm going home."

Kitty whirled round on Jock Anderson.

"We're the first! Do you hear? Buck up, my lad, and we'll scoop the chocolates yet! It's a jolly fine box!"

They ran off, noisy and laughing.

Caroline sat back with a sigh of relief.

Fifty yards up the lane Jock Anderson gripped Kitty by the elbow.

"Was that Caroline Leigh?"

"Yes. Why? Have you fallen for her in the dark? You'll be one of a crowd if you have."

"Shut up—I'm serious! What's she doing all by herself in the dark like that?"

"I don't know. What's it matter?"

"It looks—queer. Kitty, can you keep a secret?"

"Of course I can."

"It's not a joke—it's a frightfully serious business. I don't suppose I ought to tell you."

"*Beast*!" said Kitty.

"On the other hand—"

"Jock Anderson, you're the most deliberate, cautious, disgustingly Scotch person I've ever met, and if you ever want me to speak to you again, you'll tell me at once."

"The Van Berg murder," said Jock Anderson.

Kitty gave a faint scream.

"Who? What? Where?"

Jock shook her, none too gently.

"Stop that row! If I tell you, you swear you won't let on?"

"Yes—truly."

"Well, did you know a man called Jim Randal?"

"When I was a kid. He's been away for ages. He's Caroline's cousin."

"That's it! Well, they think he did the Van Berg murder."

"Mr Van Berg isn't dead?"

"Next door to it—and they've got a warrant out against this Randal fellow."

"How do you know?"

"I heard the inspector talking to my uncle. Now look here—what's she doing in that car? Whilst you were gassing, I went round to the back and put my pocket torch on the number plate, and I'm prepared to swear that's the car that passed us a mile out of Ledlington just before we took that wrong turning you were so cocksure about."

"I wasn't!"

"Oh, *weren't* you? No, shut up—don't rag! What I'm trying to say is this. When they passed us, there was a man in the car. Where's he got to?"

"Jim Randal was drowned—" said Kitty Lefroy in a slow, bewildered voice.

"No, he wasn't—he was seen and recognized in Ledlington this morning. That's why they've got the warrant out."

"O-oh!" said Kitty in a thrilling whisper.

"And I believe she's waiting for him," said Jock Anderson.

"O-oh!" said Kitty again.

"And what I thought of was this. We've got to see who she's waiting for. I've seen this Randal fellow's passport photograph—my uncle's got it. I suppose you wouldn't recognize him?"

"I might," said Kitty. "Caroline has photographs of him all round her room. She's potty about him—always has been."

"Good girl! Then here's our plan of campaign. You go back and say I've gone to get the clue by myself—say you're fed up or any old thing you like—say we've quarrelled. That ought to be quite convincing. Then get her out of the car by hook or by crook. This is essential, because I've got to put it out of action."

"How?"

"What does it matter how? There are dozens of ways. I can break the petrol pipe, or cut the leads from the coil. That's my job. You've only got to get her away from the car. Say you're cold and want to walk up and down, or something like that. If she's really helping this Randal fellow, she won't like to make a fuss for fear of rousing your suspicions. Now get on with it!''

"Suppose it isn't Jim Randal," said Kitty. "Suppose she just didn't want to walk to the Tower, and it's one of the Lester boys or Roger Blake—they're all mad keen about her.''

"Then we shall be in the soup," said Jock comfortably.

Kitty giggled.

"I say—what a lark!" she said, and disappeared down the lane.

XXXIII

KITTY LEFROY STOOD AT THE CORNER OF THE PARKING-ground and choked with laughter. She had to wait until she could choke it down. As soon as she thought she was fairly safe she approached Jemima.

"Hi, Caroline! Joyous reunion! Why haven't you got your lights on?"

Caroline wasn't dreaming now. She had been waiting with every nerve stretched for Jim's footstep. Kitty's voice stabbed her with disappointment and fear.

"Why have you come back?" she said.

"Don't you want me?" said Kitty, and felt a giggle rise in her throat. "I've turned my ankle, so Jock sent me back. Anyhow, we've had a simply blazing row, so he can just go and find his beastly clue himself. I say, who have you got with you? Is it Roger, or one of the Lester boys?"

"No," said Caroline.

"Aren't you mysterious! The Secret Escort, or Caroline's Conspiracy, by A. Non! I say, that's rather bright, isn't it, and straight off the bat!" She allowed the giggle to escape. Then, leaning with her elbow on the door of the car, she gave an exaggerated shiver. "I suppose you haven't got a thermos or anything? I'm simply frozen." It would have given Caroline the greatest pleasure to box her ears. They were so conveniently near too. She restrained herself, and said,

"I'm afraid I haven't."

"Then let's walk up and down. I'm fruzz—absolutely. I shall be a stiffened corpse if I don't keep up my circulation."

"I thought you'd sprained your ankle?" said Caroline.

She was beginning to be afraid of Kitty Lefroy. The horrid little wretch was up to something—guessed something—knew something. What had she guessed? How much did she know?

The horrid little wretch giggled again.

"Oh, it's better. I think exercise will be good for it. You know"—with a burst of frankness—"I didn't really twist it at all. Jock was such a beast, I wouldn't go with him. Come on and walk, Caroline."

"I don't think I want to."

Kitty giggled again.

"No, you want to go home—don't you? It was awfully stupid of me to forget. Don't let me keep you if you want to get off."

Caroline drove her nails into her palm.

"I'm not in a hurry," she said. "I thought I'd wait a bit and see who else rolls up—it's rather amusing."

"Well, come and walk. I think you might, to save me from being a stiffened corpse. Come along, or I shall think you've got a mysterious assignation. Have you? Do tell me if you have."

Caroline opened the door and jumped out.

"What rubbish you do talk, Kitty!"

Kitty flung a vigorous arm round her waist and began to dance her along.

"You said that exactly like a school-marm. If you're not

frightfully careful, you'll get elderly before you know where you are. That's just the sort of way that all the elderlies talk. 'Oh, Kitty, think before you speak!' and, 'My dear child, don't make so much noise!' and, 'My dear Kitty, did no one ever tell you that doors were made to shut?' I do loathe elderlies! I think people ought to be poisoned off at twenty-five. Don't you?''

Caroline couldn't help laughing.

''That would only give me another three years.''

''Do you mean to say you're twenty-two? How grim! And you're not even engaged? I think it would be awful not to be engaged before one was twenty. But I think getting married's the most awful rot. Don't you?''

''If I get out of this, we'll get married''. . . . Jim's voice and Jim's words came back to pierce her heart. For a moment she couldn't speak. Then she turned back towards the car.

''I'm sorry Kitty, but I don't want to walk any more.''

Something in her voice stopped Kitty's flow of talk. They walked back across the darkened field. And then, just as they came up to the car, someone moved between them and the hedge.

''Hi, Jock—is that you?'' There was relief in Kitty's tone.

But it was Jim Randal's voice that answered,

''I'm afraid I'm not Jock.''

As he spoke, he opened Jemima's farther door and got in.

Caroline got in too on the other side. After all, what did it matter what Kitty thought? She switched on the lights and leaned sideways to say,

''Why don't you go and sit in your car, Kitty? You'll find it warmer.''

She turned back and pressed the starter.

Kitty stood clear and crammed her handkerchief into her mouth. It was really the most frightful jest. She only wished she could see their faces.

''What's the matter?'' said Jim.

''She won't start.''

''She oughtn't to be so cold. Shall I tickle the carburetor?''

"Please."

Kitty was in ecstasies. She came nearer, and inquired in a muffled voice,

"What's up?"

"It's all right—she'll start now." Caroline pressed the starter again. It whirred, but there was no response from the engine.

Jim Randal went round to the front of the car and began to crank her vigorously. The little car bumped and rocked. The engine remained lifeless.

He came to the far window presently.

"Have you got a torch?"

"No."

"Jock has," said Kitty, leaning on the door again. She lifted her voice in a piercing scream. "Jock! Hi! Jo-ock!"

"Coming!" Jock Anderson's voice came from the other side of the hedge. He called again, and turned the corner, running.

Caroline's heart went as dead as Jemima's engine. What was behind all this?

"Hi, Jock!" said Kitty. "Caroline's car won't start. Where's your torch?"

A brilliant beam of light cut the darkness and played on Jim Randal. Caroline saw his face for a moment, and caught her breath. There was something written on it which she did not understand. Now, when everything was going wrong and she felt at the end of her courage, he looked as she had not seen him look this side of seven years—gay, confident, and ready to meet the world.

"Sorry," said Jock Anderson. He turned the beam of his torch away.

Caroline sat back and closed her eyes. She felt weak and helpless, and she wanted to cry. She heard Kitty chattering and Jock answering her, then an exclamation from Jim. He came back to the window.

"Caroline, it's no go."

"What's the matter?"

"It's the coil. We'll have to ask for a lift."

She switched off the lights, slipped across, and got out on

his side. For a moment they stood close together between the car and the hedge. In that moment his hand covered hers and pressed it hard.

She stood on tiptoe and put her lips to his ear. She said in a soundless whisper,

"That boy is Jock Anderson, the Chief Constable's nephew. There's something wrong."

She heard him say, "It's all right."

They came out into the open.

Kitty and Jock were close together, whispering. The torch played on Jim again. Kitty ran forward.

"The next clue is the Heart and Hand at Hinton. We can all go on together—it'll be much more fun. Hurry up—there are more cars coming!"

Jim slipped a hand through Caroline's arm. They crossed to the other car and he helped her in. She and Kitty had the back seat. Jock Anderson took the wheel. They passed a couple of cars in the lane, and Kitty screamed out,

"We've beaten you! You'll have to hurry!"

As soon as they were out on the main road Jim spoke.

"I'm afraid I don't want to go to the Heart and Hand."

Jock Anderson said nothing. Kitty gave a stifled giggle. Jim spoke again.

"I don't think you're deaf, Anderson, but perhaps you don't speak unless you've been introduced. Let me introduce myself. My name is Randal—Jim Randal."

"Well?" Jock Anderson's voice was defiant.

"Well, I don't want to go to the Heart and Hand, but I needn't take you out of your way. I suppose Major Anderson's still just across the road—I don't seem to see him moving house."

Caroline sat up straight and stiff. The blood thumped in her ears. Nobody spoke.

"I've got business with Major Anderson," said Jim in the most ordinary voice in the world.

Jock Anderson found his tongue.

"I was going to take you there anyhow," he said roughly.

Kitty leaned forward, elbows on knees, quick breath nearly choking her. What was going to happen next? Would he try and hit Jock over the head and grab the wheel? And if he did, would it be any good her trying to scrag him? And if she did, what price Caroline? She somehow couldn't see Caroline in a rough-and-tumble. And what was the odds they came a glorious smash in the ditch?

"*What a lark!*" said Kitty ecstatically. She did not say it aloud, because Jim was speaking again.

"You needn't have bothered to put Miss Leigh's car out of action—He cut the leads," he explained over his shoulder to Caroline. Then, "I don't know if she'll want to run you in for it, but I expect it's actionable all right. We can ask your uncle—he's sure to know."

The car swerved.

"I should think you'd have enough to ask him on your own account," growled Jock.

"Oh, we'll get down to you. I daresay you won't mind waiting."

The drumming sound in Caroline's ears ceased. She was very cold, and there was a sick weight on her heart. She went on sitting up straight. Her hands gripped one another desperately. Since they had come to the end, she must keep her head up. Above all, she mustn't faint. It would be dreadfully hard on Jim if she fainted.

Beside her Kitty drew a long breath of disappointment and sat back. There wasn't going to be a scrap after all. Of course you never knew—he might be waiting to get Jock off his guard. She had better keep her eyes open.

A car passed them without dimming. The light swept over them all and was gone again. She saw the back of Jock's head, Jim Randal's profile, and, as she turned to get the glare out of her eyes, Caroline. She took Caroline's face back into the darkness. What did she want to look like that for? It spoilt the lark. Suddenly she wished herself out of the whole thing. It wasn't amusing any more; it was a bore, and rather horrid. Caroline like a ghost, with her eyes wide open, staring into the blinding headlights. It made her feel as if someone had poured cold water down the back of her neck.

She squared her shoulders and began to whistle *Smile, darn ya, smile!* The clear, shrill sound filled the car.

XXXIV

THEY CAME INTO HINTON, AND STOPPED AT MAJOR Anderson's gate. The house faced the Heart and Hand across the village street, a circumstance which had oppressed the landlord for twenty years. A man may be sober, honest, and law-abiding, without finding it agreeable to have the eye of the law for ever trained upon his premises.

"I haven't seen a drunken man in Hinton for fifteen years," Major Anderson was wont to say.

He lived in a low two-storeyed house which was hardly more than a cottage. It held himself, a quiet elderly sister who kept cats, and sporadic nephews and nieces who turned things upside down and left rather a blank when they went away. A narrow flagged path led from the gate to a hideous little porch set with panes of blue and amber glass.

The party of four had reached the porch, when the door of the house was opened, showing the lighted hall. The man who had opened it spoke over his shoulder.

"Very well, sir, I'll report in the morning."

Major Anderson came into view.

"Just a minute, Gray." Then, as he caught sight of his nephew. "Hullo, Jock—you're back early. Who have you got with you? I can't see."

Jim Randal took Jock by the shoulder and put him out of the way.

"I expect you've forgotten me, Major Anderson," he said. "I'm Jim Randal."

Caroline followed him into the hall. There was a dead silence for a moment. Kitty and Jock came in and the door was shut. Then Inspector Gray moved forward and spoke.

"If you are Mr Randal of Hale Place, I must ask you to accompany me to the police-station."

Jim looked past him at Caroline.

"It's all right—don't worry," he said.

Then he turned to Major Anderson.

"I came here to make a statement about the Van Berg affair, sir."

"A voluntary statement?"

"Yes. I want to make a statement—I came here to make one."

Major Anderson opened the door behind him.

"Come into my study. Jock, you'd better take Kitty and Miss Leigh home."

Caroline turned piteous eyes on him.

"Major Anderson, please let me come in. I want to make a statement too. I know some of it better than he does."

She came up to him. He surely couldn't have the heart to keep her out. She blessed the inspector when he said,

"I think we'd better have her in, sir."

And then there were four of them in the small smoky room, with its neat writing-table and its comfortable shabby chairs. Caroline sat down on one of them, and the door was shut. The inspector was speaking to Jim.

Caroline shut her eyes. She felt odd and light, like a soap-bubble that is just going to fly away. Everything shook a little—the chair, the floor, her own body, her thoughts. She shut her eyes.

When she opened them again, the inspector was sitting at the writing-table. He had a sheet of foolscap before him and a pen in his hand. Jim was sitting opposite to him, and Major Anderson was standing with his back to the mantelpiece. He was frowning as Caroline opened her eyes. He said,

"Before you make a statement I had better tell you that Mr Van Berg is expected to recover consciousness any time during the next few hours."

The inspector dipped his pen in the ink. It was not for him to interrupt the Chief Constable, but he was full of disapproval. The law had been complied with; Mr. Randal had been warned. Let him make his statement. If he ran his head into a noose, so much the worse for him, and so much the better for the law.

Major Anderson's frown deepened. He had known Jim Randal since he was eight years old. He had dined at Hale Place four times a year for fifteen years. He had kissed Caroline in her perambulator. He didn't care a damn for the inspector. He was going to do his duty, but he wasn't going to stretch his duty. He wasn't going to have Jim Randal bucketed into making a statement without knowing what he was up against.

"One moment, Inspector," he said. "Now, Randal—you say you want to make a statement. Before you do so I think you ought to know that I saw Mrs Van Berg this morning."

"Yes?"

"She says that on the night of the sixth of August she came down between eleven and twelve o'clock to get a book. She heard voices in the study, and she now says that she recognized one of them as yours."

"Yes," said Jim—"I was there. I think you had better let me make my statement. There really isn't any time to lose. Meanwhile let me tell you that the man who shot Elmer Van Berg and lifted the emeralds is Jim, or Jimmy, Riddell, and I left him twenty minutes ago having an interview with his wife up at St Leonard's Tower. Here's his description. Five-foot-eight or so—slim—wiry—two teeth missing in front—long nose—long chin—palish—between thirty and thirty-five—"

"Jimmy the Eel!" said the inspector.

"Well, you'd better look slippy or he'll get away. His wife's maiden name was Nesta Williams. She's a cousin of the housekeeper at Packham Hall, and she's living with a brother, Tom Williams, at Happicot, Sandringham Drive, Ledlington End."

The atmosphere in the room had changed.

"Jimmy the Eel!" said the inspector under his breath.

Then, "We'd better get hold of him. Excuse me, sir." He lifted the telephone and spoke into it.

They waited until he had finished. Jim looked at Caroline and nodded reassuringly.

The inspector was giving instructions about Jimmy the Eel. Jim struck in once.

"His original idea was to get to Glasgow, lie low there for a bit, and then get abroad. But I think he's more likely to hang around here now—you'll see why presently."

The inspector nodded and went on with his instructions. Presently he hung up the receiver.

"Now, Randal," said Major Anderson.

"Well," said Jim, "I landed at Liverpool on the first of July—but if you've been taking an interest in me, I expect you know that. I was in the wreck of the *Alice Arden* on August the eighth, and until about half an hour ago I hadn't the remotest idea of what had happened between those two dates—" He paused, and added, "with one exception."

A wave of excitement swept over Caroline. The colour rushed to her cheeks. The room stopped trembling.

"Look here," said Jim, "can I tell this my own way? I'll sign a formal statement afterwards if you want me to, but I'd like to tell it to you first just as it happened. Can I do that?"

"Yes," said Major Anderson. "Carry on."

"Well then, I was in the wreck of the *Alice Arden*, and I understand that I was taken to the Elston cottage hospital, where I kept on repeating the name of Jim, or Jimmy, Riddell. They weren't sure at first whether I was saying Riddell or Randal, so they sent out a broadcast message with both names. Next day Mrs Riddell rolled up, identified me as her husband, and carried me off to Sandringham Drive. I don't remember any of this myself, but I gather that that is what happened. Now I come to what I do remember. I woke up next day in a perfectly strange room. A perfectly strange young woman came in and assured me that my name was Jimmy Riddell, and that she was my wife. Well, it was a bit of a knock-out. I couldn't contradict her, because as far as having any memory was concerned I might have been a new-born baby. The only thing I remembered—and I didn't know whether I was remembering it or not—was someone holding up a string of square green stones under a bright light. That kept on getting clearer and clearer all the time—I used to see it whenever I shut my eyes. And there was a fog, and a voice talking in the fog—talking about the emeralds and Jimmy Riddell. It worried me to death, because I couldn't make out whether it was my own voice or not." He paused.

Major Anderson said, "This is a most extraordinary story, Randal."

The inspector said nothing. His light, rather prominent eyes remained fixed on Jim's face.

Jim went on again.

"I'll cut it as short as I can, but you've got to understand the sort of state I was in. Nesta Riddell showed me a marriage certificate. She said we'd been married on the twenty-fifth of July at the Grove Road registry office in London, and she told me that I had shot Elmer Van Berg and stolen eight very valuable emeralds on the night of the sixth of August. She wanted to know what I had done with the emeralds. She said I was on the *Alice Arden* because I was on my way to Glasgow. She said I'd hidden the emeralds before I went, and she wanted to know where they were."

Major Anderson took a step forward.

"Really, Randal, I don't know whether you hadn't better see a doctor. This is the most extraordinary story!"

The inspector shifted his light stare to the Chief Constable.

"I think I should let him go on, sir."

Jim Randal laughed.

"I know it sounds extraordinary, but I'm perfectly sane. I'd like to go on if I may."

He went on.

"I went to the public library and read up the Van Berg Case. I couldn't believe I'd gone to see a man as a friend, talked with him, had drinks with him, and then shot him."

Major Anderson made an abrupt movement. Jim turned towards him.

"Bits of my memory were coming back. It was like seeing pictures—little brightly lighted pictures. I could see myself drinking with Elmer Van Berg. I knew that I called him Elmer, and that his wife's name was Susie. And when I remembered all that, I got the wind up, because it seemed as if I must have done it—and there were my finger-prints on the glass I'd used. I fairly got the wind up. I saw a poster, 'Man Wanted by the Police,' and my one idea was to get out of Ledlington. Well, I started out across country without any idea of where I was going. I kept trying to think things out, but it was all a muddle. The most damning thing was that Nesta Riddell really did think I'd got the emeralds—there was no mistake about that."

Major Anderson coughed. The fellow was incriminating himself, getting deeper and deeper every minute. Temporary insanity—that would be the best line for the defence to take. Unpleasant business—very.

Jim restrained a smile and went on.

"I wandered about, and I slept a bit, and then I got into country which seemed familiar. To cut a long story short, I fetched up at Hale Place, and when I got there I remembered everything except the time between the first of July and the thirteenth of August—which was when I waked up at Happicot."

The inspector made a note of the dates.

"I got into the house and I stayed there. You can understand that I wanted time. I made up my mind to wait for a week and see what happened. You see, there were several things that might happen. I might remember—or Elmer Van Berg might recover consciousness—or the police might lay hands on the real criminal. I knew I was exposing myself to suspicion, but I decided to wait. For one thing, I still wasn't sure whether I wasn't Jim Riddell." He looked from one to the other. "Have you got that clear? Except for some very compromising flashes of memory which gave me pictures of the emeralds and of Elmer, my recollections stopped short at July the first. There was all July and a bit of August for me to have called myself Jimmy Riddell, turned crook, married Nesta Williams, burgled the emeralds, and shot Elmer Van Berg. You see my point?''

He got no response, Major Anderson wore a worried frown. The inspector's face was perfectly blank; he might have been thinking deeply, he might have been on the point of dropping asleep. Neither his heavy features nor his pale stare gave the slightest clue to what was passing in his mind. He had written half a dozen words on the sheet of foolscap which lay before him. His pen remained poised.

Jim went on speaking.

''During the time I was at Hale Place the house was twice entered—''

''Entered?'' said Major Anderson sharply.

Jim nodded.

''There's a room there called the Blue Room. It has five windows like slits. The burglar came straight to this room on both occasions. The first time I surprised him. He charged me and got away. The second time he got what he had come for—the emeralds.''

''*What*?'' said Major Anderson.

''The emeralds were at Hale Place?'' said the inspector.

''They were hidden in the Blue Room. He got away with them, and I followed him to Hinton by the field path. He caught the last train into Ledlington, and I just missed it. I came on in the morning and watched for Mrs Riddell—I had some information which led me to suppose that he had come to her for money, and that she would meet him with it, probably after dark. I watched the road all day. In the evening Miss Leigh met me. She had her car, and thanks to her I was able to follow Mrs Riddell when she came out. She had taken her brother's motor-bicycle. We followed her to St Leonard's Tower. Miss Leigh remained in the field, whilst I went on to the ruins. I overheard an interview between Mrs Riddell and the man. They quarrelled. She had parked the money somewhere, and absolutely refused to hand it over unless he showed her the emeralds. In the end he gave way. They were on one side of the Tower, and I was on the other, with one of those narrow slits between us. He struck a match, and there were the emeralds dangling about a yard away from me." He paused.

"Well?" said Major Anderson.

Jim laughed.

"I grabbed them."

He dived into a pocket and flung a glittering heap of green and pearl upon the inspector's foolscap.

"There they are!" he said.

XXXV

MAJOR ANDERSON CAME FORWARD AND LEANED ON THE table. Caroline looked up from the tangle of green and pearl and saw his face. Something that was written there brought her to her feet. She came and stood by Jim, and as she put a hand on his shoulder, the inspector said,

"Well, sir, I think that settles it."

Caroline began to shake. Why had Jim told them all those things? They weren't going to understand. The things they were thinking were like a fog in the room. She felt as if it were stifling her. Jim's hand came up and covered hers. It was strong, and warm, and heavy. He said,

"Go and sit down, Caroline."

And then, to the inspector,

"You'd better let me finish. I've only got half way."

"Let him go on," said Major Anderson in a hard, tired voice. It was a good thing old James Randal was dead. Nice woman Mrs Randal. Not many of her sort left nowadays—sweet voice; pretty ways; womanly. That was it—not many womanly women left. A good thing she'd gone—a thing like this would have killed her. The fellow must be mad of course. A damned bad business.

He watched the inspector pick up the shining heap. It straightened into a double pearl-strung chain linking the eight square emeralds so lightly that they seemed to hang in the air. They were as magically green as a black cat's eyes. The inspector let them fall upon a piece of blotting paper.

Major Anderson went back to the fireplace and said curtly,

"Go on, Randal."

Jim moved his chair back a little. He wanted to be able to address the Chief Constable without appearing to ignore the inspector.

"Now we're really going to get down to it. I snatched the emeralds and made off just about as hard as I could go, and all in a flash, whilst I was running, my memory came back. You know the way a blind goes up with a click. It was like that. I won't bother you with how we fetched up here. I want to tell you what I've remembered. To start with, I wasn't Jim Riddell, and I hadn't married Nesta Williams. My business over here was to try and interest various important people in a new steel process which I had invented. Elmer Van Berg was one of them. He'd been nibbling at it out in the States, where I'd known him pretty well. He's the sort of man who gets red-hot keen about a thing and then drops it—not a stayer—you've got to strike while the iron's hot. Well, he'd cooled off. On the sixth of August I had a telephone conversation with him. When he heard that certain other people were interested in my process, he warmed up a bit. I can't mention names, because it's all very confidential. The upshot of the talk was that he wanted me to go down and see him. Well, I was leaving for Scotland next day and I didn't want to put off going, so I went down by train to Hinton and walked over to Packham. I was glad to get the exercise."

"What train did you take?" said the inspector.

"The eight-twenty. It got into Hinton at ten-fifteen. I believe it is due at ten-ten. I walked over to Packham, and it took me about an hour and a half. I went round to the library and knocked on the window, and Elmer let me in as we had arranged. We talked, and we had drinks, but we didn't come to any agreement.''

"Did you quarrel?" said the inspector.

"It depends on what you'd call a quarrel. We didn't agree. If you don't agree with Elmer, he tries to shout you down. There's nothing in it, but it's noisy while it lasts.''

"You parted on bad terms?" said the inspector.

"Oh no, we didn't—he blew himself out and calmed down. We had another drink. He told me about all the shows they were going to, and about the emeralds. He said his wife was going to wear them at the Rackingtons' in a day or two—tableaux for some charity—so he'd got them in the house. He asked me if I'd like to see them, and I said yes. He took them out of his safe and showed them to me. That was the bit I remembered—his hand under the light, and those eight thumping big stones. I said they must be worth a fortune, and he said they were. Then I said good-night and went out the same way I'd come in. I let myself out. He was over by the table swinging the chain on his finger and worshipping it. He's crazy about stones.''

The inspector spoke again.

"You left him like that?"

"I left him like that. No, I haven't finished—not by a long chalk. I'd missed the last train handsomely, so I walked into Ledlington.''

The inspector's eyebrows twitched.

"You walked into Ledlington?"

"I did.''

"Twenty miles?"

"Why not? I told you I was short of exercise.''

"Mr Van Berg didn't ask you to stay the night?"

"Yes, he asked me.''

"Why didn't you stay?"

"I didn't want to. I wanted to get back to London—I'd my boat to catch.''

"So you walked to Ledlington?"

"Yes. I took the first train on up to town and went on board the *Alice Arden*. You know about the wreck, so I can skip all that. I was washed overboard and flung up on a piece of rock. I don't know why I wasn't battered to bits—there was an awful sea running, and a fog, so that you couldn't see your hand before your face. It didn't take me long to find out that the tide was coming in. I didn't think much of my chances, because I didn't think my rock was above high water mark. I could hear people shouting and screaming. I shouted as loud as I could. Presently something bobbed up and hit me. It was a man. A wave fairly slung him at me, and I grabbed him. At first I thought he was dead, but he wasn't. He began to cough and choke, and curse and cry. He was out of his head with terror. I held on to him, or he'd have been off the rock a dozen times. The fog was so thick that I couldn't see him, and he couldn't see me, and, as I said, he was clean out of his wits with fright. I couldn't make out whether he thought he was dead, or whether he was just afraid he was going to die. Anyway he was talking-crazy. I don't think he ever stopped, and it was all, 'Jimmy Riddell,' and, 'Eight green stones—like a kid's green beads.' He must have said that hundreds of times. It was like having a gramophone record going round and round in your head. I couldn't stop him—he just went right on: "Jimmy Riddell,' and, 'A kid's green beads,' and, 'No one knows where they are except me.' And then a piece about, 'Five windows—like slits—' and, 'The finest emeralds in the world.' " Jim paused and looked from one to the other. "Do you see? I said it was like a gramophone record going round in one's head. Well, that's just what it was. All those things he kept on saying stuck in my mind, and when I'd lost my memory and didn't know who I was, there they were, and I didn't know what to make of them. I said them in my sleep, and they made Nesta Riddell think I knew all about the emeralds." He pushed back his chair and got up. "I can't tell you anything more. That's the last I remember— being on the rock, and the tide coming up. They say they found me on a ledge, but I don't know how I got there. And I suppose Jimmy Riddell must have been picked up by the life-boat. He wouldn't have given his real name."

The inspector's eyebrows twitched again.

"You say the emeralds were hidden at Hale Place. How do you account for that?"

"I can't account for it. The five windows like slits are in the Blue Room at Hale Place. The emeralds were hidden there."

"How?"

Jim hesitated for the first time. . . . . Oh well, it was bound to come out. He said,

"There's a secret hiding-place in the room. The emeralds were there."

"Can you explain how Jimmy Riddell knew of the secret hiding-place?"

"No, I can't."

Three words had stayed in Caroline's mind: "His real name." Jimmy Riddell's real name—*Jimmy Riddell's real name*—

She got up and came to the table, her eyes very bright, her cheeks flaming.

"His real name—" she said—"Jimmy Riddell's real name—do you know it?"

The inspector shifted that light, impassive stare. It rested upon Caroline and took in her colour, the excitement in her eyes, and the slight tremor of her hands. She was bareheaded, with bright tossed curls. Her hands were bare too.

The inspector spoke.

"His real name—well, it isn't Riddell. He's had a lot of aliases—Rudge—and Ray—he generally sticks to an R. As far as I know, his real name is Rudd."

"Oh!" said Caroline.

Jim turned to her with a puzzled look.

"What's all this?"

"Emily," said Caroline breathlessly—"Emily Rudd! Oh, Jim, don't you remember?"

A half memory jigged through his mind. It was like a leaf blowing. He couldn't catch it. It blew away and was gone.

"Emily Rudd?"

Caroline caught him by the arm with both hands.

"Yes—yes! You must remember! Nanna used to call her a tallow-candle piece and a prying good-for-nothing. She didn't like her—none of us did. And oh, Jim, one day when I'd been playing in the Blue Room—you know I used to go there and play, and hide things in the secret place, and pretend Cavaliers and Roundheads and all that sort of thing—well, one day I wanted something for a game I was playing, and I opened the door quickly, and there was Emily in the passage, and the door wasn't quite shut either. Nanna always said she pried and listened at doors, so she might have found out about the hiding-place and told her brother. She did have a brother, because I remember Nanna saying he was a bad lot."

They were intent upon one another, Jim upon Caroline, and Caroline upon Jim.

Then Major Anderson coughed.

Caroline's hands dropped from Jim's sleeve.

"That's how he knew!" she said triumphantly. "Emily must have told him."

She looked at Major Anderson, but he avoided her eyes. She turned back to the inspector, and met a chilly stare. During a cold, dragging pause it came home to her that they didn't believe her. They didn't believe her, and they didn't believe Jim. But they must believe. They couldn't listen to Jim and not believe what he said—it wasn't possible.

During that dragging pause the impossible became possible.

Major Anderson broke the silence.

"Well, Inspector?"

The inspector laid down his pen.

"I shall have to ask you to accompany me to the station, Mr Randal."

Caroline's breath stopped for a moment. All her colour died. Her eyes were very wide open. She turned to Jim and slipped her arm through his.

The inspector put a hand on the table and stood up, and just as he did that, the telephone bell began to ring sharply at his right hand. He pushed his chair back, and Major Anderson came to the table and took up the receiver. He said,

"Yes—yes—speaking," and then beckoned to the inspector.

"Station for you," he said, and went back to the hearth.

Caroline leaned against Jim and wished that he would put his arm round her. What did it matter about Major Anderson and the inspector? She would be glad and proud to have his arm round her if everybody in Hinton and Ledlington and Hazelbury West were looking on. She loved him with all her heart and soul. That was what he had said to her—"I love you with all my heart and soul." But he wouldn't put his arm round her. She heard the inspector say,

"You're sure?" And then, "Who knows him? . . . . . Lockwood? . . . I'd like to speak to him. Ask them to wait—I'll be along in a minute . . . That Lockwood? . . . Are you sure of the identity? . . . . All right—I'm coming along."

He hung up the receiver and addressed the Chief Constable.

"They've got Jimmy the Eel at the station."

"How?"

"This treasure hunt, sir. Mr Blake went after a blue to St Leonard's Tower. He says a man attacked him in the dark. He thought he was a lunatic because he kept on saying 'Give them back!' and using language. Mr Blake shouted, and the two Mr Lesters came up. The man let off a revolver, but no one was hurt. They managed to secure him and brought him in to the station. Lockwood says he's Jimmy the Eel."

Jim took a step forward.

"You didn't believe me just now, but that part of my story is corroborated—you'll admit that. And for the rest, I would like the inspector to make a note of the fact that I made a statement of what took place between myself and Elmer Van Berg, after being warned by Major Anderson that he was likely to recover consciousness at any moment."

The telephone bell rang again. Caroline had the strangest feeling that it was ringing in her head. She closed her eyes and heard Major Anderson say,

"Hullo!"

There was a pause. She knew that the bell had stopped, but for all that, she could hear it still. Major Anderson's voice became a little far away sound—little and far away, but quite distinct. He said,

"Yes?" and, "You have?" and then, "He's doing

well?" . . . . "Good—good! I'm very glad to hear it. Look here, Lefroy, I want the statement as soon as possible. . . . Yes, I've got a special reason. Can you give me the substance over the 'phone? . . . . . You're sure of that? . . . . . And he's quite sensible? . . . . . All right. The inspector's here—I'll keep him."

He put the receiver back on its hook.

"That was Dr Lefroy, Gray—speaking from Packham Hall. Mr Van Berg has recovered consciousness. I'd like a word with you in the dining-room. It's all right, man— Randal isn't going to run away."

The words came to Caroline's ear as small and sharp as pin-pricks. And then the click of the door as it opened, and a little thud as it fell to again. She tried to open her eyes, but the tears welled up in them and she couldn't see. Jim's arms were round her now, both of them, and he was kissing her blind eyes, and her wet cheeks, and her soft trembling mouth. A warm, golden happiness flowed over her. The tears ran down her cheeks. It didn't make you unhappy to cry when there was someone to kiss the tears away.

"Caroline—my darling! Don't cry! It's all right—it's all over—there's nothing to cry for."

Caroline heard her own voice.

"I w-want to cry."

"Darling, don't! Don't cry like that! You're breaking my heart."

"I'm so happy!" said Caroline on a sob.

"Then stop crying."

She lifted drenched eyes to his.

"I thought he was going to take you away to prison."

"So did I. But he won't now, so there isn't anything to cry about."

"That's just why I'm crying."

"Because you've got nothing to cry about?"

She nodded vehemently against his shoulder. The tears and the happiness were having a very reviving effect.

"If you'd gone to prison, I wouldn't have cried. I'd have told everyone we were engaged, and I wouldn't have cried a single tear. Oh, Jim!"

"Oh, Caroline!"

"You're sure it's all right?"

"Yes. If Elmer's recovered consciousness, I'm clear. If he'd died—well, we don't need to think about that, darling."

Major Anderson rattled the handle before he came back into the room. Three nieces had brought his education up to date in this respect. Having opened the door, he allowed Dr Lefroy to precede him. The inspector followed.

Major Anderson went up to Jim with his hand out.

"My dear Randal, I can't say how pleased I am!" He shook hands with him heartily. "Van Berg's statement corroborates yours in every detail. He recovered consciousness about an hour ago. Lefroy was there and got a statement from him witnessed by himself and the two nurses. Now what we want is your statement in writing."

Dr Lefroy was shaking hands too.

"Does Van Berg say what happened after I went out?" said Jim.

Kitty Lefroy's father was a big hearty man with a well-preserved brogue.

"Say? He says everything. And you may be thankful he does, my boy, by all accounts. He says you let yourself out, and he stood there looking at the emeralds and thinking they were the finest in the world, and all of a sudden he heard the window creak and he thought you'd come back. And it's lucky for you he turned round and saw that it wasn't you at all. He'd the emeralds in his hand, and he turned sharp round and saw a man with a cap pulled down over his eyes and a revolver in his hand—a gun, he called it. The man said, 'Put 'em up!' and Van Berg says he was hanged if he was going to let the emeralds go like that, so he charged him. That's all he knows. The fellow must have shot him down as he came on. Fortunately, he can describe him."

"The description tallies with yours," said the inspector. "Now if you'll kindly let us have that statement—"

Half an hour later they drove back to Hazelbury West in Jock Anderson's car. Jemima was to be retrieved in the morning by that ill-used and rather sulky young man. It was a piece of the foulest bad luck that his own well laid scheme should have gone agley, whilst the Lesters and Roger Blake blundered into glory.

Jim drove. It is to be feared that he had one arm round Caroline. The roads were dark and empty. It would be midnight before they reached the cottage.

"And I expect Pansy Ann will have been ringing up the police," said Caroline.

"Let her!" said Jim. "They're our bosom friends—we love them, and they love us. And only a few hours ago we skulked in lanes and hid behind hedges! I somehow don't think I'll go in for being a crook. It's a dog's life. Besides, you wouldn't marry me if I was a crook."

"'M—" said Caroline.

"Does that mean yes or no?"

Caroline laughed.

"It doesn't mean either."

"What does it mean?"

She snuggled up to him.

"If you were a crook, it wouldn't be *you*—but I'd marry you whatever you were."

They drove into the little garage, locked in the borrowed car, and passed through the dark garden, where the bushes looked like black hummocks.

"Pansy Ann will be wild," said Caroline.

She slipped in her key and opened the door.

Pansy Arbuthnot was sitting at the table, which was littered with sheets of stiff blue writing paper. There seemed to be at least a dozen sheets. They were all covered with Robert's upright, formal writing. As the door opened, Pansy picked up the first sheet again. It began: "My dearest Pansy." It was wonderful to be Robert's dearest Pansy. She gazed absently over the top of the sheet at Caroline.

"It's frightfully late," said Caroline, "but—"

"Is it late?" said Pansy Ann.